BOSSY
Brothers

LUKE

NEW YORK TIMES BESTSELLING AUTHOR

ja HUSS

ABOUT THE
BOOK

Two hot men seeking a fun, flirty girl with a sense of adventure. You in?

My life changed the day Zach Boston walked into it. And we've been inseparable best friends and lovers ever since. But he's almost seven years younger than me and I remember all too well what my twenties were like - A new adventure every day, non-stop partying every night, and a new girl (or guy) whenever I got bored.

That's why Zach and I always have a third.

Girls are how we've kept it fresh all year.

We've gone through dozens of them since we got serious and I'm not saying I don't enjoy the dynamic of a threesome, because I do.

But when this cute girl with pink hair comes sailing into our lives and upends everything—I don't know if we'll survive it.

Bossy Brothers: Luke is the final book in the Bossy Brothers series and features a sweet and sexy MMF ménage with two hot, committed men and a pink-haired gossip reporter desperate for a scoop. But when she stumbles into more secrets than she can handle, her boys need to call on all the Boston and Dumas brothers to keep her safe.

CHAPTER ONE

LUKE

The music in the club is thumping and heavy with bass. Neon lights flash across happy faces, bodies barely covered, sweaty and writhing in the heat of a Saturday night in Miami.

I'm slumped up against a wall, sipping some very nice whiskey and watching Zach Boston grind his hips against two mostly naked women. He's captured between them and both girls are smiling with the thought of what this might lead to.

Zach Boston might not be the most attractive guy in this club, but he's definitely in the top three. His hair looks more blond than brown under the flashing lights, his normally fair skin is tanned from spending the better part of a year here in Florida with me, and his tight white t-shirt shows off all the muscles in his upper body. Don't even get me started on the faded, ripped jeans. I fucking love his ass in those jeans.

"You should just talk to him."

I turn my head to the left and notice that a girl has joined me along the wall. She's dressed head to toe in neon pink.

Well. I use the term 'head to toe' generously. Her firm, round breasts nicely fill out a cropped, tie-front halter that leaves almost nothing to the imagination. Her shorts are definitely short. In fact, let's just call her outfit a bikini. She's small. A little bit tiny, actually. But her tits and hips are nice and round. She has long, pink hair with bangs that frame an amazing set of blue-violet eyes. She reminds me of an anime character I was obsessed with when I was fourteen, so internally I tag her Princess Euphemia.

Everyone I meet gets a tag instead of a name. I hate remembering names. Even Zach had a tag for a week before I decided he was gonna be a permanent fixture in my life.

I called him Slick because he's quick like that. Got an answer for anything. Even if you're not asking questions, Zach Boston has the answer.

"What?" I yell back at Euphemia over the music.

She points at the undulating mass of bodies in the center of the club. "You're looking at that guy." She pauses here to see if I have anything to add. But I don't, so she continues. "The hot one. With the two girls. Two." She holds up two fingers in a peace sign. "One for you. One for him."

I chuckle and shake my head.

"What? Are you gonna stand here and deny that wasn't what you were thinking?"

I side-eye her, but just sip my whiskey instead of answering.

She hooks her arm in mine, like we are the best of friends, then blinks her large eyes up at me. "You're not gonna get any action standing on the edge of things. You have to put yourself out there."

"Like you are?"

She hides a grin. "I'm here, aren't I? Talking to you."

"Ah." I nod knowingly. "So it's really you picturing yourself between him and I, then. Isn't it?"

She doesn't even bother to blush. Just says, "Maybe."

I look back over to Zach, wondering if he'll choose between the two girls or bring them both over here. We don't often invite two girls home with us. That feels a little too swappish, and that's not what we're looking for.

We like the tag team. One girl between us at a time.

Euphemia is leaning up on her tiptoes now, trying to reach my ear. If I weren't slouching against this wall, she'd have no hope of doing that. But as it is, she manages. "He's hot. But younger than you."

I scoff. It's true that Zach Boston is the real baby of that family. He's only twenty-three. But I'm not *that* much older. I might be turning thirty this December, but I'm not there yet.

"Maybe even… a little out of your league," Euphemia continues.

"Trust me. He's not out of my league."

I feel her shrug. "He so is. I know him."

"You do not."

"So do. I was with him last weekend. He fucked me into this Sunday."

I sneer down at her.

"What? You don't believe me?"

"What's his name?"

"Like I'd tell you. Get your own moves, buddy."

Ha. "You're the one who told me to go put myself out there. Now you're gonna get all jealous?"

She smirks, but doesn't look at me. Just pretends to be interested in everything happening around us.

"Whatever." I take my attention back to the packed dance floor and try to shrug off her grip.

"Zach," she says, her hands tightening around my biceps as she once again leans up to get closer to me. "His name is Zach."

"How do you know that?"

"I told you. I was with him last weekend. He asked me to meet him here tonight. But I got held up, so I was late. I guess he started without me. But it's OK. I'm not the jealous type."

I realize I'm looking at her again, but catch myself and turn my head to the right to think this through.

Was he with this girl last weekend?

Dumas Water Adventures—my part of the family business—goes *off* during the summer. We are busy every day, all day long. But I was getting a little bored with renting out hydroboards and doing jet ski tours, so this year I added a floating beachside bar and bought a new yacht to run overnight dive trips. I also, for the first time ever, hired a shitload of people to help me out so I could concentrate on the new yacht. Last weekend was my first official overnight client. Zach was gonna come along, but he partied pretty hard the night before and was nursing a wicked hangover, so I told him to stay home.

"What did you guys do?"

"Hmm?"

Oh. Now she's acting like she's not interested in me. Fucking girls. This is why I prefer men. Girls are so sneaky. Always playing games. Like what is her deal? Does she know I'm *with* Zach and she's just… what? Testing the waters? Insinuating that he's cheating on me?

He's not.

We don't have that kind of relationship.

He likes girls and, hell, I like girls too. So we're always dating girls. In fact, the whole time we've been together, we've dated approximately… I pause to count them up.

There was Christine. Lydia. Shawna. Bella. Mary Jane—whatever happened to her? Sheila. Cathy. Kathy with a K. Lisa and her BFF Ryella—that was the time we decided that the twofer wasn't our thing. Then there was Margo. Then Natalie. Then Tina and her boyfriend—which was interesting. I chuckle a little at the memory. Won't do that again, either.

But my point is, we've dated a lot of people.

Just… not separately.

Well, occasionally Zach will go out, find a girl, and bring her home so we can share her.

Hmm. I turn my head and look down my nose at Princess Euphemia again. She's still smirking up at me. Did he invite her here so we can share her?

I glance back at the dance floor to watch Zach writhe against the two hot-as-fuck women. They are both blonde and very tan. One is wearing a neon-yellow halter and skirt so short, it doesn't even pretend to cover her panties. I've tagged her Dandelion. The other one is wearing straps. That's it. Just straps. Which is also her tag. They criss-cross her breasts, barely hiding her nipples. Then there's a thin strip that disappears between her legs.

I was already picturing us with them. And now I have to readjust for stupid Euphemia here.

Pink-haired girls are never a good idea. Trust me, I've dated a few and even though they are pretty fun— and maybe even a little bit my type—they are always nuts. And this one looks like she plans on living up to the stereotype.

"Want me to introduce you?"

"What?" I actually laugh.

"I told you. I'm not the kind of girl who gets jealous. And I get the feeling he's open to the plural stuff."

She's right about that. Zach likes dynamic relationships.

She takes my hand and starts tugging me towards the dance floor. I set my glass of whiskey down on a passing tray, because even though I didn't come here looking for a pink princess tonight, if I play it right, this night could end up being very fun.

Euphemia stops abruptly and I bump into her. Then she's pressing her breasts up against my chest and leaning up on her tiptoes to reach my ear. "Just… pretend we're together. OK?"

My hands automatically grab her hips and I sway her a little. "We are together."

She pats my chest. "Good answer. I wanna play a little game with him. Make him jealous."

I lean down in her ear now. She smells really good. Like jasmine and blackberries. "What if he's not the jealous type?"

"Make him jealous."

"Make him?" Hmm. That's an intriguing twist. "OK." She turns, ready to head over to Zach and his ladies. I pull her back. "But are you sure you wanna play this game?"

"Games are fun," she coos. Then she tugs me into the swarm of sweaty bodies until we're dancing right up next to Zach.

Dandelion is grinding against his ass while Straps holds on to Zach's face with both hands like she's about to kiss him. She even leans up to do that, but Zach pulls off a slick dance move and spins her around.

I laugh. No one hears me because the music is too loud. And Euphemia is too fixated on reaching Zach to pay attention to me.

Zach catches my eye, then spots Euphemia and shoots me a confused look.

I hold up one finger, shooting him the 'give me a sec' sign, and he begins dancing again.

That's another thing I love about Zach Boston. He's a willing participant in just about everything. You could walk up to Zach and say, *Hey, I'm gonna jump out of a plane this afternoon. You in?* And he'd be all, *Fuck, yeah, I love wind.*

You could wake him up in the middle of the night and say, *I think I'll build a chicken coop in the backyard. You in?* And he'd be all, *Fuck, yeah. Fresh eggs every day. Let's do it.*

So this? What I'm setting up right here? This is nothing compared to the shit he's up for. Hell, he'd be into taking all three of these girls home. But three? Nah. That sounds complicated to me. Besides, Dandelion is a little rough around the edges for my taste and I have a feeling that she and Straps are a two-for-one deal.

So I'm happy to give pink-haired Princess Euphemia a try tonight.

Besides, he must already like her if he told her to meet up with him for a repeat session.

Euphemia is talking to him now. Zach concentrates on her for a few moments and Straps starts tugging on his arm to make him look at her. But Zach is giving Euphemia his full attention. Then he laughs and looks at me.

I wink at him and the game begins.

Zach leans into Straps's ear and says something. She looks mad. Then she slaps him, grabs Dandelion's hand, and pushes her way through the crowd.

Euphemia and Zach turn to me. Then Euphemia leans into my space and says, "Come on. He's in."

I grab her and force myself to look uneasy at this new development. "In for what?"

She leans way up into my ear now. "Us. Both of us." Then she pulls back and winks. "I told you. You just gotta put yourself out there."

Zach grabs her hand and begins tugging her through the crowd towards the outer edges of the club. Euphemia has my hand, so I get tugged along too. And I can't help myself. I am grinning. Excited about what kind of act Zach is planning.

I come up with my scenario as we walk, then he's pushing his way through the back door of the club. This takes us out into an alley just a few blocks away from the Miami Beach Marina where my yacht is docked.

The thumping bass follows us out, but the club door closes and it takes a moment to get used to the new hushed version of the music.

Zach lets out a long breath and whips his shirt over his head. Euphemia and I both pause to study the cut muscles of his back and the way the sweat drips down the line of his spine. She glances at me and grins. Pretty much waggling her eyebrows.

I agree with a nod. And then Zach is facing us again. "Posie!" he yells. He opens his arms and they embrace in a hug. "I thought you ditched me!"

"Posie?" I mumble. Hmm. That's pretty sweet. Kinda like her perfume.

She pulls back, still gazing up at Zach's unbelievably handsome face. "I got caught up."

Zach's blue eyes slide over to me. "This guy?"

I hold my breath. Waiting to see how we're gonna play it.

Posie jumps in without missing a beat. "My boyfriend, Andy."

"Andy, huh?" Zach winks at me.

I offer him my hand. "Nice to meet you…"

"*Zach*," he says. All flair. So slick.

We shake. "Zach." I say his name and look him in the eyes. And God damn, I could look at him forever.

Posie butts in. "Yep. I told you, remember? That I had a boyfriend? Last weekend when we hooked up."

"Don't actually recall that, but whatever." Zach lets go of my hand and takes a step back. He checks me out. Which, I'm not gonna lie, still feels good. Because Zach might be one of the top three good-looking men back in that club, but I'm definitely top two. "Nice to meet you… *Andy*."

"Back at ya, *Zach*."

Zach turns to Posie. "Well, what are you two up to this fine evening?"

She grabs my hand and swings it a little, shrugging her shoulders like she's shy. Then she looks at me and tsks her tongue. "You tell him, Andy."

I point to my chest and laugh. "Me?"

Posie leans up on her tiptoes and cups her hand around her mouth, like she's gonna tell Zach a secret. But her words are loud enough for the people down the alley to hear. "He's... *curious*, Zach. So I thought... maybe..."

She doesn't finish. Plays it off as embarrassment. So I decide I'm in. "Jesus, Pose. You don't need to announce it to the world, babe. And I'm not that curious." I say this last part to Zach.

"No?" Zach asks.

"Nah... well, you know. Just a *little* curious."

"Well." Zach tucks his shirt into the waistband of his jeans at the small of his back, freeing up both his hands. He points towards the ocean. "My boat is docked just a few blocks away."

"Your *boat*?" Posie looks at me and grins. That look says, *Jackpot! He's got a boat!*

"Yep," Zach says. "You two wanna come back to the boat with me? Have a little drink? Do a little dirty dancing?" He grabs Posie's hips and grinds against her.

Posie is all over this offer. She's already saying, "Yes. Absolutely. Let's go!"

But fuck her. She's not getting two fine men such as ourselves without a fight. "No. Babe. Come on. I'm not—"

"What?" Posie is incredulous. She points her finger at my face. "Oh, you *are*."

"Hold on, hold on," Zach says, positioning himself between us. "If Andy here is uncomfortable, that's cool." He looks at me and licks his lips. And his next words are softer. Lower. Very fucking sexy. "How could I make you more comfortable with this, Andy?"

I stare at him. Take him all in. Let all the things I love about Zach Boston run through my head.

Posie tugs on my hand. "He's fine. Aren't you, Andy?"

"Well," I say, then I look over my shoulder at another alley. It's narrow. Probably not an alley, actually. Probably a little walkway that leads to that building's back door. I look back at Zach. "Maybe we could just..." I think he's holding his breath. Dying to know what I'm gonna say. "Maybe we could be curious over there." I nod my head to the dark alley.

"What?" Posie doesn't like this idea. I'm sure she was already picturing herself on *my* boat. *Come on, Posie. Keep up. You're the non-player character here, babe. Not me.*

"Over there, huh?" Zach asks. He draws in a long breath and looks over in the direction of the alley as I study his abs and the way his pants dip low enough for me to see the happy trail of hair leading down to his cock. Which, I notice now that I'm looking at it, is slightly hard. He turns his attention back to me. "All right."

"Wait. What?" Posie is lagging behind here. But we give no fucks about her. Zach grabs my hand and leads me into the darkness. Posie has hold of the other one, so she follows me.

When we get in the alley Zach pushes me up against the side of the building. The bricks are rough and jagged against my back. And then, before any of us has a chance to say anything else, he grinds his hips against mine and kisses me on the mouth.

I hesitate for a moment. Playing my role. Giving Posie a chance to wonder what Andy will do. And then I open my mouth, grab Zach's hair, and kiss him like he's the love of my fucking life.

Zach moans into it, his cock hard now. Pressing against mine as it grows.

"Jesus," Posie mutters.

I reach out, blindly, grabbing her arm so I can tug her towards us.

"Ooooo," she coos, obviously delighted at being included.

But Zach is already reaching for one of her hands. He places it over his cock and gives it a squeeze.

I do the same, and suddenly poor Posie has two gigantic cocks on her mind.

"Come on, Posie," Zach encourages. "Let's make Andy's first time memorable."

Then he's pushing on her shoulder, indicating he would like her on her knees.

"Umm…"

"Don't be shy, Pose," I say. I'm breathing hard. And I narrow my eyes a little to make her think I'm filled with lust. Which I am, but it's a little more than that. I'm trying my best to be Andy the curious first-timer. "I'll only get this chance once."

She narrows her eyes right back at me. But she's not pretending to be in lust. She's having ideas. About me, for sure. But also probably about Zach. "Are you sure you want to do this, *Andy*?"

"Oh, I'm sure." I glance at Zach. "If I'm gonna let a man touch my dick, I want it to be this man."

Zach kisses me again. And holy fuck. His mouth. It's magic. I love the way he kisses me and it shows, because I moan a little. Zach pulls back. "Come on, Posie. Touch us, at least. Have fun with it. And then, one day, when you and Andy are bored with each other—you've got six fucking kids always demanding your attention, and you haven't been out on a real date since the last baby was born—you two can pull this night out, get yourselves all worked up, and fuck like you're in your prime again."

I'm not sure this does it for her, because poor Posie scrunches up her face, probably thinking about that post-pregnancy body Zach just gave her.

"Ah, don't worry, Posie," Zach croons. Then he grabs her, spins her around, and pushes her up against my chest. "We're gonna take care of you. You need a little pick-me-up before we really get going? Hm?"

He's so fucking slick. Because Posie melts into me. And then I'm reaching around her hips, and Zach is pressing his fingers between her legs, and the minute both our hands meet in the middle, she lets out a long breath that turns into a soft moan.

Zach leans forward, his mouth right up next to her ear. So close to mine, I get the urge to kiss him. "How's that feel, Posie? Good?"

"Um…" She hesitates. Clearly it feels good. So this hesitation is about something else.

"What?" I ask. "It's not turning you on, babe? You like it, right? And this guy—what's your name again?"

Zach almost laughs. But he's an amazing player. And clearly, he's into this game. "Who cares about names, right, Andy? We're all here for the same reason. Make Posie happy. Don't you want us to make you happy, Posie?"

"Um…" She still hesitates.

My eyes go wide in disbelief as Zach stares at me. Jesus Christ. Why is she here if she's just gonna back out when things get interesting?

Zach keeps playing. "Say yes, Posie. And I'll show you and Andy here a real good time. I'll make it a night to remember."

"Say yes," I encourage her, one hand sliding up to grab her breast as the other one joins Zach as we play with the wet folds between her legs. "I'm so curious, Posie."

Zach turns his head, unable to hide the smirk. Posie's head is turned the other direction, so she doesn't notice. But he recovers quickly. "He's curious, Posie. Aren't you curious too? Don't tell me you've never—"

"I haven't," she blurts. "It was kind of a joke. I'm not sure—"

I push her off me and slide along the wall. "All right. Well, the game's over then."

"What game?" Zach asks. He backs off her as well and now he's standing in the middle of the alley looking hot as fuck, with the outline of his long, hard cock pushing up against his jeans. If Posie doesn't pull her shit together soon, I'm just gonna drag him back to the boat and proceed without her.

I look at Posie. She wants to say something.

I'm not a hundred percent sure what she wants to say. The truth would be a nice change. And for a moment I think she will. She's gonna blow my cover as Andy the bi-curious boyfriend and admit to whatever the hell she's really doing here.

But I'm wrong.

She doubles down and takes a deep breath. "OK, well." She straightens out her shorts that really look more like a bikini. "I'm up for this. For sure." She looks at me and smiles. "I want you to have an amazing first curious experience, Andy. So… my answer is yes. With one condition."

"Name it," Zach says.

"Not here. Not in this alley. You mentioned… a boat?"

Zach's poker face right now would win awards. "Yeah. I have a boat."

Posie looks at me, still a bit nervous. But I've done this with enough girls to recognize that she's warming to the threesome idea. Then she takes her gaze back to Zach. "Let's go there."

Zach grins a sexy smile in my direction. "How about you, Andy? This good with you?"

I pan my hand in the direction of the marina. "Lead the way, Slick. I'm all in."

CHAPTER TWO

ZACH

Even though the night is hot, the sea air feels cool on my back as we walk down the dock leading to the boat. I glance over my shoulder at Luke and Posie. If I wasn't in on this little charade we're pulling, I would still know it was a setup.

Posie's eyes are shifting all over the place. She's either very nervous or taking in all the details. Either way, it's not hard to tell she's uneasy. It's like she isn't even trying.

Luke grins at me though. He's putting in some effort. And I have to admit, I quite like the curious first-timer angle we're working here.

I saw the two of them talking while I was dancing. Luke isn't much into the club scene. He only goes so we can wrangle up a girl to join us for a night of fun. So I like to watch him watch me.

I met Posie last weekend. I was a little under the weather, so Luke told me to stay home while he took a group of people for an overnight trip. It was mostly a hangover from Friday night and not anything major. So when Johnny's friend Chek called me and said he needed backup for a meeting in Miami because Johnny was busy with the new baby, I told him I'd watch his six.

That little side job only took about an hour, and then I figured fuck it, I might as well hit up a club while I was in the city.

That's where I met Posie.

She was some good fun. But I was really just stringing her along so she would agree to meet up with me again tonight. Get Luke in on this action.

We've dated lots of girls. Most of them are one-time things. We get a lot of tourists out here and I guess they figure what happens in Key West stays in Key West.

Last year we had a regular girl but she was only here for the summer and went back to school, never to be heard from again. And while the one-nighters are fine, I would really like to get us a regular girl again.

Even though this girl is Luke's type and that's why I hooked up with her in the first place, Posie is probably not a contender for said position. Oh, she's got a hot little body with nice big tits, but she's not entirely upfront about things and there's definitely a side of liar to her. But those things can be mitigated for a weekend of fun.

They make her interesting, at least.

Here's what really fascinates me about Posie—this whole Andy-is-my-boyfriend thing. That right there says she's a player. And say what you will about players, the game is damn fun.

I like the game.

Luke likes the game.

And it's not easy to find a girl who likes the game the same way we do. Even that semi-regular one we had last summer was getting tired of the game. Her mind was on the future. The game is about the present. You're not a true player if you're always thinking about the future.

I live happily in the present, thank you. The future can suck my dick.

I stop at the bathing platform at the stern of the boat and wave Posie forward.

Her eyes are big as she boards, definitely soaking up the details.

This yacht was made to impress. Sleek lines. Modern finishes. Kitchen. Three living areas. Amazing flybridge. Four fucking cabins, including a separate master, the VIP suite, and two guest cabins, not to mention a totally separate crew cabin that sleeps four.

This baby right here set Luke back almost eight million dollars. But I could tell that he wanted more out of life than renting hydroboards to tourists. So when he asked for my opinion about buying a yacht and offering up overnight charters for dive trips, I said, *Fuck, yeah. Let's do it.*

And it definitely impresses the women.

"Wow." Posie is properly impressed. "When you said boat… I don't know what I was thinking, but it was not this."

I shoot her an indulgent smile. "It's nice, right?" Then I push past her and Luke, who is hanging back a little, still playing wary-first-time-curious Andy's part. "Who wants a drink?"

I don't wait for answers, just go right into the bar on the far side of the dining room table and grab three glasses and a bottle of champagne from a drawer. The cork is popped, the glasses filled, and then I hand them out. "To a fun night," I toast.

Posie sips her champagne, but her eyes are busy taking in the interior of the boat.

Luke downs his champagne in one gulp and I almost can't stop the laugh. He holds it out for a refill. "Give me some more courage. I'm having second thoughts."

"What?" Posie says, dragging her attention back to Andy. "No, you're not."

"Hmm," I say. "You're pretty invested in his curiosity, Posie."

She tosses her long, pink hair. "Well"—she smiles sheepishly, actually blushes too—"I'm curious as well."

"About?" I ask.

"You know." Her eyes dart between me and Luke. "A threesome."

"So you've never done one?"

"Of course not." This comes out a little bit haughty. Like only tramps and whores do threesomes.

I catch Luke throwing me a look out of the corner of my eye. I don't think she's won him over yet. But that's OK. I'm kind of in charge of this night so he's gotta play along now.

"So why now?" I ask. I'm talking to Posie, but I'm looking at Luke.

"It was his idea," Posie says. She's really checking out the interior of the yacht. Like she's about to start taking notes.

Jesus Christ. That is funny. She's really gonna take this all the way and blame this little tryst on poor Andy? I eyeball Luke again. "Well, Andy? What say you?"

He shrugs and moves closer to Posie so he can take her hand. "I don't know. I think we should go, Posie. This is probably a bad idea."

"What?" She narrows her eyes at him. Yep. She's a little hot-pink liar. "No. We're here, *Andy*. And this was *your* fantasy. Right?" She makes a face at Luke. One of those top-secret looks that couples often have that says volumes without words.

Except they aren't a couple. Luke and I are. So... yeah. He sends me one that says, *What the hell are we doing with this one?*

I send him one back that says, *Motherfucker. Do I ever get shit wrong?*

His secret-look answer is actually a list of all the shit I've gotten wrong over the past year since we started playing this game. But I just walk over to Posie, push her a little so she has to take a step back, and make her sit down on the couch. Then I point to Luke. "Andy. Sit your curious ass down on that side of her and I'll take this side."

"What are you doing?" Posie protests.

"This is the best way to ease in to things, Pose. Trust me. I know what I'm doing. I've been dealing with curious men my entire adult life. I've got a system."

She snorts. "You're like... what? Twenty-three?"

"I am. But age is just a number."

Luke chuckles, but he's sitting down on the other side of Posie now and his hand is already rubbing her bare thigh, so she doesn't catch his blatant amusement.

She looks down at Luke's hand as I sit down on the other side of her and begin fondling her breast.

"Whoa," Posie says. "Hold up. I thought this was about you two?"

I place one hand on her cheek and direct her attention to me. "Listen to me, Pose. Andy here is used to girls, right? This is his first time with a man. He needs you in the middle, babe. OK? You're the…"

Luke points at me. "Gateway drug."

I laugh. I can't help it. "Exactly. You're the gateway drug, Pose. You keep curious Andy's feet firmly on ground terra familiar. Right? He plays with you. I play with you. Then… ooops. I play with him. You play with him. And pretty soon, we're all playing with each other. No. Big. Deal."

"Sounds good to me," Luke says. Then he takes Posie's chin between his thumb and forefinger and turns her head towards him. "Does it sound good to you?"

"Um…"

I take her hand and center her palm over my hard cock. She sucks in a deep breath, but doesn't squeeze it.

"All right. Well, forget it then. Sorry, Andy. You'll have to get curious with someone else. It could've been fun. Could've been a lot of fun. But. Only works if everyone is on board. Do you want me to walk you out?"

"Wait. What?" Posie's face is pure panic. "You're kicking us out?"

I shrug. "If you're not comfortable, Posie, it's best to stop it now."

"Can't I just watch?"

"I dunno. Andy? Is that your idea of curious?"

"No," Luke says without hesitation. "Nope. Not at all. We talked about this, Posie. Remember?" It takes all my self-control not to laugh at that. Fucking Luke comes through for me every single time. "I told you I needed you to participate. Like he said. You're the gateway drug. It puts me at ease."

Posie takes a deep breath and I'm fully expecting this charade to be over now—she has clearly reached some kind of predetermined limit. But she breathes out the word, "OK."

My eyebrows shoot up. "Really?"

She nods. "Yep. Let's do this."

I glance at Luke and he is finally smiling. He's not as into the girls as I am. And I'm sure he's probably tired of playing these games with me. But he's a good sport. And even though this Posie girl is kind of his type, he's obviously getting the little-pink-liar vibe off her as well.

But. She is hot. Can't deny that. So Luke and I share one more secret look and then it's on.

We both angle our bodies, making Posie the center of attention. Her fast breathing turns into downright panting as Luke and I both slide our hands up her thighs and meet in the middle once again. He begins kissing her neck and tugging her shortie-shorts down her legs and slipping off her strappy sandals as I untie her crop top and expose her breasts. A phone falls out, disappearing into the cushions.

"Jesus," Posie moans, kicking her shorts aside as I remove her top. She is fully naked now.

It's a lot of action to be coming all at once. And if she's truly never done this before, the stimulation she's about to experience will get overwhelming real quick.

I take one knee and Luke takes the other. Then we open her legs. This is a practiced move we use all the time and Posie gets nervous when her pretty pussy is suddenly exposed.

She shaves it. Which I like, but I know Luke prefers a nice trim. Still, it's not enough to deter him. He slips two fingers easily inside her and begins to slide them in and out.

"Fuck," Posie moans. "Oh, shit."

"I think she likes it." I laugh.

This makes her open her eyes and look at me.

Is that suspicion? Is she on to me?

I grab her breast and lift her nipple up to my mouth to keep her focused on what really matters.

Sex.

Then I nip her hard enough to make her squeal and squirm.

Luke stands up and her eyes fly open. She watches him unbutton his shirt and toss it over his shoulder. Then he slips his pants down and kicks them aside.

Every one of the Dumas brothers is tall—all of them are well over six foot. They are very hard from working on the ocean. Luke's chest is nothing but muscle. His shoulders are broad and his upper body tapers into his cut hips.

He's got a giant cock too. Thick, and long, and pretty much porn-star beautiful.

Posie can't take her eyes off it. Even when he kneels down between her legs and grins. She bites her lip with anticipation. I open her legs wider and spread her lips apart with two fingers just as Luke's mouth descends. His tongue darts out, licking her soft folds. And when the tip of it drags along my fingers, a chill runs through my body.

I take Posie's hand and place it on top of Luke's head and begin to use her to guide him. "Oh, God," she moans.

Luke's eyes dart up to Posie's face. He grins as he licks her and I slip my finger down the crease of her pussy and begin to play with her clit. Luke's tongue darts over the tip of my finger, licking me and her at the same time.

I suck in a breath of air through my teeth and stare down at him. If you had told me last year that I'd have this relationship with Luke and random girls, I'd have laughed it off. I didn't plan it, I didn't go looking for it, and I didn't have any expectations the very first time Luke reached for my cock underneath my jeans and gave it a good squeeze to see how interested I was.

I was curious enough about what he wanted to not stop it. I was curious about all of it, really. And Luke was the perfect guy to experiment with.

Last year my life revolved around my cousin Jesse. I was his personal assistant and he relied on me to keep him on his new straight and narrow path. He's more like a brother to me than a cousin. Hell, the guy practically raised me after my father died. And since my trust fund went missing and I had no safety net, that was no small thing in my eyes.

But now he's married to Luke's sister, Emma, and Jesse doesn't really need me anymore.

Which is great. This left me free to explore other things.

Like Luke Dumas.

Luke straightens up and eases his body forward between Posie's legs.

She moans about the switch in position. "Don't stop."

"Trust me," I say, grabbing her face and turning it my direction just as Luke slips his cock inside her. "We're just getting started."

Her back arches as Luke fills her up, her mouth open and her eyes closed as he begins grinding his hips. Slowly fucking her.

She closes her eyes and begins to wiggle a little.

I unbutton my pants and slip them down my legs. "Touch me," I tell her. "Jerk me off."

She opens her eyes and doesn't hesitate. Her grip on my cock is firm and confident.

"That's it," I murmur, placing my hand over hers. "Just like that." Our hands pump up and down my shaft. But my eyes wander over to watch Luke's dick slide in and out of her wet pussy. He's leaning forward a little, both hands gripping her firm, round breasts. She has a hot fucking body. Very tiny. But shapely too. Not too skinny either. She's kinda perfect, actually.

Luke drops his head down and begins kissing her neck.

This is a signal for us. When he starts kissing her neck, I start kissing her neck. We do that for a few seconds. Me enjoying the rocking rhythm of the fucking that's happening, Luke getting off on the idea of me watching him with her.

But then, as if on cue, we both migrate our kisses to her mouth. And we're kissing each other.

"Oh, fuck," Posie moans. "Fuck."

It's turning her on, that's for sure.

I grab Luke's hair and grip it tight. I love kissing him. His lips are hard and punishing. And his tongue is demanding and insistent.

Then we are both kissing Posie and she is moaning and writhing as Luke fucks her and I stick my fingers deep in her pussy, right along the hard shaft of Luke's dick.

"Oh, my God." Posie's words are really nothing more than a soft moan. She's going to come. It's quick. But that's OK. It's her first time. And we like to get them excited like this early. It means she'll be up for more. And barring some very unexpected string of events, there *will* be more.

"Come, Posie," I say, encouraging her. "Come on…" Shit. I almost call him Luke. "Come on Andy's dick. He's so curious now. There's no telling what he'll be up for next."

I don't even think Posie is listening to me. She's so wrapped up in being fucked by a six-foot-three Dumas man with a cock as long as her forearm, I could've called him Luke and she probably wouldn't have noticed.

Her body goes stiff for a moment, her pouty lips parted and her eyes closed. I withdraw my hand from her pussy and stick my wet fingers in her mouth. She immediately starts sucking on them. Her lips seal around my knuckles as I push my fingers in and then slide them back out. Luke begins to pound her hard, his hips slapping against her ass and thighs as he holds her legs open in a wide V.

He's got a rhythm going. *Slap. Slap. Slap.*

And Posie says, each and every time, "Fuck. Fuck. *Fuuuuck.*"

I still have a hold of her hand and we're still jerking me off. So I grip her tighter and get that going faster, matching the beat of the slap and the fuck.

She lets out a long, keening scream and it's so fucking erotic chills run through my whole body.

And even though I had no intention of coming this way—and I'm pretty sure Luke didn't either—we do come. Posie's back bucks and her hand grips my cock so tight, I almost fucking die of pleasure. The rush of semen spills out, hitting Luke's shoulder just as he groans and grips her hips tight, pulling his cock out of her pussy and spilling all over her stomach.

There is a long moment when we're all motionless and silent.

And then it's over. Luke and I stand up. She looks confused.

I catch Luke's eye and wink at him. He responds by picking Posie up, throwing her over his shoulder, and taking off towards the stairs that lead to the lower deck where most of the cabins are.

"Wait!" Posie exclaims. "What are we doing?"

I'm following them. So she's looking at me when this comes out. "We're gonna take this downstairs, sweetheart. And do it right. Andy's curiosity hasn't been quenched just yet."

"You—" But she stops. It's ridiculous to even bother.

She knew Luke and I were together when she approached him.

"Shhh," I say, putting a single finger to my lips. "Just go with it, *Posie*."

I stress the word. Because that's not her real name. This bitch is crazy if she doesn't think I do facial recognition background checks using secret contacts on every single person I meet.

My last name is Boston. This is just what we do.

And I know exactly who Posie is and why she's here.

I just don't care.

I think she's sexy and she's putting a lot of effort into this little scheme.

I'm gonna see it through 'til the end.

Downstairs, Luke heads towards the bow where the VIP guest cabin is. It's not as nice as the master—which is sequestered on another part of the yacht—but it's high-end and impressive. Windows on both sides of the curved bow-shaped room. TV behind us as we enter. And while the bed isn't really big enough for the three of us to sleep comfortably, it's definitely big enough to fuck on.

He throws her down on the bed and she squeals. It's a delightful squeal too. And it makes me grin.

I turn to Luke and pull him towards me. Then I point to Posie and say, "Watch closely."

She gasps as we kiss. Luke's hand is immediately wrapped around my cock. Jerking on it just the way I like it.

"Oh, you two are fucking hot," Posie says. She scoots forward on the bed, so she's closer to us, and opens her legs. I'm thinking the whole Andy pretense is over now because she doesn't seem to wonder how we went from curious to full-on 'this is happening' in the span of twenty minutes.

Her hand slips down her stomach, right through the mess of semen Luke just unloaded on her, until it reaches her pussy. She's still very wet from the sex we just had upstairs. She strums herself, biting her lip and moaning as she watches Luke tug on me.

I grab her by the arm and pull. "Get on your knees."

Posie rises to the occasion without comment, falling forward until she's between us.

Luke shoots me a look and grins as he places a hand on the top of her head and guides her mouth down to his thick, hard dick.

Posie absolutely goes for it. She even looks Luke in the eyes as she opens her mouth and places the tip of his head on her tongue.

Well, she's got his attention now. That's for sure.

I press myself forward until my hip is bumping against Luke's. He's still got a hold of my cock and he pushes it towards Posie's face. She opens her mouth as wide as she can, but there's no way two huge cocks are going in there at the same time.

Still, she does her best. She grabs both of us, pushes the length of our cocks together, and gives us a simultaneous hand job.

"Fuck," I mutter. I'm starting to think Posie might be a dirty little whore. Because she suddenly seems to know exactly what to do with two men at once.

That whole thought turns me on.

Every bit of it.

She rubs the tips of our dicks against her lips, her little pink tongue darting out to lick them every few seconds. Then she pops mine into her mouth and sucks.

I close my eyes and moan. Luke leans in and kisses me, his tongue darting around mine, like he's the one licking the tip of my cock.

Posie lets my cock slip out of her mouth and does the same to Luke. He bites my lip, showing *me* his excitement instead of *her*. Then he whispers a message into my mouth. "Let's fuck her."

I push her aside and she falls back against the bed, startled. Luke grabs her by the arm, stands her up, and waits for me to crawl onto the mattress. Then he pushes her down on top of me. I grab her hips, place her over my cock, and slide two fingers down between her legs so I can prime her pussy for entrance.

"Oh, my God." She's starting to understand what we plan on doing.

I hug her, pulling her down onto my chest so her ass is a little bit up in the air. And then I watch Luke look at it with lust as I whisper into her neck, "Ever had two cocks before, Posie?"

She sucks in a breath and holds it, her shoulders bunching up to ward off the chill my words send through her body, then shakes her head.

"Would you like to give it a try tonight?"

She hesitates.

But Luke and I have been here before. Posie isn't our first curious girl.

If you're a girl, and it's your first time in a two-man threesome, you always hesitate.

Luke pushes his hips into her ass and begins to grind. He's a rough man. He likes things hard. But he can be soft when he wants to. And he knows that the only way to get a girl to not only agree to do this with us once, but come back for more, is to be gentle.

So when he drags a fingertip up and down her spine, he's gentle. And her whole body erupts in chills.

I grin. Because this little move works every single time. Without fail. They melt when big, tough Luke Dumas goes soft.

Me too, actually. I like this side of him.

He's a lot softer with me than he is with the girls. And this is why I stick around. So I eat this shit up just as much as Posie does.

"Jesus Christ," she moans, sitting up a little. Just enough to make her large breasts bounce from her heavy breathing. "You guys... you're..."

"Yeah," I say. "His name isn't Andy."

She giggles a little. Which makes her tits bounce even more. And that makes me grab them and bring a nipple up to my mouth.

Luke leans over her. All the way over her, pushing her breasts down onto my chest. Her nipple falls out of my mouth, but that's OK. Because her lips are right there and I like the heavy weight of their bodies on top of me.

Luke's mouth joins the kiss and then three tongues are tangled together.

"Say yes," Luke demands.

And she does.

They always do.

He backs up, pumps his cock a few times as I lift up her hips so my own cock can find her dripping wet entrance, and then I ease her down on me.

She moans and bites my shoulder.

Then Luke is grabbing my balls between her legs. His fingers slip inside her pussy, rubbing along my shaft, getting it all nice and wet before he pushes the head of his cock up against me.

It takes a little while to get her properly ready for two thick, hard, monster cocks, but the moment he's fully inside her—when I can feel his shaft moving alongside mine like we are one—that's why I do this.

This is why I stick around.

I love sharing with Luke.

I love the feeling of both of us being inside the same person.

It's slow at first. We take turns. He pushes in while I ease back to give him room. She can't do anything but moan and cry out with pleasure.

He pulls her hair.
I choke her a little.
And then we fuck her hard.

CHAPTER THREE

POSIE

Ladies, I'm warning you now.

If you keep reading, you'll need to change your panties.

Twice.

One for each of the rock-hard men I'm fucking at the moment.

That's how I'll start the article.

Well. Probably not. But it's definitely got a hook.

The only problem is... I'm having a hard time concentrating on the details and the entire experience is starting to become a blur.

Zach Boston is underneath me. His huuuuuge cock! Inside me!

His partner—not Andy, obviously—behind me. His also huuuuuuge cock! Inside me!

Their hands are all over my body. Not-Andy is pulling my hair and slapping my ass. While Zach is palming my throat in that sexy, dominant alpha-male way.

It's so... I don't even know how to describe it. Intoxicating? Passionate? Both.

And it's very, *very* clear that everything about this night is coordinated. These two are a team and this is not their first rodeo.

But I don't even care. I am lost in a sea of lust and there's no amount of rational thinking that can pull me back.

Not even after we're done and the new guy is face down on the mattress with his back to me do I give one wild fuck that I'm here for a reason and that reason had nothing to do with letting two men fuck me silly.

The reason I'm here is... Zach Boston.

Everyone knows who he is.

Oh, sure. Jesse Boston is the spotlight hog in that family. But Zach is the baby prince. The one I grew up lusting over. He might as well be a real member of the royal family, that's how much gossip time I've spent on him.

But it wasn't public shaming like the press always did with his cousin-brother, Jesse Boston.

And it wasn't some boring business report like they did with his middle cousin, Joey Boston.

And it wasn't some wild accusation of underworld crime deeds like it was with his oldest cousin, Johnny Boston.

No. Zach Boston doesn't even know he's famous. He has no idea that I've been running a secret, underground fan group for him for almost a decade.

Yes. A *decade*.

I've been fantasizing about this moment since I was thirteen.

Well. Not this exact moment. And guy number two never made an appearance. But the dancing, the yacht, the champagne! OMG. This is the best night of my life and when the fan group finally hears about this, they will go in-*sane*. As of this afternoon we have thousands and thousands of members who are counting on me to bring it home.

Of course, they're gonna have to wait to hear about this until my article publishes.

In the beginning it was all pretty innocent. Some fun memes as I perfected my mad Photoshopping skills. Some putting myself in his pictures to make us look like a couple, some innocent fake-wedding videos, and some stalking, of course.

But it was just fun. It didn't get serious until the day six months ago when I was just minding my own beeswax waitressing in a dead-end diner at a dead-end

Kansas airstrip in the middle of nowhere when Buzz Hollywood came calling.

They want a story.

They tracked me down via the fan group and offered me this sweet gig as Zach Boston's full-time stalker.

They need a giant, front-page, world-rocking story. And they want me to get it for them.

And come on, OK? No girl in her right mind is gonna turn that offer down. I mean, they are funding me, for fuck's sake. I have an expense account. I have travel provisions, and an Uber discount code, and something called a per diem meal allowance.

I am *legit*.

And not only that—look at where I'm at! In the belly of a beautiful yacht, with Zach Boston spooning me! He *spoons*, bitches.

Oh. My. God. I almost can't stop snickering.

"Shhh," he moans, leaning into my neck. "Be good, now, Pose. Go to sleep. We can figure it out in the AM, babe."

I didn't even say anything.

It's like... he can *sense* me. My deepest, inner emotions. Like we're soul mates.

I snicker again.

"Stop it, Posie. We're tired. Just sleep."

I sigh, completely content.

I mean, was I worried that their dirty plan might be too much?

Yes. Yes, I was.

Literally quite scared, actually. But... wow. Sometimes you gotta push through the fear and just grab that bull by the horns and go for it.

I am so glad I went for it.

"Posie?" Zach's whisper has a stern edge to it.

"Hmm?"

"If you don't stop thinking so loud, I'm gonna kick you out. Because Luke is a light sleeper and right now, he's wondering why you're still here."

Fuck.

"But if you relax, and go very still, and be good, he's gonna drift off and forget about you. And that means I get you all to myself until morning."

Panty change, ladies! He's a romantic too!

I'm just about to squeal about that when he bites my ear. "Understand?"

I nod, but hold in my excitement by pressing my lips together. I don't need that stupid Luke messing things up for me now.

I'm in.

I. Am. In. And I'm gonna write the best fucking gossip story about Zach Boston and his lover. The whole world will be talking about me!

Well. Everyone will be talking about them, not me. But my name will be on the byline. And even though I'm already the queen of Zach's fan club, I'll be like… a legend in there when this is all said and done.

A legend.

And bonus perks of being a star gossip reporter— I get spooned by Zach Boston.

And wow. That's really good stuff. I have to admit, he's the real deal. I could fall for Zach Boston.

I was super obsessed with him back in my early teens, but it did waver as the years went on. Mostly because Zach has always been an enigma. Always playing last fiddle to the other Boston brothers. And then he just kinda disappeared for a while. So did Jesse.

Of course, I now know that Jesse was getting clean and Zach was helping him. Which I find adorable, by the way.

Zach Boston. You are so perfect.

I sigh again, then catch myself and hold my breath. Waiting to see if I'll be chastised.

No. But Zach's arms wrap a little tighter around me, his hand absently playing with my breast.

He's snuggling me.

I'm being snuggled by Zach Boston.

I bite my lip and stifle all my girlish giggles.

This is a dream come true.

I'm going to give Buzz Hollywood the best front-page gossip story about the real Baby Boston and from there, my whole life takes off!

I envision my own yacht one day. Maybe even bigger than this one. I envision a house in Malibu, a pied-à-terre on the Upper East Side, and maybe a little time-share on one of the private islands here in the Caribbean.

Time share? Who am I kidding? I'll buy the whole island!

I stifle another giggle.

Yep. Things are definitely looking up.

Zach Boston is going to be the best thing that ever happened to me.

I wake feeling disoriented. And when I realize we're having an earthquake, I sit up and look around.

It takes me several moments to recognize the bedroom on the yacht, then rationalize the movement I felt wasn't an earthquake, but that we're moving on the water. Fast.

There are windows on both sides of the bed. Long, dark, tinted windows that span the lower portion of the front of the yacht. And the waves are crashing against them.

From my position, I'm going backwards, and I suddenly get seasick and have to turn around real fast to hold down the urge to hurl.

Where are we going?

Did they kidnap me?

Holy. Fuck. I really hope they're kidnapping me. That would definitely spruce up this article. Because I can't really detail the kinky sex, right? I mean, it doesn't have to be family-friendly but it can't be porn.

I rub my hands together. OK. That's the mission today. Get more on them. *Them*, not me *and* them. Just them.

I sigh and picture what my article might look like online. The big Buzz Hollywood banner over the top of the page. Then a very artsy, trendy black and white photo that says 'mystery' all over it. Then, of course, a catchy headline. You gotta have a catchy headline.

I pause to think one up on the fly. Something like… *Bad Boy Cousin's Secret Life with Big Sexy Luke.*

I did a little research on him—I know his name, at least. Luke Dumas. And how he fits into the big picture. Sister of Jesse's Boston's new wife. So he's Zach's what? Cousin-in-law?

Wow. That's definitely dirty. I might need to work that into the title.

But the way I see it, Luke Dumas is just there. Right? He's nice-looking. Very handsome, actually.

And he's one of those adventure types. He owns the Dumas Water Adventures business. Jet skiing. Waterskiing. That parachuting skiing shit, whatever it's called. Things like that.

So I figure Luke is just convenient. He and Zach met because of the wedding. Maybe. No, there was probably an incident before that. Something I don't know about, but definitely need to look into. Because I need to chronicle this side of Zach Boston. His private side. Not the side with his cousin Jesse. I want something much deeper than that.

I want soul-searching.

Headline: *How Zach Boston Rose from the Shadows to Become the Sexiest Man Alive.*

That's a keeper.

He's up there with all the sexiest men. So that headline isn't just a fantasy.

Nothing about what I'm doing these days is just a fantasy. It's all real. I'm actually getting paid to be my crazy self.

I sigh and get up, looking around for my clothes. "Hmm." I hum to myself. "Where are my clothes?"

My outfit barely qualified as clothes. But it did the trick. Got Luke's attention. The minute I saw Zach walk into the club with him I knew he'd be a problem. But my plan worked perfectly.

Clothes? Are you here?

Oh. Now I remember. They undressed me upstairs last night.

I have to bite my fist to stop the squeal that really wants to burst out of me.

I take a moment to pull myself together. I need to be professional. This is my chance. My big moment. And, if I play my cards right, I can write the gossip story of the century and hook Zach Boston while I'm at it. Then, this time next year, I will write an article for Buzz Hollywood about us.

Our wedding.

Headline: *Genius Gossip Reporter Posie Payseur Weds Sexiest Man Alive Zach Boston.*

I want to faint, that's how amazing my life is right now.

Hmm. Maybe I will use a different name for the byline? I could start a new subplot about my mysterious self. Readers would be all... *Hmm. Who is this new Buzz Hollywood reporter we've never heard of documenting Posie's wedding to the Sexiest Man Alive?* (In flowing, Pulitzer-winning prose, I might add.)

I'll have to think on that.

I fan myself and suck in a deep breath as I go out into the hallway. I can hear the rattling of kitchen things as I ascend the steep stairs naked. And I really hope there's no one else on board except the hot men, because appearing in front of strangers naked would be awkward.

The stairs curve up and when I reach the top, I'm facing the dining room. Who knew boats had dining rooms?

"There she is."

I whirl around and find Zach standing in the entrance to the kitchen, also naked. He's seriously my soul mate.

"Looking for your clothes?"

"Yeah." I sigh. "Sure."

"They're over there." He nods his head towards the living room on the other side of the dining room. Then he flips an egg in the skillet on the stove. "You want eggs? I'm making everyone eggs."

I nod, still sighing as I look him over. He's so hot.

"Does it bother you?"

"What?" I ask.

"That I'm naked? I'm kind of a nudist when I can get away with it. And we'll be back in Key West in twenty minutes, so I'll have to put clothes on then. Trying to make the most of my freedom until that happens."

"Uh-huh." I nod my head.

"But you can put yours on." He nods in the direction of my clothes.

I suck in a deep breath and walk over to him. "When in Rome, Zach. When in Rome."

He smacks my ass with the spatula. Hard. And I skip ahead a step and squeal.

"I like you, Posie."

"You do?" Now I really am going to faint.

He grins at me. That grin. Oh. My God. I see that grin in my dreams. And now he's aiming it at me.

Last weekend we had fun in an alley. Which was why I wasn't gonna let him off the hook last night. Alley sex is fine for a one-time thing. But on date two, no. I need a mattress.

And boy, did he overdeliver or what? This yacht is amazing.

"Luke's up on the flybridge." Zach's attention is back on the food, but he points his spatula to the ceiling. "Heading back to the marina. We've got a party of ten today. So…" He shrugs.

I don't know what that means. I don't even care.

I'm naked. Standing less than a foot away from Zach Boston. Who is also naked. And who fucked me last night. With his partner. Which worked out pretty well.

And he spooned me last night.

There are so many Buzz Hollywood gossip stories in my future.

I'm smiling super big when he glances down at me. "You look happy."

I sigh. "I really am."

"So you're not… upset?"

I furrow my brow and frown. "About?"

"We played you, Posie. Last night? Andy? Ringing any bells?"

"Well." I twist a long strand of pink hair and shrug. "Actually, I played you. It was my idea. You guys just went along."

"Really?" He laughs. And God, his laugh is super-deep and sexy. He clicks his tongue. "Well, you've got a dirty fucking imagination, Pose. I really"—he pauses to look me in the eyes—"*really* like that about you."

"You do?" I hope I don't sound too excited. But this is great. He likes me. He really likes me.

Or. Wait. He likes my dirty imagination.

Hm. That's not quite the same, is it?

"So what are your plans for today?"

I shrug and act all demure and shy. "Oh, I don't know. I was hoping we could… you know. Do it again." I waggle my eyebrows at him.

"Yeah?"

"Oh, hell yeah. Right now, if you want."

"Luke's driving. So raincheck."

Luke. I don't need Luke. Zach is the one who counts.

"And we've got the party of ten today. So…"

"I'm sorry. What is that? Party of ten?"

"We've just added the charter thing to the business. Hence, the amazing yacht. And Luke and I have to scoot a party of ten out to a pop-up party and hang out until they're ready to leave."

Luke and I. Hm. He clearly sees Luke as a partner. Interesting. I might have to plot a way to get rid of Luke. He's not really part of my Big Plan.

"Where do you live?" Zach asks. "You never told me last weekend."

"Me? Oh. Um. Well, I'm just visiting. So. Hotel."

"Back in Miami?"

"No, actually. On Key West."

"Really?"

"Yep. Near Mallory Square." What is that look he's shooting me? Suspicion?

"What do you do for a living?"

"I'm a writer."

"A writer. Cool. What do you write?"

"Words."

He laughs, then lifts the eggs up with his spatula and sets them down on a plate that has four pieces of buttered toast on it. "Words, huh?" Then he picks up the plate and walks out of the kitchen and crosses the full length of the yacht. He shoots me a wink, then turns and starts climbing the outside stairs, disappearing from view.

I scurry outside and climb the stairs as well. But I don't go out on the upper deck—just hang back and watch as Zach takes the plate over to Luke.

He puts it on the console next to him and then leans down and kisses Luke right on the mouth.

It's hot. I'm not gonna deny that. Especially when Zach is still naked and his nearly hard dick is swinging between his legs.

But it's even hotter when Zach's eyes find mine.

Like he knew I would follow him and watch.

Like he enjoys the thought of a voyeur.

They pull apart and talk for a few seconds, saying things I can't hear over the sound of the engines, and wind, and waves.

I back down the stairs and lean against the door frame between the living room and the back deck. My eyes lock on Zach's body as he comes back down.

He stops in front of me and grins again. "Looking for a quickie?" His eyes track down my body very slowly, lingering for a moment before coming back up.

I shrug, playing it off. "I thought Luke was busy driving the boat."

I say this not because I want Luke to join us. I say it because he's made it clear that they are a team. And even though I plan on breaking this team up, I know better than to try that on day one.

Zach erases the distance between us in a heartbeat, his hands on my breasts as his hips grind against my stomach. "We're five minutes away from the marina. Do you want a quickie or not?"

I nod. "Hell fucking yeah, I do."

He picks me up, sets me down on a side table that might be hiding a grill inside, and opens my legs. There are other boats around us. And we are not hidden. But if Zach doesn't care, then neither do I.

His cock is fully hard now. And a moment later, he's inside me.

He reaches for my hips, scooting me closer to the edge so he can fuck me and hug me at the same time.

I can't even describe how good he feels. His arms around me. His hips slowly pushing forward and back. Filling me up.

His head sinks down into my neck and he bites my earlobe. Then he whispers, "Better come quick, Posie. Because I'm gonna be done in less than a minute and I don't have time to take care of you. But don't worry. I'm gonna take you home tonight. And then Luke and I will make you squeal all night long."

I picture them. Us. As we were last night. Just as Zach picks me up, walks into the living room, and backs me up against a cabinet.

I can't think straight.

I literally lose track of myself.

But he's right on task. Fucking me harder now. Thrusting upward until I squeal.

"Yeah," he says. "You like that, don't you?"

I do. But I'm not really able to articulate anything right now. I'm thinking about last night, and his promise to take me home with him.

And then his hand slips under my leg and begins playing with my pussy as he continues to fuck me.

That's it.

That's all it takes.

I bury my head in his neck, dig my nails into the muscles of his shoulders, and we moan together as we come.

There are several long seconds of heavy breathing and then Zach starts chuckling.

"What's funny?"

"Nothing. Just… I like you, Posie. Seriously. You're fun. You wanna party with us today?"

"Um… sure. I guess. I'm gonna need clothes though."

"I got you covered." He sets me down and points across the room. "Go down those stairs. That's the master cabin. There's a hall locker and inside there's a few things random girls have left behind. Grab a bikini. That's all you'll need for today. Then we'll go over to

Luke's brother's office and take a quick shower while Luke takes care of the clients and the housekeepers clean up the yacht."

"Take a shower in an office?" I'm confused. And did he just admit that he keeps bathing suits from random girlfriends?

"He's a fisherman. Runs Dumas Deep-Sea Fishing. So he's got the cushy office with the shower."

"Um. OK." I think I should've done more research on these Dumas people. I didn't realize they were all so connected. I mean, up until last winter I didn't even know they existed. Maybe if I had been obsessed with Jesse instead of Zach, I'd have paid more attention to them when he announced his elopement. But I never was impressed by Jesse Boston.

I go downstairs and just like he said, I find a locker in the hallway with a few bathing suits neatly folded inside. There are other random items too. Tank tops, shorts, hair bands, and a floppy hat. Even shoes.

Zach and Luke are players. And they're not even shy about it.

I pick a bikini, put it on, then peek into the master cabin. It's nice. Bigger than the cabin we were in last night. And better appointed. It's clear that they spend a lot of time on this boat because the closets in there are filled with clothes.

I close the door real fast when I hear someone bounding down the steps.

Zach appears, still naked. He points at me. "Mint-green bikini. Nice. Goes well with that hair." He pushes past me, opens the closet, grabs a pair of shorts off a shelf, and pulls them up his legs while simultaneously slipping his feet into a pair of skater shoes. "Let's go."

I hastily grab at my shoes as he drags me through the living room and slip them on as Zach pats Luke on the chest and tells him we'll be right back.

Luke is shooting me squinty eyes.

I don't think he likes me and this might turn into a problem. Because it's very clear that Zach likes Luke. So I smile at him.

Doesn't help.

He definitely doesn't like me. And I'm pretty sure that inviting me along for this party thing going on today wasn't his idea of a good time.

But Zach doesn't seem to notice Luke's squinty eyes, and he drags me past a waiting group of young women hauling cleaning supplies. "We'll be back in thirty," Zach calls out.

He leads me down a dock. We're in a marina. Smaller than the one in Miami, but it's very busy. Even though it feels like it's barely six AM, this place is filled with people. Zach waves to all of them as he passes, chatting as we walk, but not stopping.

At the end of the dock he leads me over to a door that says 'Dumas Deep-Sea Fishing,' which I assume is Luke's brother's place. He uses a key code to unlock it and then swings the door open.

I walk through into the dark. "No one's here."

"No, they already left for the day. The shower's back here." He leads me through another door and into a locker room that has a wall of shower heads on the far end. "No time for playing. Unfortunately." Zach shoots me a grin. "But you're good for a while, right?"

"I'm good?" Did he just ask me if my sexual appetite can hold off for a few hours?

He slips his hands onto my hips and grins down at me. "You know. With the sex. I've gotta run home real fast and grab a few things. Otherwise I'd stay and fuck you in the shower."

"We literally just fucked. Like ten minutes ago."

"So you're good, right?"

I pat his chest. "I'm good. You just go home and do your thing."

"I'd take you home. We have a really nice shower at home. But Luke, ya know?" He juts his chin in the direction of the boat.

"He's not into me, is he?"

"Well… he is. Just… he mostly does this for me. Which I totally appreciate. But I like you, Posie. I really like you and I think you should maybe stick around for a while. Be our little fuck toy. I mean that in the most respectful way possible. We like to play. And we like to fuck. And we like to have a girl do that with us. And I'm thinking you're that girl, Posie."

"Wow." I nod. Because do I care that he's including Luke in this? Does it really matter if Zach is the real prize?

"I offended you."

My eyes shoot up to his. "What? No. Why would you say that?"

"I called you a fuck toy."

"Oh. Right." He did. I *should* be offended. But to be honest, I didn't even hear that part. My mind was firmly stuck on the words *I think you should maybe stick around for a while*. "No. I'm not offended. For reals. I'm so into this game we're playing. It's completely my thing."

He leans down and kisses me. Right on the lips. "I knew I liked you." Then he smacks my ass and walks off. "I'll be back in twenty minutes."

I just stand there. My fingertips press against my lips.

Zach Boston just kissed me goodbye.

God, he's so romantic.

CHAPTER FOUR

LUKE

I'm standing on the flybridge watching the offices down at the other end of the dock, waiting for Zach to come back. It's a hot, clear day and the ocean is fairly calm. I'm actually looking forward to this charter since the group is only booked until six this evening and that means that Zach and I will make it home for Saturday night dinner with the fam.

We've missed them for several weekends in a row and my mother has limits on how many we can skip before she starts trying to publicly shame us.

Emma gets off easy because she lives all the way up in the city and she's always working. But sometimes Jesse drops in just to make sure we don't forget he's one of us now.

Zach does that for me too. If I have a late night but he's around, he'll go have dinner to keep Mom happy.

But I think we'll make it tonight. And I'll just be honest here—I love my mother's cooking. It's taco night. She sends out the menu every Tuesday.

No one skips taco night unless world-ending shit is happening.

A gang of college-age boys appears on the deck, making their way towards me. My clients. They are all very young. Somewhere between eighteen and twenty-one. They are loud, and shirtless, and smiling.

They booked me for a ride out to a pop-up party. This is kind of a new thing over the past few years. At least, that's when I started hearing about them.

They don't happen on islands, but at sandbars. Most of which are pretty transient. Here one day, gone the next. No address. No facilities. No government. Just a set of GPS coordinates.

This is why people like them. Especially college kids.

I don't know who organizes the pop-up parties, but they are definitely organized. They are invitation only, but everything is free if you're one of the invited. The ones I've heard about have a lot of party favors to choose from. Anything from drugs, to alcohol, to sex workers.

"Hey! Are you Luke?"

I nod to the ringleader as he and his entourage stroll up to the slip. "That would be me. And you must be the Snake and Apple Club."

The ringleader looks up at me and grins, but takes a moment to let my words sink in. Not like *he's* thinking about them. More like he wants *me* to think about them.

It's a weird name. I'll give him that. But whatever. Does it look like I give a fuck what the college boys call their little club?

"That's us," he finally says, still grinning as he points to his friends and names them off.

I forget every name but one immediately.

His.

Bart.

Pretty stupid, but also fitting. He's about six feet tall, maybe one-eighty, and he's got dark brown hair and piercing dark eyes that catch your attention immediately and make you want to take a second look at him.

He's well-mannered, athletic, and tanned. But he's soft too. I can just tell. I've seen my share of rich assholes on spring break and that's exactly what he is. I tag him… *Chuck Bass*. Then have to tuck down my amusement and be professional. "Welcome aboard, Bart. Come on up here to the flybridge and we'll settle up the paperwork."

"Sounds good. Where do you want my boys?"

"They can make themselves at home. Bar and fridge are stocked." I don't bother telling him which parts of the yacht are off limits. Those places are all locked up tight.

The boys get excited and disappear into the saloon, while Bart climbs the narrow stairs that lead up to the flybridge. "Whew!" Bart exclaims, taking in the living area, the view, and the helm console. "This is *niiiice*, dude. How much this set you back?"

It's a pretty rude question, but fuck it. "Eight large."

"*Daaaamn*, son. You must be making bank. I might need to get me a piece of the adventure biz."

I smile at him. *Son.* I refuse to roll my eyes. I don't need this money, but Dumas Water Adventures is a friendly establishment. So I'm not gonna make a big deal. He's not the first pretentious, over-privileged rich kid I've had to deal with.

This makes me chuckle.

"What?" Bart asks. "What's funny?"

"Oh. Just thinking about my partner in crime. You remind me of him."

Bart looks around like I've got Zach stuffed under a lounge pad. "Love to meet him. Where is he?"

"He'll be along."

Bart smiles at me. I am so fucking familiar with this smile. It's not Zach. Not specifically. I've just met enough rich assholes in my life to recognize the smugness in that grin. If Chuck Bass were a real person, he would literally be Bart. "Where do I sign?"

"Right. I've got the paperwork over here." I point to the flybridge bar. Bart walks over and takes the paperwork I hand him. He reads it. He reads it far too carefully in my opinion. "It's a standard waiver," I tell him. "In case anyone gets drunk and decides to swim with sharks against my professional advice."

He nods. Then signs without comment. "No problem, *Luke*. I've got my guys on a tight leash. So you don't need to worry about any of that. But it's always good to know our captain has our best interest at heart." He reaches for the black tank that's tucked into the waist of his shorts. But it's not just one shirt, it's several. He tosses me two of them and then tucks the third back into his shorts. "You and your partner will need to put those on when we approach the party. And"—he pulls a folded square of cloth out of his back pocket and hands it to me—"fly this flag."

I take all that crap and look at it.

"It's an invitation-only party. The flag gets us into the cove and it's your choice if you want to wear the shirts, but you gotta show them off to *partake*."

"How's that work?" I ask. "Invitation only? Because most sandbars around here are in public water."

"The islands around the cove are all private." He hands me a slip of paper. And when I glance down at it, I recognize GPS coordinates. "And it's not around here. There *will* be security so just fly the flag, OK, Luke?"

I press my lips together and nod back a smile. "Sure thing, *Bart*."

He grins back. "OK, then. I'll just join my boys below and let you handle the rest."

He leaves the way he came and just as he disappears down the stairs, I hear Zach greet him.

I don't walk over to the edge of the aft deck because I don't like Bart. And the more contact I have with him, the more that dislike is going to manifest. This is an easy job. We don't even really have to entertain these boys. I'm taking them to the pop-up party, hanging around all afternoon, and then they come home with me, or they don't.

That's it. That's the extent of this contract.

No waterskiing today. No jet skis. No parasailing. Hell, they're not even spending the night on the yacht.

So it's in my best interest to just pretend Bart isn't here.

The boys downstairs get loud and my anger with them builds when I recognize the sound of men commenting on a beautiful woman.

Posie.

I'm not sure I like the girl—in fact, I'm pretty sure I *don't* like her. She's good for a night of fun, but beyond that, she's no one to me and I've got a list going of suspicious things about her right now. However. I like the attention these boys are giving her even less.

I force myself to let Zach handle it.

Which he does. Good-naturedly. Because that's the easy-going kind of man he is. And then Posie appears, coming up the stairs to the flybridge. She forces a smile but I can tell she's not thrilled with our clients either.

"Everything OK?" I ask.

She nods, but looks over her shoulder as she walks towards me. "Your *clients*?"

"Don't worry about them. This is an easy job. You can just hang out up here with me if they bother you. Zach will keep them out of the way."

She sighs as she pushes past me, then takes a seat on the L-shaped bench across from the helm and points to her outfit. It's a very revealing mint-green bikini that really contrasts nicely with her long pink hair. "Zach gave me this."

I'm just about to offer her a cover-up from our collection of random girl things down in the master cabin when Zach appears holding such a garment. He walks straight over to Posie and drops it into her lap without comment. He's actually looking at me, not her. "Let's get this day started."

I salute him. Because that was code for, *These boys are assholes.*

The next twenty minutes is mostly just me navigating our way through the marina and out into the channel. Posie stays right where she is, but Zach, ever the charming host, hangs out downstairs with our... guests.

Bart wasn't kidding when he said the pop-up party wasn't local. It's a good four-hour trip and I'm already calculating what time we will need to leave to get home in time for dinner when Posie gets up off the bench she's been lounging on and takes the helm seat to my left. "What's wrong?"

I glance at her. Princess Euphemia. It was a good tag last night, but right now she's no Princess Euphemia. Now she's just Posie. And don't get me wrong, Posie is a very pretty girl. She's got a super-hot little body. Tiny, but curvy at the same time. Big tits. Little waist. Round hips. She's a mini-bombshell. Especially with that unruly, long pink hair.

But there's something off about her. She knows we played her last night, but she doesn't seem to care. And that bothers me. She should at least ask questions about us. *Do you do this all the time? What kind of relationship do you guys have? Why are you letting me come on this trip?*

And my answers would be—*Yes. A casual one that I would like to make more permanent.* And... *Not my call. You are Zach's project.*

Instead I say, "So... how long are you planning on hanging out with us?"

"What do you mean?"

"I mean... it was fun and all. But I hope you're not imagining something more... lasting."

"Hmm."

"That's it? That's all you have to say?"

"Zach and I seem to be getting along pretty well."

"So said the last dozen girls who have taken a day trip with us on a boat."

"Wow. That was rude."

"It's not rude. It's just facts, Posie. And I'm just trying to prepare you for the inevitable end."

She gets up and walks away.

She doesn't go downstairs. It's pretty clear by this time that those boys are all drunk. She stays up on the flybridge. But she sits down on one of the loungers positioned on the aft deck, as far away from me as possible.

And that's where she stays for the rest of the trip.

As we approach the cove where the sandbar is, Zach comes up to fly the flag. Posie helps him and they chat together easily.

What I said *was* rude. And I meant it to be rude. Because you know what? I'm kinda sick of sharing my boyfriend with random girls. The sex is fun. But I like them to go home afterward. I don't want them hanging around our cottage, or coming on boat trips, or interfering with our life.

This is a problem because it's very clear that Zach enjoys having the girls around. He might even use them as a buffer between us.

I don't want to think that, but after a whole year of dating like this, it's getting hard to deny.

The banter and laughter between Zach and Posie as they fly the flag is pissing me off.

Am I jealous?

Let's put it this way—I've asked myself that question dozens of times over the past year since Zach and I started this… thing. It's a relationship for sure. He's been living with me—or actually, that's not true.

He came down to Key West to visit. So he got one of the cottages on our street of vacation rentals. It was next to mine. My whole family lives on the same street on Key West just a few blocks away from the marina. But Zach and I were friendly immediately so I started staying at his cottage. And pretty soon, I had moved in over there and my parents were renting my old place out to tourists.

So technically—and as stupid as this sounds because these cottages all belong to the Dumas family, which is *me*—I moved in with *him*.

I'm staying at *his* place.

I think about that for a moment.

"OK, we're all set." Zach slips into the seat to my left and I snap out of my introspection. "Where the hell are we? It felt like it took forever to get here."

I point at one of the large display screens on the helm. "Well, that's Cuba right there, so. Yeah. We covered some water today." I glance at the clock. It's nearly eleven. "We'll need to leave by three to make it home for dinner."

Zach bumps his shoulder into mine. "Dude. It's taco night. I have this dinner on my calendar. We're not missing taco night." He laughs. And I really like his laugh. "I'll let Bart know what time we gotta bounce. I don't imagine they're gonna need a ride home though. He and his boys were all talking about what happens tonight. Where the hell did these guys hear about us, anyway? They're all from New England."

I like the way he says *us* when he talks about the business. Even though this is my business, we're a team. "They called the dive shop and my dad handed them off to me because we got this new boat."

Zach's hand goes around the back of my neck and then he's leaning in to kiss me on the mouth. It's a hot enough kiss to make me think about getting hard. But he pulls back, kinda fisting my hair, and whispers, "I like the way you say 'we,' Luke Dumas. Like we're a team."

I side-eye him. "We are a team."

He kisses me again. "Fuck, yeah, we are." And then he pulls back and glances over his shoulder at Posie, who is pretending not to watch us. "And now we have her too. She's gonna be some fun, Luke. Trust me. She's about to get… interesting. You'll see."

I doubt that. But I don't say anything. And Zach doesn't stick around for any more discussion about it, so whatever.

I slow the yacht down until we're just floating, then wait as six security guys approach the starboard side on jet skis.

They all appear to be wearing the same black tank top that Bart gave me. The design on the front is a primitive, folksy design in red and cream of a coiled snake, head pointing towards the sky, mouth wide open with fangs penetrating the flesh of a half apple.

I don't recognize the design, but the theme is hard to miss.

Temptation.

Things are about to get interesting all right.

But I highly doubt it will have anything to do with Posie.

CHAPTER FIVE

ZACH

Bart greets the security team by jumping into the water. It's pretty shallow here. Still deep enough for a yacht this size, but you can see the white sandy bottom of the ocean very clearly. Even after all Bart's friends jump in after him and stir the sand all up.

Posie follows me downstairs now that the leering eyes of those college boys are safely fixated on other things, and I wait as the security team leader approaches the bathing platform.

He cuts his engine and floats, so I guess we're gonna have ourselves a little chat. The boys are already clambering onto the backs of the other jet skis, and the ones who aren't are swimming with speed towards the cove entrance.

"Hello," head security guy says. "What's the draft on this monster?"

I glance up, looking for Luke. Because I have no fucking clue what our draft is.

Luke stands on the flybridge and calls out, "About seven feet."

"OK. It's too shallow on this side to be safe all day," security guy says. "So I'm gonna need you to go around to the other side of that island where there's a back entrance to the cove. It's deeper over there." Then he slips his fingers into his vest pocket and pulls out another black flag, reaching up to hand it to me. "Fly this one under your banner and they won't mess with your approach. Drop anchor anywhere you want inside the channel. Not along the outside of the island. Got it?"

I take the new flag and salute. "Loud and clear, boss."

"All right then. Enjoy the festivities." He salutes back, starts his engine, and then scoots off.

I look up at Luke. "Well. This is an elaborate setup for a pop-up sandbar party, don't you think?"

"Yeah." Luke nods. "But it could be fun." And then he relaxes. I know he's not into Posie the way I am. And, to be clear, my fascination with her comes with a lot of conflicts. But she's a hot little number and Luke and I have been going through a weird patch. It's not boring. At all. Everything about Luke is exciting.

It's more like… we're both starting to wonder what comes next.

If nothing else, being around Posie lights the fire up in my opinion. And even though Luke would never admit it, he knows her being here makes things more interesting.

But we're gonna have fun today. That's all I know.

All kinds of sexy, sandbar, pop-up party fun.

And Posie is gonna be a big part of it.

I put the new banner up underneath the other one while Luke slowly guides the yacht around the island. They are just plain black flags. No design on them at all. The top one is large and rectangular. Regular flag shape. But the second one is a pennant.

While I'm up there on top of the flybridge, I carefully stand up and take a look around, trying to see what's really going on here.

The channel between the two islands is nice and wide. And even my amateur eye can spot a cool reef along one side of the larger land mass. It's next to a small waterfall running down the steep face of a cliff. Luke must spot it too, because he eases the yacht that direction. It's deeper than the rest of the channel, and none of the boats here are as big as our yacht, so they are staying closer to the sandbar.

I look over my shoulder and scan the channel to do a quick headcount. There are about three dozen boats here and more motoring in. About ten times the number of people though. Lots of fucking people. All young too. It's like Spring Break, except it's the middle of November.

That gets me thinking.

If these are all college kids, why aren't they in school?

Thanksgiving isn't for two more weeks. And even though it's the weekend, Bart and his crew flew down from New England. Probably Boston. I didn't ask, but they have a Harvard look to them. And that's not really a day trip. You don't fly six hours one way to spend one night in the Caribbean.

That's not even something I would do.

Luke backs the boat in stern first, then sets the anchors the way he likes them. I pinch Posie's ass and make her jump out of the way.

"Hey!" she squeals.

"Sorry. Flippers are in here." I point to the bathing platform transom.

"Oh. We're gonna dive?"

"Fuck, yeah, we're gonna dive." Luke jumps down onto the platform with us. "If we were staying longer, I'd turn this place into a playground. But…" He swipes his hand across his brow. "Looks like these people got it covered."

He's right. There is a large floating platform in the middle of the channel and about half a dozen pontoon boats serving food and alcohol. There's another platform where a bunch of people are stacking wood—presumably for a bonfire tonight. People are kayaking, and diving, and Seabobbing all over the place. There are even dogs here.

This is no pop-up party.

This is an event. And by the looks of it, they have them regularly.

I toss the flippers and masks onto the platform. "Who do you think runs this?"

Luke whips his shirt off, takes in a deep breath as he tosses it up to the cockpit area, and then shrugs. "Dunno. Some rich fuck with more money than he knows what to do with, I guess."

I narrow my eyes at his comment because he's always saying shit like that.

I know I shouldn't take it personally, but I kinda do. Because I'm one of those rich fucks. Maybe I don't have money the way my cousins do, but I was brought up in the same house. And it's not like Luke is poor, either. He's got no room to talk. This is an eight-million-dollar yacht. And yeah, he didn't buy it cash or anything, but still. I couldn't qualify for a one-million-dollar loan with a bank, let alone eight.

So what if he's a self-made man? He's one of us now.

"How do I look?"

I glance at Posie and chuckle. She's got her mask on and her voice is all nasally from being pinched. "Hot, baby. You look fucking hot."

This makes her blush.

And dammit, I know she's a sneaky little liar, but I don't really care. She's damn cute. And she's fun. Not to mention sexy.

I glance over at Luke, who is sitting on the platform adjusting his flippers with his back to me. At least she's not always bitching about people with money.

"Have you ever snorkeled, Pose?"

She shakes her head. "Nope. But I'm up for just about anything." She pulls her mask down so it's hanging around her neck. "And I'm a quick learner. Just give me bullet point tips and I'll be a champion snorkeler in ten minutes."

Luke snorts. "Whatever. It's not that simple and you're not that smart, honey."

Posie is taken aback at the mean undertone of his words.

"Luke," I say.

"What?" He looks over his shoulder at me.

I side-eye him. "Are you in a bad mood today?"

"No, why?"

"Because you're kinda being a dick to Posie."

His eyes dart to hers. They narrow, then quickly relax. "I'm joking. You know I'm joking, right?"

Posie shrugs. Manages a smile. "Sure."

But he's not joking. She might not know it for sure, but she feels it. And anyway, I do know it for sure because I've been dating this dude for the better part of a year.

I shoot him a look that says, *Be nice.* And he just shrugs and slips into the water.

"He doesn't like me," Posie says, once he's underwater.

"Posie," I say, pausing to look at her. "*I* like you. That's all that matters."

She blushes again. I like that blush. And I actually do like her. It's not a lie. I just… have her here on less than honorable intentions.

I scoot down to the platform and put my feet in. "OK, here are your bullet point tips. Ready?"

She nods and sits down next to me. "Hit me."

"One. Your mask has to fit right." I pull it up onto her face and make sure the seal is perfect. "Two." I grip her shoulder and squeeze it gently. "Relax. Take nice, even deep breaths. Three. Don't kick your feet around too hard. Let your fins do the work. Four. Stay on the surface and you'll never have to hold your breath. And five. If you do dive, stay close to Luke, Posie. He's been diving since he could walk. He would not let you get hurt. I promise. He's not that kind of guy."

She nods. "OK. And thanks. I know I'm pretty much a complete stranger to you guys and me being here wasn't in the plan. But I'm glad I am." She pauses to look at me. "Really. I'm glad I am."

"Come on," I say. "Let's go see some cool shit."

I take her hand and we slide off the platform and into the blue-green water of the channel.

I'm not an expert diver. In fact, before Luke and I got together I could count on one hand the number of times I've been diving. Jesse made me get SCUBA-certified because he was pretty much in charge of my life as a teen and we spent a lot of time on his racing yachts. But it was his thing, not mine.

Now though, it feels like *our* thing. Me and Luke dive. We dive a lot, actually. Once or twice a week, at least.

I go back up to the surface with Posie and flank her as we swim over towards the waterfall with our faces in the water. Luke is already down near the sandy bottom, poking his head around various things on the small reef that he finds interesting.

He looks in my direction, then pushes off the bottom and shoots up to the surface.

I poke my head up and tread water while Posie continues swimming. "What's up?" I ask Luke once he surfaces.

Luke is smiling as he pulls his mask down. Then he points to the cliff. "Wanna jump off?"

I laugh. "Not especially."

"Why not?" He swims over to me, still grinning. "It's not that high." He studies the cliff wall, his eyes tracking all the way up to the flat ledge at the top where a thin sheet of water spills over the side. It's not a rushing waterfall, by any means. But it's legit.

Luke is into adventure. I like that about him. But do I really want to climb up a slippery rock cliff and throw myself off it?

Uh. No. Doesn't sound particularly fun.

I'm about to tell him that when a Seabob comes bursting up from the water and Bart shoots past us, splashing water in Luke's direction. Bart turns the underwater scooter around and slowly glides up to me with a wide grin that tells me a whole lot about what just happened here. "Hey, boys," he says, positioning himself between Luke and me. "Enjoying the party?"

Luke is immediately tense. He's not even hiding his dislike for good old Bart here. So I take over. "Sure.

It's pretty great. We were just discussing jumping off the waterfall."

Bart looks over at Luke, who is treading water and forcing himself to be silent. "Sorry, bud. No cliff-jumping for the hired help here. Insurance reasons. You understand, right?"

Jesus Christ. I shake my head at Luke, begging him not to make too much of a scene. *Bart is baiting you. Do not bite.*

Luke casually looks up the side of the cliff, then over to Posie, who still has her face in the water, oblivious to the potential confrontation over here with the men.

"That your girl, Luke?" Bart nods his head to Posie.

"She's ours," I say, taking over.

Bart smiles big. "Nice. Well, what about you, Zach?"

"What about me?"

"You wanna meet the frens? Expand your social circle a little?"

"Sure," I say, then look over at Luke. "Let's get our Seabobs out and go join the party."

"We only have two," Luke deadpans. "What about…?" He nods his head to Posie.

"You can ride with me, Zach." Then Bart whirls around, showing me his back. "Grab on."

Oh, fuck. Like… why? Why me? Why is this dude messing with us like this? He's fucking flirting with me in front of Luke. On purpose.

"Yeah," Luke says without even blinking. "That's a good idea. You go with him, Zach. I'll grab Posie. We'll meet you over there in a few." He nods his head towards the floating platform in the deeper water where people are gathered.

He's pissed. I can tell.

He was pissed about Posie earlier and this Bart stuff is about to send him over the edge.

But I'm not about to have a fight with my boyfriend *here*.

Fuck that.

So I grab hold of Bart's shoulders and before anyone else can say another word, we take off towards the party.

CHAPTER SIX

POSIE

I'm studying the reef below me, trying my best to ignore what's happening on the other side of the little waterfall lagoon with Luke, Zach, and Bart, but at the same time desperately trying to hear what they are all saying.

Bart is definitely coming on to Zach. And Luke is pissed.

Hell, I'm pissed. Zach is mine. He's the only reason I'm here. I can deal with Luke. He could turn out to be a big, ol' sexy bonus, even if he is kind of moody and distant.

But this Bart guy?

No. He was not part of my plan.

Suddenly Luke is below me in the water, his dark hair waving around his face, his finger pointing up.

I stop snorkeling and pull the mouthpiece out, then slide my mask up my face so I can see him better when he pops up in front of me. "What's up?" I ask.

"We're going to the party." Luke nods his head in that direction. "Zach is already over there. With *Bart*." He adds a little extra malice to the name Bart.

Luke's eyes track over to the floating party platform where dozens of people are crowding. We both watch as Zach and Bart come to a stop in the shallows of the sandbar. Bart leaves his Seabob in the water and pushes Zach, making him stumble and laugh as they both wade their way towards the platform.

"Hmm," I hum. Then I look at Luke. "Are we going to allow this?"

"We?"

"Hey, I wouldn't be here if he didn't want me here. And at least I'm on your side. Bart there, he's just some random rich kid looking to get laid by the first shiny thing that catches his eye. Which would be Zach."

Luke frowns at me. "You're no different, Posie. Zach and I are partners. You're his version of shiny. He's with me."

"He's with *Bart*, Luke. And like I said, Zach wants me here. So looks like you need a little help in holding onto your man. I'm offering to be that help."

Wow. I'm not really sure where that came from, but I like it. It's gonna be a good quote for the article. One of those big ones in the middle of a wall of text. The kind with ginormous quotation marks framing it.

Anyway. Back to reality.

"But," I continue, "I can just as easily stay on the yacht until we're ready to go and you can handle things all by yourself, if that's what you prefer."

He glances over at Zach again. And Zach is laughing and smiling, like he's completely unaware of the drama going on over here.

"I like him, Luke."

Luke's attention snaps back to me. "So? You're no one, Posie. Just another girl we picked up in a club. Do you have any idea how many times we've done that? Dozens."

"But I'm still here."

"For today. Trust me, after we drop you off at home tonight, he'll forget all about you and just start hunting down another girl."

"To spice things up? Is he bored with you, Luke? Is this how you keep him?"

I'm pissing this guy off. It's probably a bad idea. I'm hours away from the mainland, he's like six-foot-three, almost twice my weight, and he's my ride home. So it's a very bad idea to pick this fight with him.

But he needs an ally. And I'm his only option. If I'm gonna position myself as a permanent fixture in Zach Boston's life I need to jump the hurdle called Luke first.

And this stupid Bart guy is the perfect way to unite us so I can make that leap.

"You have no idea what you're talking about. Zach and I have a lot more between us than sex. Our families are connected. Our business is connected. There are bigger things on our minds than who we're sleeping with. This is just Zach being Zach. It's just a game. But trust me, when it comes time to go home, he leaves with me, Posie." He pauses. Then points his finger at me. "And I'm on to you."

I scoff. "Whatever."

"I see you, Posie. I have seen plenty of girls like you over the past year. You all think Zach is a prize to win. And don't bother playing dumb. You know his last name is Boston. That's the only reason you're here, isn't it?"

For a moment I panic, thinking Luke knows who I really am. He knows about the contract I have with Buzz Hollywood. He's figured it out.

But then he says, "You're looking for status. Money. You want to party with him, and get your picture taken, and use him to get something better. Climb some ladder you don't have access to. Discard your boring, pathetic life and reinvent yourself a new one."

"Wow," I say. "You get mean when you're jealous."

"I'm not jealous."

"Stop it, OK? I'm not here to steal him from you. I just like him. And I like you too. Enough to share. And isn't that what he and you do? Hm? Share?"

Luke doesn't react. Like at all. So I keep going.

"If we team up, then Bart doesn't have a chance. Zach likes you, Zach likes me. He has a life with you—as you pointed out—and I'm the new flavor of the week. One he's barely had a chance to taste. He wants us. We don't need to fight over this. Yet."

I pause to see if he'll say anything about that. But he holds his words in, so I finish.

"We need to get him out of here. Because Bart over there?" I nod my head towards the crowd. "He lives in Zach's world. Not ours. He's one of the ruling class. You don't need to talk to him to figure that out. He's dripping with privilege. Just like Zach. They are of the same kind. And maybe Zach does love you, but this is his world, Luke. He's not Zach, one half of your yacht charter service. He's a Boston. He *belongs here* in this exclusive, secret pop-up party for the rich and bored—and we *don't*."

Luke lets out a long breath. Like he was holding it in while I talked. He's gently waving his arms in the water. And I can feel the slight current his flippers make as we tread water in the middle of this beautiful waterfall cove.

He knows I'm right. Luke has a precarious hold on Zach Boston for now. But for how much longer?

They don't have much time left by the looks of it. I'm no expert in relationships but I've been in enough of them to see the signs of one winding down. The bond between Luke and Zach is based on a lot of things—but it's not love.

Mutual attraction, sure.

Family ties and all that business junk. Fine.

But that's not eternal partner type stuff.

So all I have to do is hang around long enough to watch it break and then be there when Zach needs somewhere to turn.

Wow. I'm sorta ruthless when I'm focused.

Who knew?

I feel like this whole experience is just the challenge I needed to level up in the maturity department.

Luke is still thinking about my brilliant monologue. But I already know I've won him over. We team up to get Zach away from Bart—because that part of my speech wasn't a lie. Bart is... what? Wooing him? It's possible.

I didn't come this far and get this close to the real Baby Boston just to lose him to some stuck-up rich jerk called *Bart*.

"So what do you say?" I extend my hand up out of the water, offering it to Luke. "Wanna be on the same team?" I shoot him a wicked, devilish grin.

He does not reciprocate the smile, but he does shake my hand. "Fine. But only for today. Once we get back on the yacht, deal is over."

I could say a lot of things back to that remark. But I know when I'm ahead. And that's the best time to quit. "Fine with me."

"I don't want to take the Seabobs over there. Maybe these rich punks are fine with just throwing their fifteen-thousand-dollar toys into the water as they party, but I'm not. So we're gonna leave all the gear here and swim over."

"You're the boss."

It's not that far of a swim, but it's definitely a decent bit of distance. So even though I have already agreed, I eyeball the open water between here and there. I don't know how you calculate distance on the water. But I have an idea that it's deceiving.

Luke sighs. "What's the problem?"

"How far is it? In like... distance I can relate to?"

He looks over at the party, does some kind of quick calculation in his head. "Maybe... two hundred yards."

"Two football fields?"

"Surely you can swim two hundred yards."

"Don't judge me. That's far."

He actually laughs. "You're not gonna drown, Posie. There's a sandbar. We can probably walk the last hundred."

"Oh." I nod. "OK. I'll be fine."

He sighs, already tired of me and we just got here. He takes my gear, locks everything up, and then jumps back into the water. "Ready?"

I nod and take off.

We're not even halfway to the sandbar when I noticeably start lagging behind Luke. He doesn't look back until I'm really behind, and then he treads water, waiting for me.

"Do you need a lift?" He asks the question in a way that leaves no doubt in my mind that he's not really interested in helping me out.

So I say, "Yeah. Thanks," and grab onto his shoulders with a grin.

He huffs about this and says, "Don't grab my shoulders. I need them to swim. Hold on to my chest."

I don't feel bad that he's piggybacking me the last leg of this journey. He's the one who offered. Besides, Luke might be a jerk, but he's all muscly and hard. And sure, his personality is lacking, but he was pretty hot in bed last night. So being this close to him gets me thinking about that. And before I know it, he's standing up on the sandbar, shrugging me off his back.

I drop into the soft sand and take a look around. The music is loud over here. An upbeat thump with no singing. Just a club mix. And there are a lot more people than there were the last time I checked. Maybe… over a hundred now.

All of them are tan, and beautiful, and happy.

Luke points to Zach, who is on the beach with Bart. They are standing in front of a tiki hut holding drinks and laughing at something a large group finds funny. "There he is." Luke takes off, wading through the shallow water that only comes up to his waist. But I'm a good foot shorter than him, so it's up to my shoulders and he leaves me behind.

Someone suddenly grabs my arm and turns me around. "Lyssa?"

I stare at the man. Boy. Not sure. Like Bart, he is something in between. Cropped blond hair, blue eyes, and perfect athletic body.

"Sorry." He laughs. "I thought you were Lyssa."

"Nope," I say, trying to tug my arm out of his grip.

But he holds on to it. "Well, that's OK. You'll do. You wanna party with me?"

"Uhh… No."

"Wut?" He chuckles like he probably didn't hear me right.

"No. I'm with—" I look around for Luke, but the crowd is dense in my immediate vicinity. In fact, the crowd is all men in my immediate vicinity. And they are all looking at me, and wading towards me, and—

Then they're flying off in two directions as Luke bursts through, pushing them aside. He offers me his hand from a distance that is too far away to actually take it. "Come on, Posie. We're going this way."

"Posie," the first guy says. "That's a hot little name. You're a hot little number, Posie. I think I'm gonna keep you."

Luke is suddenly removing the jerk's hand from my arm. "You will not be keeping her." He says this simply and without any malice. Just the facts. Luke is a huge man. Especially compared to these college boys. He towers over this one by several inches. "She belongs to me."

It's convincing. I mean, if I were that guy I'd be convinced. But he's not convinced. "She's here, right?"

"What?" Luke scowls at him.

"So she belongs to no one. She's *meat*."

"What?" This time it's me saying that. Then I look around at all the women. Each one is surrounded by several men. Some of them are topless. Hell, some of them are completely naked. Hmmm. It's entirely possible that they are all… hired help.

"I think you've got the wrong idea." I say it politely. Sweetly. Just letting him know this is all just a little misunderstanding.

"No," he says. "I don't." And he reaches for me again.

Luke pushes him. Just one hand. One palm flat on his chest. And this kid goes reeling over backwards into the water.

And that's when all hell breaks loose.

CHAPTER SEVEN

LUKE

I can honestly say I've never kicked anyone's ass in the ocean before, but hell, there's a first time for everything.

I don't know who this rich, dickface asshole thinks he is, and I don't care that Posie isn't really mine and I barely like the girl—no one acts the way this douche did without learning a lesson before he goes on his way.

My fist crashes against his jaw in a knockout punch I learned way back in my early days when bare-knuckle boxing in the back alley behind the dive shop was a regular thing for me and my brothers.

Dickface goes stumbling backwards into the water. The world goes silent. Like someone pushed the mute button. And time goes slow for a moment as little tendrils of scarlet red seep into the sea. I feel like I'm in the middle of an artist's interpretation of violence. Something very cinematic. Something very... *Fight Club*.

But then the real world rushes back and everything speeds up and becomes loud.

Posie is splashing around in the water behind me. I think I might've knocked her over in the tussle. And then five guys come at me.

Some quick deduction tells me this is the Dickface crew.

But I grew up with Alonzo and Tony Dumas. I'm the baby of the family. I learned to take a punch long before I learned how to dodge one. And if these guys think I need a fair fight to win, they didn't grow up with the brothers I did.

I trip the closest one with a foot sweep under the water. He goes sideways, arms flailing like an idiot. I get the next one with a left-handed uppercut to the jaw. He goes backwards, heels up in the air as he sinks under. I almost take a second to laugh.

But the next one has connected with my face and I turn in that direction, get him with a left hook to the side of his jaw, and then use my right elbow to get the guy coming up behind me.

In a handful of seconds, I've taken out four of the five. The last one is glancing around like he can't believe this is happening and he's got one of those privileged, incredulous looks on his face. Then his blazing blue eyes meet mine and I shake my head in a warning just as the first guy surfaces from the water, sputtering and spitting out blood.

"You don't want any of this," I tell the last guy standing. "Trust me."

But he's either stupid or a much better fighter than I take him for, because he comes at me. It only takes another moment to decide the answer to my question is... stupid. Then I bow my head like a bull and ram him in the stomach while he's mid-swing in a punch that never had a chance in hell of connecting with my face.

We both go under. But I'm pretty good underwater. So that's not enough to stop the fight. I grab him by the hair to keep him steady, and then clock him a good one right in the eye just to make sure he comes out of this scuffle with a souvenir.

But I only get in the one punch.

All the other dudes—or maybe it's new dudes—are back in action. Pulling on me. Kicking me. I come up for air, gulp it down, then hold my breath as they force me back under.

Kicks. Punches. Knees. Elbows.

But the funny thing is, it all feels so different underwater.

Still, that breath will only hold me so long and I'm spewing out bubbles—maybe starting to worry a bit—when I'm suddenly pulled out of the water.

I shake my head to get the hair out of my eyes as I inhale deeply and then realize Zach is pulling me through the water and out of the circle of angry assholes.

Bart is running interference. And this pisses me off so bad, I try to go back in and finish those stupid little rich fucks off.

Zach tugs me hard. "What the hell are you doing?"

"Me?" I scoff. "I didn't start that shit. That one right there was trying to take Posie. Said she was *meat*."

"What?" Zach looks over at his new BFF Bart.

Bart holds up his hands in surrender. "Sorry." And that douchebag is actually laughing. "I should've explained."

"Explained what, exactly?" I ask. "That all the women here are toys?"

Bart laughs harder. "Jesus Christ, Luke." He elbows Zach, a gesture that implies they are both friends and in on the joke. And they are neither. "He's kind of uptight, right? How about we get him a drink?"

"Fuck that!" Original Dickface says. "Do you see my lip? I'm bleeding! I have a modeling gig on Monday."

I roll my eyes and groan. "A modeling gig? You fucking pussy. Get the hell out of my face before I—"

"Luke!" Zach says. "That's enough!"

"That's enough? He called Posie *meat*. He was trying to take her away against her will."

"Whoa, whoa, whoa!" Another guy—also of the rich asshole variety—wades up to us in the water. "What's the problem over here?"

"I'm handling it, Chandler," Bart says.

Chandler. It figures.

Chandler hooks an arm around Bart's neck and shakes him up a little. All good-naturedly. He laughs as he does this. "No offense, little brother, but I think you could use some backup." Then Chandler directs his gaze at me. "What's the problem, big guy? We got an issue here?" He squints his eyes at me. "Do I know you?"

"No," Bart says. "They own the yacht over there. That was our ride in."

Chandler takes a moment to eyeball my boat. Then he whistles. "*Daaaamn*, son. That's one nice ride you got there."

Again with the 'son' thing. Weird. And fucking stupid. I'm waiting for him to ask how much it set me back, but he turns to the Dickface crew and says, "Take off, Niles. There are plenty of women to go around. You don't need to get greedy with this man's"—he eyes Posie with a little too much interest—"lovely better half." Then he shoots me a wink.

Zach elbows me, cautioning me not to roll my eyes and make things worse.

Niles. For fuck's sake. Don't these people believe in normal names? He glares at me, his lip still bleeding. But the blood is diluted from the water, so it's just a trickle of pink down one side of his chin.

He looks like a fuckin' idiot.

Zach leans in and whispers, "Stop snarling at him."

I turn away and start walking through the water because I'm still angry that the fight got broken up.

It's not exactly Posie that set me off. But it's not exactly not Posie, either.

What she said to me back at the yacht—*Is he bored with you, Luke? Is this how you keep him?*—well, that hit closer to home than I'd like to admit.

Zach Boston *is* getting bored with me. He's been living a fairly quiet life down in Key West with no real direction for long enough to know that this is not his dream life the way it is mine.

I like my life. Before all the FBI drama started with Alonzo and Tara, my life was simple.

I do realize now that my brothers were protecting me from the deep, dark family secrets. But even with that knowledge, I'm happy where I am.

My business is fun. I got a new yacht that actually qualifies as a legitimate tax writeoff. I own my own cottage on Dumas Street. I'm close to my family and every Saturday night, without fail, I know that my mother is cooking dinner for me.

I am surrounded by support.

Hell, I can't actually recall a time in my life where I wasn't one hundred percent sure that the people around me had my back.

I look over my shoulder. Zach is talking to both Posie and Bart, two people he doesn't even know, trying to… what? Explain my actions? Like said actions require justification?

Posie is not on my side.

Bart is not on my side.

And Zach?

I'm not sure anymore.

This is a new feeling for me. This… aloneness. Singleness.

This is not what support looks like. Trust me, I know.

When I'm out with my brothers and we get in a scuffle with assholes we don't make excuses for each other. We just take care of business.

We're loyal. Always loyal.

And I'm starting to realize that that's not actually how the bigger world works.

I'm starting to realize that most people only like you for what you can give them.

I'm starting to realize that they see me as an opportunity.

I'm starting to realize that they are traitors and they will not have your back the way my brothers do when the shit goes down.

I sigh. Because that sucks. And I miss my old worldview. Even if it was a narrow slice of reality.

Finally, Zach, Posie, Bart, and Chandler start wading through the water towards me. Zach is smiling. He's always smiling. Nothing touches that dude. He's easygoing, and mellow, and he's never up for a fight the way I am.

He's likable. And… nice.

I used to think I was the nice, likable Dumas brother. I mean, hell, Tony really is an asshole. I still love him, but he's definitely the jerk in the family. And Alonzo is the quiet one. He keeps his thoughts to himself. He's not mean, but he's not overly friendly, either. At least not to strangers.

So I was the nice, likable one. The happy one. The one who smiles. The one people want to talk to. The one who doesn't cause too much trouble.

I was the adventurous one too. Alonzo takes bored men out to sea to catch trophy fish. Tony takes honeymooners kayaking through the mangroves and serves them sunset dinners on his sailboats. I own speedboats for waterskiing. I have a whole fleet of Sea-

Doos and jet skis. I offer parasailing, and flyboarding, and overnight adventures.

But it's a controlled kind of adventure these days. Nine AM to sunset. I did everything I wanted in my twenties. Took all the risks. But thirty looks different. Thirty looks like the beginning of a nice, comfy decade. Where I reap the rewards of my hard work and slip into a more predictable life. Most of my risk-taking behind me.

But Zach is just starting his adventure.

He's just starting to think about the risks he wants to take.

So what does that future look like?

Zach is smiling big as they approach. "Come on. Let's forget this bullshit and go get a drink."

I sigh and look over my shoulder at the yacht, then glance at the Dickface crew, who are all wading their way over to a pontoon boat serving alcohol.

"They're not gonna fuck with it," Chandler says. "Trust me. They wouldn't dare."

I look at him. Now that I know he's Bart's brother, the resemblance is obvious. Same height, and build, and dark piercing eyes.

But I don't tag him *Chuck Bass senior.*

No. He's not Chuck Bass.

He's… *Gatsby.*

Wrong hair color, wrong eye color, no linen suit or pretentious West Egg mansion out here in the Caribbean. But back home—wherever that may be—that's the world he lives in.

Not new money though, so the tag doesn't quite fit. The amount of self-assurance these boys project screams old money all the way, so I should probably call him Tom Buchanan instead. But Gatsby gets the point across with fewer syllables and no one remembers what the fuck Tom Buchanan was doing in that story.

I glance over at Zach, but he's already walking off towards the beach with his arm around Posie, looking at Bart as they laugh about something.

Chandler sighs. "Come on. I'll buy you a drink. And it won't be that weak, watered-down crap they're serving the masses." He pushes me. It's unexpected, so I stumble a little. But he's smiling when I look at him. "Bart is gonna be Bart. But trust me, your boy isn't going home with him."

"That's not what I'm worried about."

Chandler smiles. And even though it annoys me—hell, *he* annoys me—I have to admit, his good mood might be slightly contagious. "No? Great. Let's forget about him. Come on. I'll take you up to the main house. There's a lot more going on up there on the private side of things." He points to a set of stairs that lead up the side of the cliff beyond the beach. He doesn't wait for me to answer, just starts wading forward through the water. I hesitate. But when he looks over his shoulder and beckons me to follow with a nod of his head, I decide… fuck it.

Why not?

CHAPTER EIGHT

ZACH

When I look over my shoulder, I see that Luke has teamed up with Bart's brother, Chandler, and is walking out onto the sand a little ways down the beach. I know he's probably pissed at me for hanging out with Bart and Posie, but this pop-up party—hell, this whole place—it's bugging me. There's something off about it. And if we've gotta be here for the day, then I'm gonna spend my time figuring out why that is.

My entire life has gone like this. Something unusual happens and you chalk it up to... you know, fuckin'... coincidence. I did that well into my teens. But by the time I started college I was done letting these so-called coincidences upend my life time and time again.

Nothing is a coincidence in my world.

None of it.

Hell, not even Luke was a coincidence. Right? I mean... the Dumas family are a bunch of child-smugglers. And I don't give a fuck that they are smuggling those kids out of dangerous places to give them a better future, this is part of the… the *plot*. It's a plan.

And even though there was no family meeting about what happened to Tony while he was in Colorado, I know something happened.

He came back with a girl with the last name of Ameci.

And I've heard that name before. I can't place the where or the when, but I've heard that name before. She's a nice enough girl. Kinda spunky and earthy. One of those girls who wears gauzy shirts and long skirts.

Whatever. It's not really *her* that interests me. It's her *name*.

Where have I heard that name before?

Don't know. Can't place it.

I tried to pump Tony for some details, but I don't think he likes me. He literally just grunts at me every time I say hello. And then I tried to get Luke to go get some details, but that was a dead end too. They don't tell Luke anything until they have to. Hell, I know more about Luke's family business than he probably does.

We reach the beach and I realize that Bart has been talking to Posie this whole time and I just spaced out an entire conversation.

"Ohh," Posie squeals. "They have a frozen drink cart! I want one. How much are they? I don't have any money."

"They're free," Bart says a little smugly. "And does it look like anyone down here has money on them?" He chuckles. But he's not wrong. Most girls are dressed like Posie, a style I call might-as-well-be-naked, and some of them are topless. "But trust me, you don't want those drinks," Bart continues. "I've got something better in mind for us today. You in?"

I think he's talking to Posie, but when I glance over at him, he's staring at me. "In? For better drinks? Sure. Why not?" I grin at him. He grins back. I know I'm playing a dangerous game here—I'm kinda leading the dude on. But I don't care. I feel this place. It's part of the plot.

He directs us over to a path that leads up the side of the cliff. It's dirt—pretty smooth, which is good, since we're all barefoot—and switches back a few times before we reach the top.

It's breezy up here. Almost downright windy. And the fall sun is warm, but not hot.

It's nice, actually.

"Wow," Posie says. "That is some house."

I glance over to where she's looking. And yep. That is something all right. But I would not call it a house. Mansion is a much better word. Huge, in other words. Three wings. Laid out in a u-shape with a center courtyard and the biggest private pool I've ever seen.

"Jesus Christ," I mutter. "I didn't even know there was a house up here. You can't see this place from the ocean."

"Nope," Bart affirms. "We built it that way on purpose. We like our privacy."

"This is your place?" I ask. I figured this kid was rich, but this is some other kind of rich. This is... Boston brothers rich. Not that we have Caribbean estates or anything. At least I don't think we do.

"This is us," Bart says, opening his arms up wide.

"What's the occasion?" Posie asks. "I mean... this party is a pretty big deal."

She's right. This is no pop-up party.

"Well," Bart says, and for the first time today, he seems a bit... uncomfortable. "Halloween fell on a Tuesday this year, so." He shrugs. "Just celebrating late, I guess."

"No one's in costume," Posie ponders.

"No. But it gets... interesting later. Trust me. But don't worry about any of that. Not to sound rude or anything, but you guys can't stay. I wish you could." Bart winks at me. "But it's invitation only. You understand, right?"

"Yeah. It's no problem," I say. "We have big plans tonight anyway."

"What kind of plans?" Bart asks. We begin walking towards the house.

"Family dinner stuff."

"Family dinner?" He laughs.

"Yeah. Luke's family? They're big and tight. And every Saturday we go over there to eat. It's taco night. So. Yeah. I wish we could stay for your super-cool, super-invitation-only   almost-not-quite-Halloween party and all. But raincheck, right?"

Bart laughs again. "I like you, Zach. Where are you from?"

"Oh, well. Right now, I'm from Key West."

Bart points to a bar near the pool. "Posie. There are excellent frozen drinks at the bar. Feel free to go get one."

She looks at me. "You want anything?"

"Sure. I'll take whatever you're having."

"I'm having a piña colada, Zach."

"Sounds perfect."

"How about you, Bart? Can I get you a drink?"

"Sure, I'll take a Johnny Blue. Neat."

"Got it. One super-girly drink coming up for Zach Boston and super-manly one for our host."

I cringe when she says my last name for two reasons. One, I didn't tell her my last name. And two, I didn't want Bart here to know my last name.

But cat's out of the bag now. Posie tosses her long pink hair and turns towards the poolside bar and I just stare out to sea for a few moments before I look back at Bart.

He's nodding. Grinning. Then he points at me. "I knew you were one of us."

I chuckle. "What the hell does that mean? One of you?"

"You know what I mean. Boston. Jesus fucking Christ. I have heard all about you boys."

"Well, don't believe everything you hear. Almost none of it's true."

"Which parts are true?"

"I wish I could tell you," I tease. "But it's all need-to-know basis. You understand, right?" He's still grinning, his eyes sparkling with… what? Mischief? Nah. I'd call that trouble. "So what's your all-important surname? Anything I'd recognize?"

"Conner," he says, extending his hand. "Bartholomew Conner."

"Conner. Conner. Where do I know that name from?"

"Does the Kane family ring any bells?"

"Oh, shit. That's you?"

"That's us."

"Do you live up at that estate?"

"When I'm not in school. Haven't seen you there though."

"No. I don't go up. But my cousin-brother, Joey, does."

"Maisy Kane."

"Yup. She's my cousin-niece."

"That custody battle almost got ugly."

"'Almost' doesn't count," I say.

"Yeah." Bart laughs again. "Michael Conner is my cousin-brother. So I guess Maisy is my cousin-niece too. At least by marriage, anyway. Not blood."

"Huh. Small world." And now I'm pretty much ready to go. Because this cannot be a coincidence. And I suddenly have an urge to call up to the city and see how the hell these Conner boys fit in to the shit show called the Boston brothers. Because I'm one hundred percent sure that they do.

"So who is Luke? Anyone I'd know about?"

"Nope," I say. "Nope. He's just Luke."

"You're a really bad liar, Zach."

"Seriously, his family is… not one of us. At all."

But I can tell that Bart here is already putting two and two together. "Oh, shit," he says. "The yacht. The dive shop. Fuckin' ay. He's a Dumas brother. I had my assistant call the dive shop because someone at the estate recommended it to me for a charter down to the island. Our yacht is getting work done. And when she told me that didn't work out, I just assumed it was some other charter service."

"Nope. Nope, that's us. Dumas Adventures."

"So you and him are…?"

"Yep. Partners."

"Business partners?"

"No, Bart. We're lovers. So if you're being cool to me because you think we're gonna hook up today, you can stop now. It's not gonna happen."

He nods his head to Posie, who is now heading our way with a half-naked pool boy trailing behind her holding a tray of drinks. "So how's she fit in?"

"Just a fun time, that's all."

"That's all?" Bart scoffs. "So let me get this straight. Your boy Luke got all up in Niles's face for insulting your flavor-of-the-week fun time?"

"He's a good guy like that."

Bart guffaws. "OK. I'll take your word on that."

Posie is back, and we all get handed a drink.

"How about we have a seat?" Bart asks. Then he points to a little sitting area between two umbrella palm trees.

I don't want to have a seat. I want to go find Luke and get the fuck out of here. Because these Conner boys can't be good for my already too-twisted-up plot of a life.

Something weird is going on here. And now it's not about having a bad feeling or anything so esoteric as that. This is based on facts.

I wasn't there when that whole money-making ritual went down at the Kane estate, but I saw the one in the spire of the Bossy Building.

This place? This party, these people, this isolated private island? All of it screams weird middle-of-the night ritual.

And I don't want anything to do with it.

CHAPTER NINE

POSIE

Something has changed in the time between me leaving to go get delicious free drinks and me coming back from getting delicious free drinks. But I'm not sure what it is. All I know is that suddenly Zach seems tense.

Before I left, he was kind of enjoying Bart's flirtations. I'm really not the jealous type, but Bart was getting on my nerves with his over-the-top advances. Winking, and grinning, and all his innuendo.

Who the hell does he think he is? I mean, I put in time on this man. Zach Boston is mine. It's bad enough I have to share him with Luke. I'm not about to add another competitor to the mix.

So the fact that Zach is clearly trying to distance himself from Bart should make me happy. But the gossip reporter in me is buzzing inside.

There's more to this story, that buzz is saying. *And it's your job to figure out what it is.*

"How about you, Posie?"

"Hmm?" I look up at Bart and slip the cherry-colored straw between my lips to sip on my amazing piña colada. Because I don't want him to think my attention is straying.

"Where did you go to college? Did we ever see each other on some random spring break trip maybe?" He waggles his eyebrows at me.

But it's fake. He's not interested in me. He's interested in Zach.

"Oh. I went to…" And for fuck's sake. I really need to get my head in the game. Because I went to Oklahoma State. But I'm not me, I'm Posie Payseur. And Posie Payseur would not go to a state school. So I just blurt out the first elite private school I can think of. "High Court. I went to High Court College."

"No shit?" Bart looks over at Zach. "So you know each other?"

"What?" I say.

"From school?" Bart's not looking at me, though. He's looking at Zach. And my gossip-reporter Spidey sense is telling me he's looking at Zach like he just caught him in a lie.

But what lie?

"I thought you said you just met Posie?" Bart asks Zach.

Oh, shit. What did I miss?

"But you two went to school together? You both went to High Court."

Zach smiles at me. But I know his smiles. I did my research. And that smile is… yeah. He's mad about something. "We were two years apart, right, Pose? So we never saw each other there."

"Yeah." I rally. "We actually just met in a club last night." Then I laugh and slide into a self-deprecating ice breaker. "The only reason I'm here is because I woke up late and Luke and Zach were stuck bringing me along because we had to drop you and your friends out here on this amazing island. Wow. And it's so amazing. Did I tell you that already? It is."

I'm babbling. So I force myself to tone it down and just blink at him like a clueless bimbo.

This works most of the time. But I'm not sure Bart is buying it.

Zach is definitely not buying it. He's suspicious of me.

Well, of course he is, you idiot. You just claimed to have gone to school at High Court College. What are the chances Zach went there too? It's like the most elite private college in the United States.

Actually, now that I think about it, the chances are pretty damn good considering his last name is Boston.

And that's when I realize…I called him Zach *Boston* before I went to get the drinks.

And I'm not supposed to know his last name.

Shit.

"What's your last name, Posie? Maybe we know each other from some other social circle?"

Bart is smiling amicably at me. But this question feels like a trap. However, I am all in now, right? You don't just claim to have graduated from High Court College and not have a pedigreed name to back that up.

Luckily, I do. A fake one, at least. And is it really fake if it's my legit pen name?

"Payseur," I say, grinning back at him as I suck on my straw. He's not buying it. His face has gone all serious. So I bat my eyelashes. Doesn't work. My only other option is to stand up, jiggle my tits—they're nice tits—and croon, "Well, I need another delicious drink. Who's with me?"

"We'll both take another," Bart says, answering for Zach. "But this time, bring Zach a whiskey."

"Sure thing!" I blow them both a kiss as I turn. Then call, "BRB! Don't start the fun without me!"

I force myself to walk slowly towards the house, my gaze aimed at the bartender. He was sorta friendly and I could use a friendly face right now because I'm literally on a super-secret private island in the middle of the Caribbean Sea surrounded by hundreds of well-connected strangers and my ride home just caught me in a lie. And the closer I get to the pool, the deeper my realization goes regarding just how fucked I am.

"Shit, shit, shit," I mutter as I walk.

Claiming to be an alumna from High Court College was a major misstep. But how was I supposed to know Zach Boston went there?

Well. I am an investigative gossip reporter for Buzz Hollywood. And the president of Zach Boston's secret fan club.

Wait a minute. Wait. A damn. Minute. Zach didn't go to High Court. He went to that other one. The snooty-pretentious one in the city because Jesse Boston didn't want him living away from the Bossy Building.

So. That was the lie.

I stop walking and turn around, hands on hips as I stare at the seating area where Zach and Bart are. They're not paying attention to me, but I tap the toe of my foot and scowl at them with squinty eyes anyway.

Then I realize… shit. Is Zach Boston… nervous?

Yep. That's definitely Zach's nervous smile.

But why?

And why did he lie to Bart about his college?

What could that possibly mean?

I turn back around before they notice me and continue walking. Thinking. Pondering all the past happenings over the last two days. Because if you think about it—how the hell did I get here?

It's weird.

But… not all in a bad way. I mean, I am on a super-secret private island in the middle of the Caribbean Sea surrounded by hundreds of well-connected strangers.

Maybe I should expand my story?

I look around and take in the island from a reporter's perspective.

First thing I notice is that the people up here on the top of the island are different than the people down below.

Even though this entire party is invitation-only, down below on the beach and the sandbar it feels like spring break. Half-naked college-age kids. Lots of drinking and frolicking. It's obviously planned—the pontoon boats, the floating docks, the carefully stacked wood that will lead to a bonfire. But pop-up party isn't far off the mark. It's definitely more than that. Pop-up parties typically imply that the event is temporary.

Not even the fun down there appears to be temporary. In fact, if I had to guess, I'd say that Bart and Chandler throw these parties on a regular basis.

Why wouldn't they? The channel between the two islands is totally private. No unwanted prying eyes. At least not from the ocean. I look up. The sky though. People could see from the sky.

The point is there seems to be two separate parties going on here. The one for the invited masses and the one up here on the top of the island for the real insiders.

And I'm here with them.

I look around cautiously as I approach the bar. There are several small groups in front of it. People being friendly and chatting each other up. But none of them are paying any attention to me.

I glance over my shoulder, making sure that neither Zach nor Bart are watching, and then I slip through the two halves of a billowing curtain directly behind the bar and find myself in a large bustling living room.

A tall, elegant woman in a long, breezy white dress is directing staff. Pointing at things. Calling out instructions as they move chairs and whatnot around. She's very blonde, but her hair is done up in a slick ponytail. And her blue eyes are so bright I can discern their color even from here.

She notices me. Forces a smile. "Can I help you with something?"

"Yes. I'm sorry to bother you. I need a bathroom." I hesitate, grimacing. "I'm having a… a feminine emergency." I whisper that last part.

"Oh." Her tight face relaxes a little. Then she smiles. In fact, she pauses for several moments. And it's just about to become uncomfortable when she says, "Yes. Of course." She snaps her fingers and points to one of the men. "You. Show our guest to the coral bathroom, please." Then her eyes find mine again. "You'll find what you need in there. Please do take extra care. We wouldn't want to mess anything up."

"Uhh. Sure. Of course. I certainly will."

The man she was talking to bows his head a little, but doesn't say anything back. Just beckons me to follow him with a single finger.

"Thank you," I breathe, passing by the elegant woman.

But she's already calling out more instructions and doesn't respond.

My guide takes me out the door, across another courtyard, and into another part of the massive mansion. We weave through two more hallways, pass more than a dozen closed doors, and then finally, we stop at another closed door. He opens it in a dramatic fashion, stepping out of the way so I can have a clear, unobstructed view of the room.

"Oh," I say. "Is this a restroom?"

It doesn't look like a restroom. It looks like a... a... well. I cock my head a little, trying to force it to make sense. A... bathhouse? Maybe? But not quite.

I turn to ask my guide if this is indeed the coral bathroom, but he's already gone. And I'm alone.

Weird. But also fortuitous. Because I'm here to snoop and these people just delivered me to the promised land.

I go inside, close the door and then calculate how much time I have to go through all those closed doors I saw on my way here before I am missed.

Not much. Maybe twenty minutes. And that's probably pushing it. I was probably only gone about ten minutes the last time I went and got drinks.

I take a deep breath and look around, desperately wishing I had my phone so I could take pictures of everything. But I'm pretty sure my phone is somewhere in the couch cushions of the yacht. So my memory will have to do.

I don't know what's up with the coral bathroom, but it's bizarre enough to be noteworthy. So I soak it all up and then commit it to memory.

The entire room is tiled from floor to ceiling. Small tiles too. Not more than an inch square. But they are not all the same color. More like a mosaic.

I tilt my head back and forth trying to make out the motif, but honestly, it must be one of those designs you need to see from above. Because it doesn't make sense to me.

There is a tub. Sort of.

It's actually a large egg-shaped… vessel? Best word to describe it. It's gold in color, but it can't be real gold.

Can't be.

Can it?

I don't want to waste much time here in the bathroom when there are so many secret rooms to peek into, but I can't help myself. I walk over to the tub and scratch my fingernail along the side.

Jesus Christ. A little bit of gold actually peels off.

I look over my shoulder and then furiously buff out the blemish.

OK, then. It's gold.

I back up and notice there's a small table along one wall with a gold cup setting on a gold tray.

Cup? More like a chalice.

Oh! My eyes cross a little as I look at the far wall and then I see the mosaic motif. Yes. It's very clear now and… what the… ewww. It's a bunch of animals being slaughtered by men with halos, all done up in a medieval style.

Gross. OK. I've had enough of the weird bathroom.

But that's when I realize there's no bathroom facilities. Not even a sink.

What the hell?

This can't be the coral bathroom. That man took me to the wrong room.

But this is good. It's very good, actually. Because now if I get caught, I can just say that he took me to the wrong room so I was just looking for the coral bathroom.

I slip out into the hall. Then pause, looking back and forth just to make sure butler guy isn't waiting for me.

He's not. And I don't hear anyone talking. So I rush over to the first door and put my ear to it.

Silence. I try the doorknob. Locked. Dammit.

I go to the next one. Locked.

And the next, and the next, and the next. All locked.

But the sixth door is open. And then I hear voices, so I quickly duck inside.

At first, I think it's totally dark. But my eyes adjust quickly and I realize there are a few very tall pillar candles lit in the corners.

It's a… church. Or something.

Looks like a church. Maybe more like a chapel. It's not big and there doesn't seem to be any windows, which is weird. There a floor-to-ceiling red velvet curtain just to my left but I don't think there's a window behind that because it's not on the outside wall of the house.

The voices out in the hallway get louder and louder. But then they pass by.

I hold still, trying to listen to their conversation, but it's very muffled.

Shit. I think they are looking for me.

And yep. The footsteps come back this direction and then pause outside the door.

Shit.

I don't know what to do, but I definitely don't want to be caught in here. So I slip behind the velvet curtain and hold very still as the door opens.

"Girl? Hello?"

I think it's the same woman who told the guide to bring me to the bathroom.

"Are you in here?"

If I wasn't currently hiding behind a curtain and in the process of acting out my gossip-reporter dream job, I might answer her. But there's no good way to explain this. So. I just shut up.

"She's not in here, Jacob."

"I'm sorry, ma'am. I put her in the coral bathroom."

"If you put her there, she would still be there."

"It's possible she wandered off."

"This is the only room unlocked—"

But the door closes and I can't hear the rest of that sentence.

I'm fucked. I'm gonna get caught. And then this very rich woman is going to figure out that I was in here when she called out for me, and then… I don't know. I'm gonna get kicked off the island. Banished. And probably get Zach and Luke in trouble too.

I lean against the curtained wall to think this through, but fall over backwards onto the hardwood floor with a thud. Because there is no wall behind me. It's just empty space.

I hold my breath and pray that they didn't just hear that in the hallway.

No one comes to check, so I push the curtain aside, get to my feet, and start feeling around in the darkness, trying to figure out what this is. It's not really a room, it's a large closet. Hangers sway on racks as I reach out, trying to find the wall.

My fingertips find a switch and a light flicks on over my head.

Hmm. It is a closet. And the hangers hold lots of… I dunno. Choir robes, I guess.

Fits. Church. Choir robes. These people must take their god seriously if they have a chapel in their private-island mansion.

Though it kinda makes sense. I mean, if you're religious and you're all the way out here at your middle-of-nowhere vacay house, you gotta pray somewhere, right?

I'm going with that.

And that's when I see the door on the far side of the closet.

Fuck, yes. I'm in luck. I switch the light off and try the handle.

Unlocked.

I know I should not go through this door. I should not be peeking through these people's house. And snooping in a church—even if it is a homemade one—has to be some serious kind of sin. But what else can I do? I can't go back the way I came and I have been missing for at least ten minutes now. Zach and Bart are gonna start wondering where I am. So priority one is getting out of the damn house.

But the moment I pull the door open I know it's a mistake.

And it's also too late to turn back because the woman is back. The door to the church opens and once again, she calls out, "Girl?"

I step in, close the door as quietly as I can, and then feel my way along the ragged rock wall. I almost trip on a step, but catch myself just in time.

Just as the door handle begins to turn, I scurry down the rest of the steps in the dark, then feel along the curve of the wall just as she opens the door above me.

"Hello?" she calls softly.

I hold my breath, my bare feet sliding along the cold, hard concrete floor until I reach another edge. I slip into an alcove and press my back against the rough wall.

Then…blink. The lights go on.

My eyes are fixated on the room in front of me. And I don't really understand how time passes in the next few eternities. Because it feels like it stops.

The woman is coming down the steps, her footsteps clicking on the stone. And my brain is concentrating on that because the consequences of her finding me here are unknown. But it can't be good. And I realize this. And I'm worried about her finding me. But there's a little sidecar part of my brain that isn't aware of her at all.

That part is concentrating on the scene in front of me.

Well. Not concentrating. It's more like… calculations. Or something. I don't know. My eyes are darting back and forth across the room, soaking it all in as the panic and fear begins to build up inside me. Trying to make what I'm seeing fit into my known reality.

My heart is suddenly thundering inside my chest.

Because nothing about this room fits into my reality.

"Charlotte?" The woman's voice is so soft I can barely make out the name. "Are you here?"

I press my lips together. Forcing myself not to move. Not to breathe. Not to do anything that would let this woman know that I am hiding down here in this secret room that I don't want to think about.

I close my eyes. Squinting them shut.

The rational part of my brain suddenly realizes that the woman is at the bottom of the stairs and I'm pretty sure that if I looked to my right, I would see her. And she would see me. So I do not move.

"Charlotte," the woman breathes. "You have to stop this." Then she raises her voice and yells, "Stop it!"

I jump in surprise and a little squeak escapes past my lips. But the woman is in full retreat, her feet flying back up the steps the way she came.

Blink. The light goes out.

And then she slams the door.

I hold my breath and count to sixty, whispering a little mantra to calm myself down. "You didn't see that. It's not real. You are not locked in. You will leave here and get the fuck off this island."

I let out the breath and immediately suck in another, still saying these words as I feel my way along the wall until I get back to the stairs. "You did not see that. It's not real. You are not locked in. You will leave here and get the fuck off this island."

I go up the steps, both hands outstretched so I can drag my fingertips along the rock wall to keep my bearings in the dark.

"You did not see that. It's not real." I exhale again, feeling for the door handle. "You are not locked in."

It twists in my hand. But I pause, listening for any hint of someone being on the other side of the door.

Silence.

I open it.

Darkness.

This is the choir-robe closet. And there is just enough light filtering through the edge of the curtain. Just enough for me to take two steps forward and quietly close the dungeon door behind me.

I feel I can't get enough air. But I force myself to breathe slowly or I might start panting. Or, God forbid, hyperventilating.

I need to get out of this house. And I need to get out right now or I will be in full-on panic mode.

I swallow hard, pull the red velvet curtain aside, and step into cooler air.

I pause. Breathe. My whole body is shaking.

Did that really just happen?

Did I just stumble into a dungeon filled with…

I can't. I can't. I cannot think about this.

Not now. Maybe not ever.

I rush over to the door, press my ear against it, but there is no sound on the other side. And even though I understand that I should be very careful at this point, I can't stop myself. I pull the door open. Slam it behind me. And take off running down the hallway in the opposite direction to the one I came from.

CHAPTER TEN

LUKE

Chandler is a talker. He never shuts up about the island, or the party, or the good time everyone is having. He leads me over to a set of stairs that climb their way up the side of the steep cliff. They are old, and wooden, and could definitely use some maintenance.

There are several small groups of people on this side of the beach, but they stay clear of the steps. Probably due to the two mercenary-looking security guards who are blocking the entrance.

They part for Chandler just before he reaches them so he doesn't have to break his stride, a telling reaction that indicates Chandler's level of authority here.

We start climbing the steps. At least they are not rickety. And Chandler is saying, "So we have these things every now and then."

I'm just going to assume we're still talking about the party. But I'm really not listening to him. I'm thinking about Bart. And Zach. And, even though I don't want to admit it, also what Posie said to me earlier. *Is he bored with you? Is this how you keep him?*

Meaning girls like her.

Or guys like Bart.

Because we have been with some men too. Not alone. We've never had a threesome with a guy who didn't come with a girl.

Is that what Zach is thinking about? Three dudes?

I sigh and rub both hands down my face.

"What's up with you?" Chandler stops on a landing in between two switchback sets of stairs. We're about halfway up the cliff.

"What do you mean?"

"I mean, you look stressed. Not trying to be disparaging or anything. But... fuck. Just hold on a little longer. I'll get you a drink."

I shake my head at him. "I'm fine."

"Dude. Everyone can see you're not fine. And if you're worried about Bart—"

"I'm not worried about Bart."

"I'm not saying you are. I'm just saying if you were, you don't need to. He's... not that kind of guy."

"Not what kind of guy?"

"He doesn't do anything long-term. If he hooks up with your boy up there—"

"They're not gonna hook up. And he's not my boy. He's only a few years younger than me."

"Ohhhh." Chandler nods.

"Oh, what?"

"I get it."

"I doubt that."

"No. I do. I'm about your age. I'm thirty-one."

"Be thirty soonish." I shrug.

"And uh… yeah. I've had my share of college boys."

"He's not a college boy. He's almost twenty-four."

Chandler sighs. "Damn, twenty-four was a good year."

"Anyway." I pan my hand to the steps. "We going up or what?"

"What's the rush? Take in the view, *Luke*. You're missing things."

"I'm not."

"Let's talk about your yacht."

I turn around and look across the channel at the yacht. It's so much bigger than any of the other boats at this party, it's a little embarrassing.

"That's quite a fucking canoe you have there."

I smile. "It's pretty pretentious. But it's new. My regular boat is a Corsair 970."

"Damn, dude. You definitely got a thing for boats. What the hell do you do for a living?"

"Well." I suck in a deep breath, let some of the tension drain off. I like talking boats. So this convo is fine. I guess. "My day-to-day stuff is mostly jet ski rentals. Got a whole fleet of those over in West. But we do all the high-adrenaline water sports. So I have speedboats too. This one"—I nod at the beast—"she's new. My dad got tired of weekend dive trips. That's our family business. Dive shop. So my brothers and I do ocean shit."

Chandler is squinting down at the yacht. "What's her name?"

"Who?"

He chuckles. "The yacht."

"Oh. Well, we have a family tradition that my sister gets to name all the boats. And she named this one *Sparkle Dreams*."

Chandler guffaws. "No."

"Swear to God. She owns a cosmetic company and this was the name of her favorite new eyeshadow last summer."

Chandler smiles at me as he leans back against the railing, getting comfortable. "What are the other boats called?"

"Fuck."

"Come on. I swear I won't laugh."

I grin. Because this isn't a bad conversation. And the names are funny. "Well, the Corsair is called *Hooker Pink*." This time I laugh with him. "And the two speed boats are *Glitter* and *Glamour*." I shrug. "She bought them for me. So whatever."

"Your sister is loaded too, then?"

"I'm not loaded."

Chandler chokes on a laugh. "Shut the fuck up."

"Serious. I fucking work. And my sister is part-owner of Bright Berry Beach Cosmetics. So. Yeah. She is loaded." I point at him. "But self-made."

"Right."

"Seriously."

"No, I get it. It's just… no one is self-made."

"She is. And so are her partners."

"Like I said, I *get* it. But there are always people behind the scenes, ya know? Pulling those strings. Making shit happen. Success is never an accident."

I'm not in the mood to argue about it. So I just say, "Well, if you say so."

"So what's your boy do?"

"He's not my boy."

"He's one of us, isn't he?"

"Us?"

Chandler points to himself. "Me. Bart. Everyone down there. Everyone here, actually. Except, apparently, you. And the security team." He waits to see if I'll say anything. But I don't. So he goes on. "But I'm just following your lead here. Like it or not, Luke, when you buy an eight-million-dollar yacht, you're one of us."

"How'd you know what I paid for it?"

He looks out across the lagoon. "I know yachts." He side-eyes me, a little bit of his dark hair falling over one of his dark eyes. "I work on the water too."

"Yeah? What do you do?"

He grins at me. Straightens up. "Well, I could tell you, but then I'd have to kill you. And I like you, Luke. So let's just leave it at that." He points at the stairs. "Shall we? I'm dying for a fucking drink."

I just stare at him for a moment, then decide, *You know what? I don't give a fuck what this guy does.* I'm sure it's illegal. You don't own places like this making legitimate money. In fact, you don't need places like this if you make legitimate money. It's very clear that this island has a purpose.

I'm not sure I want to know that purpose. I only found out this year that my family is involved with some very illegal shit ourselves. The last thing I need is to be making friends with another guy in the biz.

At the top of the stairs Chandler and I find ourselves on a covered deck, a kind of lookout point. And when I turn around to face the sea, the moment morphs in real time, going from the mundane chore of trudging up steps to the feeling of pure serenity before I can even process this change. The sound of people partying down below fades into the wind and the mist of the ocean tempers the heat of the sun.

I walk to the railing and lean against it. "Wow. That is some view."

Chandler comes up next to me but he stays silent as I look around.

I can see everything and I take my time putting it all together in my mind. Two islands—or maybe, at one time, just one that got split down the middle. They are not typical islands, either. The second one—the one the yacht is anchored closest to—is much smaller than this one. But it's like a mini-twin. Both of them are tall with steep, rocky cliffs and flat, plateau-like tops. Perfect for buildings and helipads.

The second island only has one small structure. Kind of like a shed, but made of concrete.

I look over my shoulder to compare the two buildings and find a sprawling U-shaped mansion off in the distance. That's where the party is.

"It's not bad," Chandler finally says.

"Yeah. Not bad."

"Impressed?"

"Yep. I'm pretty impressed."

"What's your place like?"

I shrug. "Key West, ya know?"

"Crowded."

"Almost suffocating. If we didn't own our whole street I don't know if I would stay there. At least, not on land."

He raises his eyebrows at me. "Live on the yacht?"

"Probably. But we do own the whole street. We run vacation rentals. My whole family—except my sis—all live on the same cul-de-sac."

Chandler groans. "I'd fucking kill myself if I had to live by my family. Bart's OK for short periods of time. But Mother? Fuck that. She's nuts."

"Not me. I like 'em. And it's family dinner night… so we're gonna have to get going soon."

"Are you fucking with me?"

"No, why?"

"You're not staying for the party?"

I pan my hand down to the beach. "Yeah… no. I've seen enough. Grew out of this kind of shit before I was even old enough to drink. I'd rather have tacos tonight with the fam. But thanks for the offer."

Now he guffaws, then points at me. "I like you, Luke."

"Most people do."

"And what about Zach? He going with you?"

"Yep."

"You sure about that?"

"One hundred percent positive."

"Maybe he wants to stay for the party?"

"Trust me." I smile at Chandler. Weird that these two brothers are coming on to both Zach and me at the same time, but whatever. We're handsome dudes. It's pretty much expected. "He's not staying behind."

"You seem pretty sure of yourself. I mean, for a guy whose boyfriend is hanging out with my brother over there."

I look in the direction he's indicating and yep, sure enough, there's Zach kicking back with Bart between two shady palm trees. "Yeah, well. Bart's not gonna get anywhere. Zach prefers girls."

"Does he?"

I turn back to Chandler. "Yep. He's gay for me."

Chandler laughs. Points at me again. "Yeah. I like you."

"He's just being nice. Zach is flirty. And Bart is flirting."

"Doesn't it bother you?"

"Why are you asking? You're flirting with me?"

"You know I am."

"Yeah." I sigh. "I'm a pretty good catch. But I'm not into this... lifestyle. I like what I have. I'm satisfied."

"And what about Zach?"

"You're pretty interested in Zach. Be my guest, dude. You wanna go flirt with him too? Make him some kind of offer? Give it your best shot. If he wants to stay with you, nothing I can do about that, is there? There is more between he and I than attraction."

Chandler is smiling at me during that whole speech. "Just checking, OK? No need to get upset."

"Not upset. But you're not just checking, Chandler. And your brother over there?" I point in the general direction of where Bart and Zach are kicking it. "He's got ideas in that head. He showed up that way. Trust me. If there's one type of person I learned how to recognize early, it's the super-rich player and you and your brother certainly fit into that category."

"Luke." Chandler smiles. "You're getting worked up."

"No. I'm not. If I was worked up, believe me, you'd know it."

This makes him pause. Because I am a huge man. Slightly over six-foot three. A hundred and ninety pounds. And while Chandler here isn't small by any means, he's no me.

"Fuck, man. Calm down. I'm just—"

"You're just trying to wind me up for some reason. And your brother over there is doing the same thing to Zach. I don't like games, Chandler. So if you've got something to say to us, you'd better come out and say it. Because if I find out later that there's more to this little… *job* than meets the eye—" I pause to shake my head. "Yeah. I'm not gonna like that."

He stares at me for a few minutes. And I swear to God, I get the feeling like he's about to spill all the secrets.

I don't really want him to do that.

I don't want to know his secrets. I don't want to get involved.

So when he sighs and says, "I just want to have a drink with you, OK?" I actually feel relieved.

I know he's lying. But as long as he keeps his little secret locked up tight and doesn't get me or Zach involved, I'm totally fine with that.

So I say, "Sure. Let's get a drink."

The mansion courtyard is the interior of the u-shaped house. Chandler and I are on one side of the U and Zach and Bart are on the other. I expect Chandler to lead me into the pool area to the bar. But he doesn't. He starts walking towards the closest wing of the mansion.

I catch Zach's eye just before I disappear from view and Chandler and I end up inside some kind of solarium or dayroom. Whatever you call that space inside pretentious houses that has a circular ceiling made of glass.

He walks over to a bar cart with several crystal decanters on a tray and begins to pour two drinks.

But that's when the door comes crashing open and Posie—of all people—skids into the room, breathing heavy and hard.

"Oh, thank God!" she exclaims. But then she spies Chandler and the words that were just about to come pouring out of her mouth get swallowed up.

"Hey, Pose." I say this cautiously. "What are you doing?"

"Girl!" A woman's voice calls from somewhere down the hallway.

Posie looks over her shoulder, pure panic on her face. Then she looks at me. "I need to go."

"Girl!" The woman appears in the doorway. She's pretty—maybe mid-fifties. Long, flowing, asymmetrical white dress that reminds me of Ancient Greece for some reason. Her hair is blonde and styled in an elaborate updo. Her lips are pink and with each step one long, tanned leg slips out of the slit up the side that goes all the way up to her hip.

She claps her hands. "What are you doing?"

"Mom," Chandler says. "What the fuck?"

"This girl! She's running from me."

"What the hell are you talking about?"

"She's our…" The woman, Chandler's mother, pauses and squints her eyes at me. Then looks back at her son. "She's our… *girl*."

"No, Mom. Jesus fucking Christ." We all turn to see Bart and Zach enter the way Chandler and I did. "That's not the girl. This is Posie Payseur, for fuck's sake."

"What?" The woman looks confused for a moment. And all that confusion is directed at Posie, who is just standing about halfway between me and the mom, glancing back and forth between us with a look of pure panic on her face. "Posie?"

"Yes," Bart says. He walks over to the woman and takes her arm, gently, slowly turning her around and pointing her back towards the hallway. "Come on. I'll take you back to the reception room. They need you, Mom. They need help setting things up."

His words drift off as they disappear.

"What the fuck was that?" I ask, looking first at Posie, then at Chandler.

"Sorry," Chandler says, walking over to hand me a drink. I take it. "That's Mom. She's…" He bobs his head a little as he studies Zach. "Not all there anymore." Then he looks at Posie. "But shit, girl. Why the hell didn't you tell us you were coming? Your name isn't on the list."

I look at Zach.

Posie looks at me.

Zach looks at Chandler.

None of us say anything.

But luckily Chandler is already walking back to the drink cart and pouring more drinks.

Then Bart appears again. Smiling. Big. Arms out wide. "Sorry, man!" He walks over to Zach and claps him on the back. "Our mom. She's a character."

Chandler says, "How come you didn't tell me Posie is a Payseur?" as he hands Bart a drink.

"Literally just found out like twenty minutes ago, bro." Then he points at Zach. "Do you know who this guy is?"

"Who?" Chandler comes at me with a drink, but this whole thing is weird enough for me to put a hand up and refuse it. Fuck that. I ain't taking shit from these people. All I want to do right now is leave.

"Zach. Fucking. Boston," Bart says.

Chandler is taking a sip of the whiskey I just declined when this comes out. And he almost chokes on a piece of ice. "What?" His new incredulous look is aimed at Zach.

"Yeah." Bart is genuinely gleeful. "Pretty fucking cool, huh?"

There are several long, awkward, silent seconds as Bart's words hang in the air.

"Uhhh…" I say. Because yeah. I'm out. "So. We have to get going." I point at Posie. "Family dinner, remember? You're still in, right?"

Posie nods dumbly at me. I don't know what the fuck is going on with her, but it's clear she's afraid of something.

"What?" Bart says. "No. Dude." He's talking to Zach now.

And this whole time Zach has just been silently looking at me. But I can read his look. And he can read mine. So Zach says, "Yeah, man. I told you. Remember? Family dinner night."

"We're having tacos," I say.

"And it's kinda far," Zach adds. "So yeah." He puts his fist forward looking for a dap.

Bart misses it. "No, dude. You have to stay. Shit is just getting started. And Posie!" He points at her. And I actually watch her suck in a deep breath of dread in real time. "Posie. You wanna stay, right? We could really use you."

Posie says nothing.

"Uhhh…" Chandler's… yeah. Got a look on his face. I don't know who this Payseur family is or why these guys are so excited to have a member here at their little not-really-a-pop-up party. But it's all too weird for me.

Chandler finally finds his words. "Well. That sucks. But if you guys gotta jet…" His player smile is back in place. "Sorry to see you go."

"No," Bart says. "We need them, Chan. This is…
this is *good*."

"Bart. Bro." Chandler sends his brother a look
that says *shut the fuck up*. "Why don't you go take care
of Mom and I'll walk our guests down to the beach?
Hm?"

Bart looks back at his brother like he really wants
to argue.

But he just draws in a deep breath and walks off
without saying another word.

CHAPTER ELEVEN

ZACH

Bart and I were just starting to wonder what happened to Posie when we saw Chandler and Luke disappear behind the far side of the house. So we went to investigate.

The awkward exchange that happened next—I couldn't explain it, even if I wanted to.

But I do know this: Secrets were being revealed by mistake. And then there was a very messy sweeping up of said secrets.

I didn't even have to think about that part of it.

Secrets are something I understand better than most and over the past year I've come to realize one thing about them.

I don't actually care for secrets.

I don't need to know all the answers. I don't want to be an insider, I don't want to be on the A-list, and I sure as hell do not want to find myself the subject of a Buzz Hollywood cover-page article.

That's why I gave Posie a long rope to hang herself.

I am a live-and-let-live kind of guy. But that little witch just outed me as a Boston. And then… all kinds of fucking secrets came flying out of nowhere. Just spilling out like a goddamned overflowing river.

And the mother? What the hell was her problem? And more importantly, how is this gonna come back and bite me in the ass?

Because it will.

I know it will.

One day—maybe not soon, but one day—I will be doing my thing and somehow this day, on this island, with these people—it's all gonna come back to haunt me.

I stew in this realization as Chandler leads us all out of the house and over to a set of stairs that takes us down to the beach. He and Luke walk up front, talking like they are old friends, and Posie and I hang back a little. I'm trying to put enough space between us and them so I can ask Posie some questions, but she's determined to stay as close to Luke as she can.

Probably to avoid said questions.

Because I know who, and what, Posie is.

Did I expect her to pull the Payseur surname out of her ass and get everyone all riled up and excited? No. But that's the fun of secrets, isn't it? You never know when they're gonna rear their ugly head and expose you.

And to be honest, I'm kinda pissed about that Payseur move.

I mean, I get it. I knew she was a dirty little liar mid-week when the facial recognition came back, but Payseur? Are you fucking kidding me?

All I know is she had better not be an actual Payseur. I will lose my fucking shit if I find out she's part of that family.

Down on the beach the mood is decidedly different than it was when we went up top less than an hour ago. The sun is already starting to drop lower on the horizon, everyone is lit, and they are all naked. Like, the only people who have clothes on are the security.

The party-goers are all fascinated by some kind of body paint station set up on the beach. They are busy drawing symbols on each other and painting masks on their faces while they dance in circles to a thumping drumbeat, which is being drummed by actual drummers. Like those giant, round, tribal drums, which totally just makes this whole thing all that much creepier.

Luke studies them as we pass by.

I force myself not to look.

We all wade out into the water and watch Chandler round up three security men on Sea-Doos.

He instructs them to drop us off at our yacht across the channel.

Then he turns to Luke and offers his hand.

Luke is polite. There's not a chance in hell he's not shaking that hand. So he does that.

But a look passes between the two of them. Some kind of hidden message.

I don't know how that's possible. They have literally known each other an hour.

But it happens. Because I see it happen. And I have those looks with Luke. I am fluent in Luke's secret-look language.

So that pisses me off too.

Then we all climb on a Sea-Doo and five minutes later, we're telling the security team thank you and waving goodbye from the sunbathing platform.

"Welp. That was… interesting." I say it to Posie because Luke is already climbing up the flybridge steps.

Posie looks at me, then turns on her heel and tries to open the doors that lead into the saloon.

It's locked, of course.

"Can you please open this? I need to find my phone." There's a little bit of panic in her voice.

"Jesus." I grab her arm and turn her towards me. "Calm down."

"I need. My phone." She growls these words through gritted teeth.

"OK." I punch in the code for the doors, then slide them open.

Posie darts away from me, heading towards the couch, feeling along the cushions until she finds her phone. "Fuck." She turns towards me. "There's no service?"

"Well. We are in the middle of nowhere." Just as I say that, the engine comes online with a low rumble and Luke is yelling at me from the flybridge to pull the anchors. "You're gonna have to wait until we get back to the marina."

"Fuck!" she says, turning away again.

"What the hell is your problem?"

But she doesn't answer me. Just walks through the dining room and disappears down below to the guest cabins.

OK. Note to self. Time for Posie to go. I've had enough of her.

Luke is still yelling about the anchors, so I put Posie out of my mind and get to work so we can leave this damn island and go home.

Taco night.

I'm really looking forward to taco night and none of what happened today is gonna ruin it for me.

After I get the anchors situated, I go up to the flybridge and plop down on the couch across from the helm. Luke is standing, leaning against the backrest of his chair, carefully navigating the beast out of the channel. The security team waves to us as we leave and motor into open waters. Luke messes with the autopilot and then turns to me.

"What?" I ask.

He just stares at me, eyes a little bit narrowed. Then he sighs. "Where's Posie?"

"Down in the guest cabin. Why?"

"Why? Why?" He huffs. "Because that shit show of a party?" He points in that direction. "What the hell was that?"

I shrug. "I dunno. But who cares? The job is over and we're on our way home for taco night." I smile at him. He can't resist my charm. It's why we're so good together.

But he doesn't smile. Instead he growls at me. "*Zach.*"

"Luke?"

"That wasn't a party. It was a…" He pauses to look back at the island. "It was… something. But it was not a party."

"Looked like a party to me."

He shoots me a fuck-you look and then walks away.

"Where are you going?"

"To check on Posie."

I get up and jog over to him, grabbing his arm just before he reaches the stairs. "Forget her. I'm done with her. She was just a fun distraction, right? But it's over now."

Again, he just… stares at me.

"*What?*"

He shrugs off my grip, grabs the handles to the stairs, and jumps all the way down in one leap, landing with a thud on the aft cockpit deck.

"What the hell is wrong with you?" I call.

He doesn't answer me. Just disappears inside the saloon.

I never quite mastered the whole jumping down boat stairs the way natural-born sailors do, so it takes me a few seconds to catch up to Luke in the dining room. "What the hell is your problem?"

"My problem?" He turns on me. "My problem is…" He looks back at the island. "Everything that just happened back there. That's my problem."

"OK." I don't know what to say. I get what he's referring to. I would just prefer to put this day behind us. Because Posie is a problem and I'm done with her. Even if she didn't raise all kinds of eyebrows back there by calling herself a Payseur and outing me as a fucking Boston, I would still be done with her.

And is now really the time to start explaining to Luke how Bart and Chandler have the last name

Conner? And how I'm practically related to those freaks by my little cousin-niece, Maisy?

Nope.

Nope. I'm so not ready to go there right now.

That's the kind of shit show I wanted to get away from.

That's the whole reason I stayed down in Key West and didn't go back up to the city with Jesse and Emma.

And it's fucking taco night. OK? I'm really trying to focus on taco night.

"Well?" Luke asks.

"Well." I rub my hands down my face. "I don't know what to tell you. I don't even know why you're looking to me for an explanation. It wasn't my party. It wasn't my idea to come out here today. It was your job, Luke. You're the reason we went there."

He narrows his eyes at me. And then in a low voice he says, "But you sure made the most of it, didn't you?" Then he turns away and walks into the kitchen, banging cupboards as he gets down a glass, then banging a drawer as he picks out a bottle of whiskey.

I follow him. "What are you talking about?"

"You know. This whole fucking year we've been hanging out I've gone along with your… *fun times*. With your… *sexual preferences*. With your… *girls*."

"Gone along?" I scoff. "Is that what you call it? Because I seem to remember you having a pretty good time with all my *girls*. And I just told you, I'm done with this one. We're getting rid of her the minute we dock at home. Then we're going to your parents' house, we're gonna eat some delicious homemade tacos, and chat with your fucking family, and drink a few beers, and then we're gonna walk down the street to our house and forget this day ever happened."

"Is that right?"

"Isn't it right?"

"Did you get Bart's number?"

"Did you get Chandler's?"

"I'm not the one who's always looking for another sexual partner, Zach. That's you."

I laugh. "You really think that I'm gonna hook up with Bartholomew *Conner*?" I scoff again. "Like… have you lost your fucking mind?"

"Bart *Conner*." Luke pauses to think about this. I'm like ninety percent certain that Luke has no idea who the Conners are or how they're related to me because this is my cousin Joey's secret problem. Maisy Kane Conner is Joey's daughter. Charlotte Kane was his baby mama before she disappeared down here in the Caribbean two years ago. And Michael Conner is Charlotte's ex-husband and baby daddy to Charlotte's second child, Malinda.

And, apparently, he's Bart and Chandler's uncle. Wonderful.

The whole thing from top to bottom is a family-tree shit show. Because my oldest cousin, Johnny, was the money-maker for all those people who live up at the Kane estate.

I cannot tell Luke any of this.

Hell, I barely understand what it means that Johnny is the money-maker for this insane shadow-government, global cabal of rich and powerful people who actually run the world. Especially since Johnny stopped being the money-maker a year ago when he came back to the city with a girl called Megan Machette and settled into a life of leisure at our family lake house while his new girl incubated a baby.

They had a girl, by the way. She's now two months old and we call her Beatrice.

Well, I don't call her Beatrice. I don't call her anything because I've never met the kid. I've been hiding out in Key West with Luke, trying to forget my place in this deranged Boston world and pretend I'm part of his Dumas normal one.

And that was going pretty good until today. It's been almost one whole year of living in a tiny cottage on Dumas Street, eating family dinners every Saturday night, and having crazy dirty sex with my hot boyfriend.

"Conner. Why does that name sound familiar?"

"Uh… because it was on your schedule today?" I offer this up hopefully.

But Luke isn't buying it. Because somewhere along the line he's heard the name Michael Conner. He heard it from me, or Jesse, or Emma—it doesn't really matter who he heard it from, he just knows it's ringing a bell. And he's about ten seconds away from asking the right questions. The ones I will have to answer truthfully. Because lying by omission is one thing but lying to his face is something else entirely. I don't do it. I like Luke. I'm not going to fuck up what we have over Michael Conner.

But that one bit of truth will unravel things. Once you pull on that loose string… well, there's no telling how fast things will come apart after that.

So I only have one option left.

Distraction.

And there's only one sure-fire way to distract a man on the verge of deciphering a secret and that's with sex.

So I walk over to him, I look him straight in the eyes, and I say, "Luke. I'm not interested in Bart. I'm into you, OK? You. Just you. And Posie is nobody. I give no fucks about Posie." Then I grab his dick through his shorts and shoot him my trademark sexy grin. "And I'm gonna prove it to you."

CHAPTER TWELVE

POSIE

I don't bother answering Zach, just head down the stairs that lead to the guest cabins.

I'm never going to tell him what's on my mind right now.

I'm never going to tell anyone.

I pause at the bottom, looking to the left. That's the bedroom we were in last night. Then I look to the right at the two smaller cabins on either side of the hallway.

I don't know what I'm going to do down here so I just lean against the wall, slide down it, then pull my knees up and rest my chin on them.

I don't want to think about what I saw in that room back on the island. I want to forget about this whole day.

But I hear it in my head.

Blink.

The lights go on.

And my whole world ceases to make sense in that moment.

Charlotte?

Whispers to a ghost. That's all that could've been. Right?

Surely there was no one else down in that room with me.

I close my eyes tight, forcing the image to go away. Blink.

The lights go out.

Yes. I like the darkness.

But then that woman… what was her deal?

I should not think about her. I should not think about any of it. But the reporter in me is already asking questions. Already adding up all the extraordinary things that were happening on that island.

In plain sight.

Those people on the beach—they weren't getting naked in some secret dungeon room. They were doing that in the open.

And the bonfire? That was some teepee of wood they had going there. At least thirty feet high.

And the body painting? Those symbols? The masks. What good is a painted-on mask? Does that hide you? Or was that not the purpose of them?

Then we have the drums.

Jesus Christ. I feel like I fell into an alternate reality. Some… alien planet where the native people were all backwards and looking to eat the unfortunate crash-landers.

Fuck. My imagination is working overtime. *Stop it, Posie.*

And I fucked up. So bad. First, I outed Zach as a Boston. I don't know what they were talking about after I left to get drinks, but I'm absolutely positive that it involved the surname Boston. That's why he was hostile to me up there.

He's mad.

And I think he knows.

He knows I'm fake. In fact, now that I think about it, I'm pretty sure he set me up. He knew last night. And this weekend was just a way to… what? Keep his eye on me? Feed me bunk info so I would write my gossip article and then get pinged by the Boston family lawyers for defamation?

But that can't be all of it. First, he wanted me to be his little toy. To spice things up with Luke. And you know what's funny? I thought Luke was the asshole this morning.

But nope. Turns out it's Zach Boston.

I need to get the fuck out of here.

Four hours. It's at least four hours back to the marina. Then I'm checking out of my hotel, leaving a message for my boss at Buzz Hollywood that I quit, and I'm getting my ass on a fucking plane back to Oklahoma.

A loud thump pulls me out of my thoughts. Then Luke and Zach are arguing upstairs.

I can't quite make out what they are saying because they are not being overly loud. But it's definitely an argument. And I hear my name.

Great. That's just great.

I hold up my phone, waving it around, desperate for some random signal. How does a yacht this big not have cell service?

There must be a satellite. Or a radio. But then I'd have to ask Luke to use his... connection of whatever the fuck. And I'm not leaving a message for my boss while they're around, that's for sure.

Maybe Zach is on to me. But I'm pretty sure he hasn't told Luke.

The argument upstairs gets louder. Not because they are screaming, but because they're right up at the top of the stairs now.

And now I really can hear it.

They are arguing about their sex life.

No. Not quite. Luke is bringing up all the things I said earlier about how Zach brings girls home to him. And that's wonderful. I'm gonna be blamed for this. I feel it coming.

But Zach is trying to remain playful. In fact, if I'm not mistaken, he's trying to distract Luke with sexual innuendo.

Clever.

Nope. Luke isn't falling for it. And now he's asking questions about me.

Great. I'm screwed. Zach is gonna blab, Luke is gonna throw me off his boat, and I'm gonna be stuck dealing with the aftermath of what I just saw in that room all alone.

I take a deep breath and hold it.

What did I see in that room?

Am I really sure that's what I saw?

I want to lie to myself. I really do. I want to convince myself it was fake. Not real. Or possibly even an illusion. Hell, I'll settle for a hallucination at this point.

But none of that is true.

It was real.

I could *smell* it.

And if I quit my job and go home—and that woman figures out that I was in that room when she went down there—will they come after me?

Oh, hell yes, they will.

And if they do, I'm going to need people on my side.

People like the Boston family.

I look up the stairs. Zach is whispering things to Luke. Presumably sexy things. But still, Luke is resisting.

I stand up, suddenly understanding what I need to do next.

Get Zach on my side.

And I'm gonna do that by helping him distract Luke. I don't know why he's doing it, but it doesn't matter. I fucked up. And I need allies.

I adjust my girls in my bikini top, fluff up my hair, and then take a deep breath.

When I let it out, I head up the stairs.

I can see them both before I reach the top. They're in the kitchen, which is directly behind the helm. It's a pretty nice kitchen with a bar that goes all the way around. Both of them are on the opposite side of the bar.

Luke spies me coming up the stairs and this makes Zach turn around.

I flash my best sexy grin and both of them pause their fight. It's probably not because of my sexy grin. They probably just don't want to fight in front of me.

"What's going on?" I ask.

Both of them huff.

I walk around the bar and sidle up to Zach, rubbing a hand up and down his perfect six-pack abs. Even though he and I are much further apart in the comradery department, he's the one trying to distract Luke with sex, and not the other way around.

Zach pushes me off him. There's not a lot of heat behind that move, but it's clear he's not interested in me.

"What the hell, Zach?" Luke asks.

"What are you talking about?"

"Don't just push her off. I mean, I get it. That's how you see people. Just things to discard. But she's a person, OK? Treat her like one."

"What the actual fuck, Luke? You don't even like this girl."

"I like her," Luke says. Then he grabs my arm and pulls me over to his side.

"Um. Guys? I'm not here to start a fight. I thought maybe... you know. Before we get back to civilization, we could..." I waggle my eyebrows at Luke.

"Oh, for fuck's sake," Zach huffs and points a finger at me. "I'm on to you, Posie. Fucking poser."

I scowl at him. "I don't know what you're talking about, but you're being a dick. To both of us." I slip my arm behind Luke's waist. He's very firm. And I can't help myself. I take a moment to enjoy his hard back muscles.

"Please," Zach says. "Do you really want me to out you? Right now?"

"What are you doing?" Luke asks Zach.

"She's not who she says she is. She's a spy."

Luke laughs. "A spy?"

"I'm not a freaking spy!"

Zach points at me again. "I know who you work for, you little liar." Then he directs his attention to Luke. "The only reason she's here is because I noticed her following me a few weeks back." He looks at me again. "Pink hair, Posie? Or should I call you Patty Ann?"

I look down at my long pink hair. "There's nothing wrong with my hair."

"It makes you stand out, dumbass."

Luke takes a step forward and pushes Zach back with a flat hand to the chest. "Don't call her names."

"Why are you sticking up for her? She's spying on us! She's a fucking wannabe reporter for goddamned Buzz Hollywood!"

"What?" Luke looks down at me. Then positions himself in a way that makes it very clear he's not on my side anymore.

Which is just great. Now they both hate me and I'm gonna be all alone when this little boat trip is over. All alone, knowing that at any moment those people back on that island might suspect I saw more than I should've. Might come looking for me.

"She was hired to spy on me," Zach says. He narrows his eyes at me. "Do you really think I can't pick you parasites out in a crowd?" He laughs. "I grew up with Jesse Boston. All the tabloid fucks followed us everywhere. I do a facial recognition background check on every person I meet. I have a fucking security company on standby, bitch. I ran your face that very first night. And guess what? Your name isn't Posie. And it sure the fuck isn't Payseur!" Then he takes his attention back to Luke. "She fucked up back there. Big time. And it did not go unnoticed. She outed me, Luke. She told that fuck Bart who I was. Then…" He's worked up now. "Then! Then she has the nerve to call herself Posie Payseur."

Luke is shaking his head. "OK. Like. That sucks. I'm sorry she outed you to Bart. But what the fuck does this Payseur name have to do with anything?" He side-eyes me. "Aside from the fact that she's a liar?"

"Payseur? *Payseur*?" Zach is kinda losing it. "They're only the oldest, richest, sickest banking family on the entire planet!"

Luke shrugs. "Never even heard of them."

"Of course you've never heard of them! That's the whole fucking point!"

"The whole point of what?" Luke is beginning to get tired of this. "I don't know what you're talking about."

Zach shoots me a look. And I swear to god, I have never seen this expression on his face. Ever.

It's… it's… *hate.*

He's shooting me hate.

He reaches out, pokes me right in the chest three times, and says, "You have no fucking idea the kind of shit storm you just unleashed."

"I didn't do it on purpose!"

"You're a liar!"

"I'm not! I didn't mean to out you! Your name just slipped out! And I don't know who the fucking Payseurs are either! It's just a damn name I saw when I was waitressing at the airport! It goes nice with Posie! I like alliteration! So kill me!"

"Your name isn't Posie!"

"Fine! I'm Patty Ann. Happy now?"

"Why are you calling yourself Posie?" Luke asks.

I open my mouth to explain, but the only thing that comes out is a long, tired breath. And then… I don't know. I just get fed up with this shit. "None of this is my fault! All I wanted to do was snoop a little! Get a little flavor to add to my article! That's it!"

"What the hell are you talking about?" Luke is getting mad now too. "So you really are a reporter for Buzz Hollywood?"

"Yes. But—"

Zach throws up his arms. "See? I'm not into her, Luke. Once I found out I was just playing her the way she was playing me. I'm not into Bart, either. I was just being nice to the guy so we could crash their party for an afternoon. The only thing I want right now is to get rid of this bitch, enjoy taco night with the fam, take you to bed, and forget we ever met two people called Bart and Chandler Conner! Is that too much to ask?"

"What?" Luke puts up his hand. "Conner. That's where we left off before you started trying to distract me." Then he looks at me. "And that's why you came back upstairs. What do you two know that I don't? Or maybe the better question is, what are the two of you trying to hide from me?"

"Listen," Zach says, placing a hand on Luke's chest. But it's not an aggressive move. It's meant to gentle him. "It's a long story and I don't want to get into it in front of her. I'm sure the Conners are part of her hit piece too, and I don't want to drag Maisy into this, OK?"

"Jesus Christ." Luke glares at me. "You're doing a hit piece on a little kid?"

"What the fuck are you people talking about? I don't know anything about some Conner family and I've never heard of some stupid girl called Maisy!"

"She's my cousin-niece!" Zach growls.

"So?"

"And that's why you wanted to come on this trip. You knew Bart was a Conner. And you figured—"

"No! What the hell are you talking about? I'm the one who's fucked here, OK? I'm the one who stumbled into some… some… some Satanic temple. I didn't come here looking for a goddamned dungeon! I don't know who the hell Charlotte is either, but she's creeping me out! And now you two are gonna go on your merry little way. You're gonna drop me off at the marina, kick me to the curb, and I'm gonna have to live with what I saw back there for the rest of my life! So fuck you both!"

I turn to leave and go back downstairs, but both of them grab me by the arm and pull me back.

"Hold on," Luke says. Unlike Zach, he's pretty calm. "Did you just say 'Satanic temple?'"

"Fuck the Satan bullshit," Zach counters. "Did you just say… '*Charlotte*?'"

I look back and forth between the two of them, unsure what to say next.

"One sec." Luke walks around the bar, goes up to the massive computer display that controls the boat, and all of a sudden the engines power down and things go very quiet.

"What the hell are you doing?" Zach asks.

"I'm putting us on pause. Because we're not all on the same page. And we need a minute to catch up."

"But…" Zach looks over his shoulder at a clock. "It's taco night. And we're hours away from home."

"Zach? Fuck the tacos. OK? I'll buy you some fucking Taco Bell on the way home. We just had a day. Understand? And when people in families like ours have a day"—he pauses, letting this sink in—"we don't just go home for fucking taco night. We need to figure out what just happened."

"What do you mean what happened?" I'm so confused. "What's going on?"

"You tell us," Luke says. "Now go back to the Satanic temple."

"I don't really know if it was a Satanic temple," I huff, so freaking tired right now. "But it was a weird church room in the house. And then that woman? She was looking for me. All I did"—I plead my case to Zach—"was ask where the bathroom was. I swear! I mean, I did hint that I had a feminine problem because I was afraid she would tell me the house bathrooms were only for family or something and make me use some porta potty—"

"Porta potty?" Zach laughs. "People who own private islands don't make their guests use a fucking porta potty, Posie."

"How would I know that? My experience with event bathrooms comes from festivals!"

"Stop being hostile to her," Luke snaps. "She's stressed."

"Why are you taking her side? She's a dirty little liar."

"So are you," I counter.

"What the hell am I lying about?"

"You led me on. You dragged me out here to the middle of the ocean. And now I'm scared."

"Scared of what?" Luke asks.

I turn to him. "Of what I saw back there."

"What did you see?"

I let out a long breath. Then I just shake my head. "I don't really know. It was just…" A shiver runs up my spine and then a sick feeling begins to grow in the pit of my stomach. "All of this is wrong. I can feel it." I move my attention to Zach. "I think I was set up. I think maybe… this whole thing was a setup. It was that FBI agent. Madrid."

"What?" They both say that at the same time.

"Did you say Madrid?" Luke asks.

I nod. "Yeah. She's the one who got me the job at Buzz Hollywood. I thought I had finally caught a lucky break. But I didn't. It was just a setup."

"All right," Luke says. "Let's go sit down and start from the beginning."

"But—" Zach starts.

Luke cuts him off with a pointed finger to the face. "If you say 'taco night' one more time, I swear to God, Zach, I'll never let you come to family dinner again."

Zach huffs. But he shuts up.

Luke directs me into the living room and points to the couch. "Sit."

I do, taking one corner while Zach takes the other and Luke fills up the middle. I angle myself into the arm so I can see them better. Then Luke says, "OK. Start from the beginning, Posie. How did you meet this Madrid?" He takes both my hands in his and squeezes them. "This is very important. Because we know a FBI agent called Madrid too. She's not on our side and if she sent you here, we might all be in trouble."

I'm very relieved that he wants to start with Madrid. Because I'm not ready to talk about what I stumbled into back on that island just yet.

"OK." I take a deep breath and look at Zach. "I really am a reporter. I went to Oklahoma State, not High Court."

"Ya don't say," Zach growls.

"Keep going," Luke says.

"My dad and I were super poor when I was a kid. And then he passed away in my freshman year of high school. So I got sent to a home—"

"Is this relevant?"

"Zach," Luke says, slowly turning his head to look at him. "Shut up and let the girl talk."

Zach throws his hands up. "We can't trust her. She's lying about everything."

"I'm not lying about this! The point is, I got sent to a foster home. And they were good people. The lady helped me apply for college and I got a scholarship to Oklahoma State. And I went, and I majored in journalism, but then, after graduation, I couldn't find a job. I tried for almost two years before I finally gave up and just went home. And home was in Kansas, not Oklahoma. I didn't have any family there, but I still had a few friends."

"OK," Luke says. "Where does Madrid come in?"

"Well, here's the interesting part. While I was gone those six years they built this airfield nearby. And when I got back, they were just opening a diner in the small terminal. It was just one of those private airfields, right? One terminal, one baggage claim. There was one commercial airline and they had four flights a day. The rest were all private planes. So I got a job in the diner as a waitress. My dad was the one who always called me Posie. So that's not my name, but it really is my name."

"So where did Payseur come from?" Zach asks.

"Well, the diner was never really what I'd call busy. I was the only waitress and we had one cook. But it was the only place to eat for nearly twenty miles. And the people who came in on the private planes had a house on the other side of the airfield. It was like the only house anywhere close. And all these people came in wearing black suits. Even the women."

"FBI," Luke says, looking over at Zach.

"Yep. FBI. I knew they were FBI and I know Madrid was one of them because she told me. She liked to chat me up as she was eating. Not a lot of women came in with them. But they all paid their bill with this special credit card. It was black with red letters that said 'Payseur.'"

"Fuck," Zach says, scrubbing his face with his hands.

"That's where I got the last name. Posie Payseur. I just thought it sounded cute." I shrug. "I swear. And then, out of nowhere, a guy comes in, not wearing a dark suit, but still looking nice, and he offered me a job."

"Buzz Hollywood?" Luke asks.

I nod. "Yep. Buzz. Fucking. Hollywood."

"You didn't think that was strange?" Zach asks.

"No. Madrid introduced him to me. So that seemed natural. But I also didn't get suspicious because…" I take a deep breath because this is where I turn into a psycho stalker.

"Because?" Luke prods.

"Well, a friend of mine from high school was in the diner one day. And we were talking about this secret online fan club we had for this guy back in the day. And I was still running it, even though she had moved on to more… IRL things, so to speak."

"Get to the point, Posie!"

"Listen," I say, patting the air in the direction of frustrated Zach. "I'm not crazy. And I'm not a stalker. It was a harmless teenage crush and by the time I went to college, the fan club was so big… like… I literally couldn't shut it down even if I wanted to."

"What the hell are you talking about?" And that's Zach too. Because I'm only looking at him right now.

"The fan club was about you."

Luke busts out laughing.

"Why is that funny?" Zach asks.

"Hold up," Luke says. "I think I've got this but let's run through it again. You and your friend had a fan club for Zach Boston in high school."

"Yes."

"And you're working at the diner in rando buttfuck Kansas?"

"Yep."

"Where the FBI hang out because they have a safehouse nearby."

I sigh.

"So Buzz Hollywood comes in while you're coincidentally talking to your"—he stops to do air quotes—"'high-school friend' about your fantasy love affair with Zach. And he says… what? 'Hey, Posie. I hear you're the Zach Boston Fan Club queen and we're in this buttfuck-nowhere town, casually eating at this buttfuck-nowhere diner, looking to hire a new reporter to do an exposé on this very guy. How would you like the opportunity of a lifetime?'"

"You don't have to make fun of me."

"I'm not!" But he is, because he's laughing.

"Fine. I was…"

"Stupid?" Zach offers.

"OK. I'll go with stupid. Because my point is… I'm not the bad guy here. It's a weird string of coincidences—"

"It was a setup, Posie."

"It was a setup," I amend, agreeing with Luke. "And it's not my fault that I was accidentally doing my snooping job on that island and ran into a Satanic temple and then got stuck ducking behind a curtain that had a secret door to a dungeon, filled with…"

Oh, God.

"Filled with what?" Luke asks.

"Well." I swallow and take a deep breath. "I'm not really sure what I saw, you guys. It was…" I make a face. "It was…"

"It was what?" Zach looks like he wants to shake the shit out of me.

"Evil." I look up at them and exhale. "That's the only way to describe it. It was just… *evil*."

CHAPTER THIRTEEN

LUKE

"Posie." I say her name calmly. But inside I want to scream at her. "We're gonna need more to go on than just *evil*."

"I know. It's just…" She looks at me. And that fear I saw in her eyes back on the island is back. "It's hard to explain."

"How did you get the name Charlotte?" Zach asks. "It's really important, Posie. Like, I cannot stress enough how important this is."

"Why is it important?" I ask Zach.

He puts up a hand. "Just hold on, Luke. Posie. Tell me how you got that name. Because I know someone named Charlotte who went missing two years ago and if she's alive—"

"She's not alive," Posie whispers.

"How do you know?" Zach asks.

Posie takes a deep breath. "Because… because there was a skeleton down in that dungeon. And the woman?" She looks up at me. "That crazy woman Bart came and took away? She followed me. She was looking for me. But I was hiding in a little alcove. I didn't realize where I was. I couldn't see anything. It was dark. But she flicked the light on before she came down the steps, and then she stopped at the bottom, and said, 'Charlotte?' Like she was asking if Charlotte was there." Posie looks at Zach. "But she was dead. Just a skeleton chained to a wall by her wrist. And written on the wall—in what I think was blood—were the words 'Charlotte was here.'"

"Jesus fucking Christ," Zach says. "What did she look like?"

"Look like?" Posie asks. "Like...a fucking skeleton."

Zach looks at me. "Then it might not be Charlotte."

"She had blonde hair," Posie says. "That was the only thing left of her. Except the white dress and what looked like a white mask. You know, the kind people wear to masquerade parties? Except it wasn't black. It was white."

Zach gets up and starts pacing the saloon.

"What's this mean?" I ask him. "Who is Charlotte?"

"She's... she was... Maisy's mother."

"Maisy? Your cousin-niece?" I say.

"Yeah. She disappeared two years ago. This is…"
But he stops.

"This is what?"

"It's… well, I hate to be Captain Obvious here, but literal Boston family skeletons in the closet."

"Dungeon," Posie whispers. Then she looks up at me. "That's not all that was down there. If it were just one skeleton chained to a wall? I could probably process that. But it wasn't."

"There were more?"

"Not bodies. Just the one. But there were photos, Luke. Really, really… evil photos."

I don't expect her to continue. And I'm not going to make her give details.

But she does this anyway. "Torture, I think." She looks at Zach and whispers, "I'm sorry. They were photos of people being tortured." She pauses. Like she's picturing them. Then she shakes her head. "I've never seen anything so… evil. Not in all my life. It was… evil."

"OK," I say, getting up to pace the floor with Zach. He goes one way. I go another. And then we turn, pass each other until we run out of room, and do it all again. "OK. Let's just… calm down."

Which is a dumb thing to say. No one is hysterical. No one is even talking.

"We need to go back," Zach suddenly says.

Posie stands up. "No. I'm not going back. If you guys want to go back, you can. But I'm staying here." She stomps her foot.

"Here?" Zach says, sneering at her. "Here is the middle of the fucking ocean. You go where we go."

"I'll get out. Give me a lifejacket and call the Coast Guard. I'm not going back. I'm not. I did not sign up for this kind of shit. I'm not good with gore, OK? I wanted to be a gossip column reporter! I'm not some… investigative war-zone, Pulitzer Prize-earning journalist! I run a damn online fan club! I was hoping to date you! Maybe… if I was super lucky, marry you next summer."

"What?" I laugh.

She whirls and turns on me. "You can laugh all you want. But I'm a nice girl, OK? A nice. Girl. I don't do this shit. I dream about weddings, and honeymoons, and weird, coincidental random meetings with famous people on tropical islands. I do not do… *this!*"

"We're not going back," I say.

"We are going back!" Zach counters. "Johnny risked his life to look for stupid Charlotte last summer and came home… weird. And now he's got this baby mama—who I do not trust, by the way—and a fucking actual baby! And he retired from the goddamned money-making business and is now living at our lake house. Something is not right about all that. And then today, I stumble into a fucking clue? I need to follow up. I need to go home and give Johnny facts. I need to warn Joey that Maisy can't stay with those Kane people anymore and he needs to file for full custody. So as much as it pains me to miss taco night at the Dumas house, we are not leaving here until I have something to take home to them."

Sometimes Zach Boston really is adorable.

This is definitely one of those times.

"Relax," I say, gripping his shoulders. "I said we weren't going back. I never said we weren't gonna follow up."

"Then we have to go back."

"Do you remember when you made fun of me for wanting the drone package when I bought this yacht?"

He looks confused for a moment. Then he laughs.

"Not so funny now, is it?"

"The drone. Are we in range?"

"Probably. We were only motoring for about ten minutes before I cut the engine."

"A drone?" Posie says. "You can't fly a drone down into the dungeon."

"No," I say. "We can't. But something happening there tonight. Something creepy is my guess. And none of that seemed to be happening in a dungeon." I point at Posie. "Go get us some sandwiches. We need to eat something."

"Fucking taco night," Zach whines.

Posie glares at me. "Did you just order me to make you sandwiches?"

"Yes. And bring us a beer, too."

Her face. I almost laugh. But I'm not really kidding. "Bitch," I say, "you're a huge pain in my ass right now. You know that? And we all have to eat. You don't have a job on this ship. So that's your fucking job. Go do it."

She points to Zach. "He's not working either. He can make sandwiches."

"He's part owner. You're the only freeloader."

Zach guffaws.

Posie narrows her eyes at me. "Is this a man joke?"

I roll my eyes. Fucking women. They are too easy. "Yes, babe. It's a man joke. But we really do want beer and sandwiches. So get your ass in that kitchen and rustle up some eats while us men figure out how to work the new toy. I mean… the high-tech surveillance equipment."

Zach laughs again.

Posie flips me off with both hands, but she does as she's told and retreats to the kitchen.

I look over at Zach. "We good?"

He lifts his chin up a little, but his smile is still there. "I'm on your side, Luke. You should know that by now."

I glance in the direction of the kitchen, then say, in a lowered voice, "What about her?"

Zach walks over to me, kinda looking over his shoulder. There's a partition between the dining room and the kitchen, but the pocket doors on either side are both open. So it's not exactly private. "What about her?"

"You brought her into this."

He shrugs. "Doesn't mean she needs to stay."

"That's cold."

"What are you talking about?"

"We can't ditch her now. Not after what just happened."

"She's a fucking spy, Luke."

"And it sounds to me like she's over it."

"Great. She can go back where she came from. Problem solved."

"No. Problem not solved. She's in danger now. And that's our fault."

He narrows his eyes at me. "You mean my fault?"

"I'm not blaming you. I'm here too. It's not about blame. It's about responsibility. We need to make sure she's safe before we let her go anywhere."

"What if she wants to leave?"

"She can't. It's as simple as that. She's a loose end, Zach. For everyone. She stays with us. So you need to be nicer to her."

"She set me up, Luke. She had a creepy fucking fan group about me. God only knows what kind of delusional bullshit is running on repeat inside her head."

"She stays with us. At least until we figure out what the hell is happening. And that's my final word on the matter."

Zach gets this defiant look on his face. I'm familiar with it. But we don't generally argue and he's not up for one right now. Not with Posie in the next room. So he just throws up his hands. "Whatever."

"Good," I say. "Let's unpack that drone."

We go up to the flybridge where the drone is stored in a locker and start pulling it out. I was excited about this little add-on. But I've only had the yacht for about a month and things have been pretty busy, so I hadn't actually taken the thing out for a test spin yet. I've had my share of drones over the years. Tony uses them a lot to take pics of his clients. They are often honeymooners looking for shit like that. But I use them for the hoverboarders and the parasailers. They like to have footage to post on Insta. In fact, that's almost always one of the first questions customers ask me. *Can we get a vid? Need to post on socials.*

Social media is the best thing to ever happen to the adventure business. Everyone wants to prove they are spontaneously badass even when the whole thing is planned from top to bottom.

Zach is quiet as we work. He's got things on his mind.

But that's nothing unusual. He's always been one of those guys who has things on their mind, but pretends not to if you ask. So I've stopped asking.

It's about his family, anyway. I know that's what he's pondering as we casually chat about the drone.

Our families have become… well, sort of a no-go zone for us. The Bostons have secrets and us Dumas brothers have secrets too. And sure, we've had to share a bunch of those secrets with each other since the FBI swooped in trying to entrap us during one of the family smuggling operations. But we still have no clue what Johnny Boston is up to. And I'm pretty sure Johnny plans to keep it that way.

So Zach and I don't go there.

Zach gets up and goes over to the helm to download the software into our system just as Posie comes up the steps wearing an apron and carrying a silver tray filled with sandwiches wrapped in plastic wrap.

She does this kind of ironic curtsey thing and smiles a very big, but very fake, smile at me. "Your sandwiches, my lord."

I grin back at her. I can't help it. And that apron looks adorable on her. It's some vintage thing I bought for Zach in a local thrift store as a joke. Mint-green, made of that organza fabric that's probably pretty useless as far as aprons go, and it has ruffles around the edges.

And Posie is still wearing her green bikini and when you add it all up with her long, pink hair she looks... cute. She looks very fucking cute.

She's definitely growing on me.

She did come off as a player at the club, but she's not in control of much, that's pretty clear. And I like the ones who need saving. Always have.

"Did the cooking exhaust you, serving wench?"

I'm not sure if that's gonna offend her or not, but I like to make crude remarks like that just to see where a woman's line is. Just to see if she has a sense of humor or if she's gonna try to cut my balls off every time I say something politically incorrect.

Posie snorts. "My lord, the sandwiches were prepackaged."

"I know, Posie. The housekeepers stock the fridge when they clean. Their mom makes those sandwiches for us. That's why I told you to go get them." Then I wink. "I wouldn't send you to the kitchen. I'm just fucking with you."

She sighs, sets the tray down on the coffee table, then sinks into the couch. "I know. I get it."

"That apron looks good on you though." Then I glance over at Zach, who is still messing with the software at the helm. "Looks good on Zach too. He's usually naked underneath when he serves me breakfast."

He glances over his shoulder at me, grinning. "Fuck you. That only happened one time."

Posie smiles, then chuckles to herself. "You guys are weird."

"We're not weird. Why are we weird?"

"What do you do? Do you guys go hunting for girls? This is a regular thing for you?"

"Why not?" Zach says from the helm. He's not looking at us.

"So… you're together? Or you're not?"

"We're together," I say. "We just like… to keep things interesting." My mood drops a level when I say this because this was Posie's argument when she talked me into being her little partner in crime this morning.

Zach is getting bored with me. And the girls are a way to keep him interested.

It might be truer than I'd like to admit.

I mean, he's twenty-three. His life just started. I'm not old, but I'm set. I've got the business, brand-new yacht, a house that's paid for, and I'm turning thirty soon. Dating Zach Boston isn't like dating a woman because I don't take care of him. He doesn't need me. To be fair, I don't need him either, but we're just at different stages in life. And if I was dating women, I could maybe find a younger one who wanted that shit. The house, the money, the stability. To be taken care of.

Zach isn't like that. This thing we're doing probably won't last. And that's got nothing to do with how we feel about each other, it's just the odds.

"OK, we're ready," Zach says, letting the topic about us and our girl habits slide away. "I programmed the GPS into the drone's navigation. What screen do you want to use?"

I get up, drone in hand, and point to the TV up here. "Put it on there. That way we get a nice clean view and we can record it."

"No problem," Zach says, fucking with the helm computer again. Another minute later, the app pops up on the sixty-four-inch screen. Then the camera comes online and I get a nice view of Posie on the couch.

"Oh, my God." She starts arranging her messy hair. "Point that thing another direction. I look like the death I saw in that dungeon."

"No, you don't," Zach snaps. "You look fine."

He's not even looking at her when he says this. So it comes off like more of a 'shut the fuck up' kind of remark than the 'you look good, babe' it could've been.

Posie and I trade glances. I shake my head at her and she keeps her mouth shut, tacitly agreeing to let me handle it.

"We're ready," Zach says. "Let's do this before the sun sets."

"It's got night vision," I say.

Zach looks at me as he finger-combs his hair. "Damn. You went all out on this one."

I shrug. "Fuck it. Go big or go home. And it's gonna pay off right now." I grab the remote, take the drone over to the flybridge's aft sun deck, and set it down. The remote has a screen on it. It's actually bigger than a nice-sized tablet and looks a little bit like a gaming control with joysticks and a track pad. And that screen is fine if you're doing something simple, but having the footage on the TV will bring everything up in 4K ultra-HD.

The drone rises and then takes off in the direction of the island. I keep my eye on it until it disappears, then go back and sit down next to Posie in front of the TV.

"What if they see it?" she asks. "Would they shoot it down?"

Zach sits on the other side of her, propping his elbows up on his knees to lean forward. "They better not shoot it down," he murmurs. "I'll be pissed. This is a damn nice drone."

I don't know why I smile at that, but I do. "I'm gonna go in high. This model can go several thousand feet up in altitude if I want it to."

"Is that even legal?" Posie asks.

Zach and I both grunt. Then he says, "Pretty much everything is legal out here, Posie. We're not in the US right now."

"Oh." She pulls her legs up and resituates herself and we all concentrate on the drone footage for a little while, watching as it flies across the sea towards the island.

I split the screen so that we have a view in front and behind.

"Damn," Zach says, grinning at me. "That's fucking cool!"

"And the sunset looks amazing," Posie says.

It does too. Deep red orange off in the distance and a little bit of purple around the edges.

I feel like maybe our little trio has arrived with this sudden satisfaction from all ends. I'm not sure where we're at, but the tension that was so thick earlier is definitely gone now.

We're not that far away from the island, so it doesn't take long for it to come back into view. I go way up high just in case any of the security people are looking at the sky.

There's little chance of them seeing us since the sun is going down, but the sea is super calm today—which means no wind. And I don't want them to hear us.

But as I get closer, I realize that I don't have to worry about that.

The drone does not have sound, but a little bit of zoom action shows me dozens—maybe even hundreds—of those huge drums lined up along the edges of the smaller island. And an equal number of people pounding on them.

"Damn," Zach says. "That's quite a show they're putting on."

He's not just talking about the drummers, either. The whole sandbar has been transformed since we left. The tide is low right now, so the sandbar is an actual beach. And there are hundreds of naked people dancing to the beat of the drums.

And in the center, on top of the floating platform, is a raging bonfire. Easily thirty feet high.

"Hold on," Zach says, getting to his feet. "What the hell are they doing with that girl?"

"Oh, shit," Posie says. Then she hides her eyes with her hands. "Tell me that's not happening."

But it is happening.

There are half a dozen naked men dragging a girl in a white robe towards the bonfire. She is kicking and screaming. Thrashing around. And when I lower the drone down and zoom in more, there is a look of pure panic on her face.

And then....

"Oh, fuck!" Zach grabs his hair and turns away from the footage.

"What? What happened?" Posie asks. She's still got her face covered.

"They threw her in," Zach says, walking over to the TV so he can get a better look. "They fucking threw her into the fire!"

CHAPTER FOURTEEN

ZACH

I just stare at the TV. Unable to process what I'm looking at.

Part of this is because it's so horrific. But also because it's on the fucking TV. Which makes it feel like a movie.

But this isn't a movie. This is raw footage of a party the three of us were just at, less than two hours ago.

"Holy shit." Posie breaks the silence. "Holy fucking shit." She turns and looks at Luke. "It makes sense now."

"What are you talking about?" I ask.

She looks up at me. "That woman. When I asked her to use the bathroom, I said I had a feminine problem."

"So?" I say. And I'm not trying to be a dick to her. But I'm still not over the fact that she outed me as Zach Boston to these freaks.

"So?" She sneers back at me. "So I was hinting I was on my period. That's like… you know, the magic words when you need to use someone's bathroom and you get the feeling they're gonna tell you to go jump off a cliff."

Luke and I just look at each other.

"Well, you wouldn't know, would you?" Posie is really making a face at me now. "What it feels like to be a woman in need of a bathroom?"

I roll my hand at her. "Can you just get on with the story?"

"Zach," Luke cautions. "Just be cool."

"I'm being fucking cool, OK? I just watched a girl get thrown into a bonfire. Excuse me if I don't have a lot of patience for her bathroom problems."

Posie and Luke share a look. And you know what? That pisses me off. He's my boyfriend, not hers. They should not be sharing *looks*.

"Anyway," Posie huffs, "it was just an excuse to snoop around."

"Oh, I get it. Two for the price of one, right? You get the Conners *and* the Bostons for your stupid Buzz Hollywood article."

She doesn't deny it, so I feel a little smug. But then Luke says, "For fuck's sake, Zach. Let her fucking talk."

"Thank you." Posie smiles at him. "But she told this guy to take me there. And she called it the coral bathroom. Which was a literal bathroom. Like… just a bathtub. No toilet or anything."

She pauses like this is the end of the story.

"So?" And that comes from Luke, so I'm glad I didn't have to be Captain Obvious this time.

"It was a ritual room," Posie says.

Zach and I look at each other. Dubious.

"It was! And I was the girl." She points to the TV.

We all look at the hovering drone footage, then immediately wish we hadn't. "Jesus Christ, Luke." I turn away, covering my eyes. "Get that off screen."

"I want more evidence," he says. "Might as well get as much as we can while we're here."

"My point is," Posie snaps at us both now, "I was her."

"You were never her," I say.

"That woman thought I was. I was this close to being her! If Luke and Chandler hadn't been there—"

"Hey, I was there too!"

She ignores me and just shakes her head. "I could've been her."

No one says anything for a few moments.

Then Posie gets up and just… leaves. Just goes downstairs. Disappears.

Luke lets out a long breath. "You don't have to be so mean to her. None of this is really her fault."

"First of all"—I put up a finger. I'm making a list—"it *is* her fault. She pushed her way into my life under false pretenses. She lied about everything. Second. She outed me as a Boston to fucking Bart. I could've done without the goddamned reminder that my family is into secret society shit up to our necks. Third. Those psychopaths?" I point to the screen. "Live at the Kane Estate. Where my fucking cousin-niece lives." I say that part slow to enunciate my point. "Do I need to go on?"

Luke takes a moment. I wait it out because Luke is kind of a contemplative guy and I sorta enjoy looking at his face when he's thinking.

Finally, he says, "OK. I see your points. But she's…" He looks over at the aft deck stairs. Then he looks back at me. "She's vulnerable, Zach."

"You didn't like her this morning. Why are you suddenly taking her side?"

"I'm not. Well, OK, fine. I am. But the reason I didn't like her this morning was because I felt like you were bringing these random girls in because you were bored with me."

I… don't know what to say.

"And I was pretty sure—" He holds both hands up. "OK. I'm just gonna be honest here. It feels like you're about done with me."

"I'm not bored. I just like…" I shrug.

"You like girls, Zach."

"So? I mean, yes. I do. But I'm… Well. I'm worried I'm too much and not enough for you at the same time."

He squints his eyes at me. Then fucks with the remote and sets it down on a side table. "Explain."

"You know." I'm still holding up my finger so I start ticking off my points. "I'm kinda lazy. I don't have a job. I don't have a trust fund. I don't have any goals. And I live in your parents' cottage house rent-free. Which pretty much makes me Jesse Boston junior." Luke laughs at me. "And my family is part of some global secret-society shadow-government cabal. That's what I mean by not enough and too much. And one day, Luke, you're gonna wake up—or actually start listening to your brother Alonzo—and decide I'm dead weight. I'm holding you down or whatever. And maybe all the other girls I brought home were for me, but this one"—I point down at the floor—"she was for you. I took one look at Posie last weekend and I thought, *Holy fucking shit. I wish Luke were here. Because even though he doesn't think he's into girls, he would love this one. She's totally his type.*"

Luke glances away from me. And for a moment I figure—welp. This is it. This is where we break up. And the next four hours are gonna be really awkward. And then I'll be homeless. And you know what? Who cares about all that? I'll be without Luke.

"I don't know what life looks like without you, Luke. I don't. Last year, I guess, maybe I could see myself somewhere else. But now?" I just shrug as Luke's eyes track back to meet mine.

He shakes his head. "I thought you were getting bored with me. I thought you brought Posie home to like… give me one last chance to be what you needed."

"Dude."

"I sometimes think I'm too old for you. Or I'm too rigid for you. Not fun enough. Not spontaneous enough—"

"Luke. You literally own an adventure business."

"I know. But it's a business."

I walk over to him and place both hands on his shoulders. "Listen. I'm willing to blame this all on you if that's what you need."

He laughs.

"Seriously. I'm not going anywhere. Are you?"

He shakes his head. "Nope. Not unless you're there. But what about Posie? We can't leave her now, Zach. She's in. Whether she wants to be or not. She can't just run away and pretend it won't follow her."

"No, she can't. She really fucked up back there when she said the name Payseur."

"Who the fuck are these people? I've never heard of them."

"Bankers," I say. "They run the fucking world."

I can tell he wants to disagree with me. And I get it. How can a family no one has ever heard of run the entire world?

But it's true.

"I figured this out while I was at college," I tell Luke. "I went to school with some distant Payseur cousin. Dated her on the low-down, actually. And when she realized who I was, she told me some shit, Luke. I'm talking she spilled some really dark secrets."

"What kind of secrets?" He's starting to look worried.

"Like... like Johnny Boston goes down to the Caribbean looking for Charlotte Kane and comes home with a chemist called Megan Machette kind of secrets."

"Fuck. Where is she now?"

"She killed herself end of freshman year."

"What?"

I nod. "Yep. And the guy she was dating who wasn't on the down-low? He killed himself too. Same night. They called it a suicide pact, but... you know. It wasn't. Because it was murder."

Luke looks at the aft deck stairs again. Then he looks back at me. "They're gonna go after Posie."

I sigh. "Maybe."

"And us?"

"Probably not. Johnny, right? People are typically very reluctant to cross Johnny Boston."

"She has to stay with us. That's all there is to it. She can't go home. Not until we figure out what's gonna happen."

"Well," I say, backing off and starting to pace the upper deck, "she's not real fond of me right now."

"No. She isn't. But you can fix that, Slick. I know you can." He walks over to me, grabs my face with both hands, and then kisses me.

I smile into that kiss. He makes me happy.

Then he pulls back and says, "You can fix it because you're the most charming asshole on this planet." We stare at each other for a moment. I get a little lost in his eyes. They are light brown with maybe a hint of green. Not as green as Alonzo's and not as brown as Tony's. Something in between. "Go talk to her," he says. "Be nice to her. Let her know it's gonna work out. I'm gonna bring the drone back, pack it up, and then radio home to tell my mom we're not gonna make it for dinner."

"Dude. It's taco night."

He laughs at me. "I know. But we need to figure this out. We need to be on the same team. Because if shit follows us down to Dumas Street, there's gonna be trouble. Go make it right with her, Zach. Tell her we're not gonna let her get hurt. She needs to hear that right now."

He's right, I guess. Even though she did weasel her way into my life, the rest of it is just bad luck. So I just nod my head and head for the stairs.

I find Posie lying face down on the couch in the saloon. I smack her ass playfully, but she just sniffles. And that's when I realize… she's crying.

"Hey," I say, lifting her legs up so I can sit down. "What's going on?"

She says something back to me. But I can't hear it because her face is in the pillow.

"I can't hear you, Posie. Turn around."

She turns her head, but only enough to see me. Her eyes are red and her cheeks are wet from the tears. "I said I don't need your pity, OK? Or your protection. I'm fine. I heard you guys talking upstairs. I'm not fucking helpless."

"We never said you were."

"He sent you down here to make me feel better. Just go away. I don't need you. And you've made it pretty clear you're not into me. So spare me the lies that are coming."

She resumes her previous position, hiding her face from me.

I let out a long sigh. "I didn't mean to make you feel bad. I was really just kinda pissed off at you."

"I get it. Thanks. No need to explain further."

"No, I do need to explain. You see, when we met last weekend, I really did like you. I knew you were kinda stalking me. Here's a hot tip for you—if you're gonna follow someone don't have pink hair."

She glares at me. "Thanks. I feel much better now."

"I'm just saying that I noticed you. And then, when you turned up at the club that night, I was like, 'OK. Let's give this a try.' For sure, I was hoping Luke would like you too. He was the reason I was looking for a new girl. I figured he was getting tired of me."

She turns over a little, listening.

Which is a good sign, so I continue. "But... I liked you. A lot. I thought you were pretty, and even though the hair is over the top when you're stalking people on the down-low, it's fucking sexy. Your whole body— like seriously, Posie. You're a hot little bitch." I point at her. "Bitch is a good word in this context. So don't get mad at me."

"Yeah, I get it."

"I liked your personality too."

"Oh, for fuck's sake."

"I'm not lying. I was bringing you in for Luke. But in order for that to work, we both have to like the girl. So that's what I'm trying to tell you. I liked you. I *really* fucking liked you. And I thought you liked me too."

"I did! I mean, I do! I'm the president of your fucking fan club, for Pete's sake!"

"I know that. I get it. But I always run a facial recognition check, Posie. And when yours came back and I realized you were lying, well…"

She flops over again, huffing air.

"I was fucking hurt, OK?"

"What?" She peeks at me over her shoulder.

"Yeah. Hurt. I wanted you. And that means I needed to be able to trust you. And when I figured out I couldn't, then I wanted to… well. I'm not proud of it, but I wanted to hurt you back."

"That's why you invited me to the club this weekend?"

"No. I invited you to the club this weekend to meet Luke. And because I liked you. I didn't realize you were lying until Thursday night. So the new plan was to just hook up with you, then ditch you at the end of the night. But you came over with Luke, playing that little game. And he looked… happy." I stop to shrug. "I like him happy, Posie. I think you make him happy. He's already feeling protective of you. He's not gonna let you leave, by the way. It's way too dangerous. More dangerous than you realize at the moment. And he and I are a team, so—"

"So you need me to like you. Because you're stuck with me? At least for a while."

"Well. I guess. But you don't have to make it sound like a punishment. I'm not a bad guy. I'm actually pretty fun and charming."

"Duh. I know you better than you think."

"So? Will you stay with us?"

She looks confused for a moment. "Stay with you? Like… what does that even mean? Here on the yacht?"

"No. I'm sure Luke means the cottage. We have a cottage and—"

I'm interrupted by the sound of the radio at the helm station on the other side of the dining room. "Home Base Mama, this is Baby Luke. You out there?"

Posie and I look at each other, then she stifles a giggle.

"Baby Luke?" his mother answers in a crackling voice. "You better not be calling to cancel dinner on me when it's already six fifteen, young man."

"Sorry, Ma. Zach and I are pretty far out. We won't be back in time."

"It's taco night." Silvia Dumas is tempting him now. Sometimes this works. If we're close enough to the marina to hustle back. But this time it doesn't because we're hours out from Key West.

Luke makes excuses as Posie and I listen. Then he promises to trim her hedges as punishment and the radio goes silent.

Posie is giggling by this time. "He's a mama's boy."

"Oh, you have no idea. The entire family lives on the same street. It's…" I sigh. "It's pretty fucking special what they have going on down there. It's not a bad place to hang out with two handsome men while you're hiding from the heat."

She looks away. Stares out the window. There's not much to see at this point. The sun is mostly gone. So it's just one great big dark blue ocean.

"You should just give in."

She side-eyes me. "Should I?"

"Yep. You really have no chance. Luke is determined to—"

There's a loud thump and Posie and I look towards the outdoor seating area to find Luke landing one of his famous stair jumps.

"I'm determined to what?" he says, walking into the saloon and standing in front of the couch with folded arms.

Luke is a massive man. Like both his brothers—and his father—he's well over six foot. I'm tall too. All the Boston brothers are somewhere between six foot and six one. But we wear it different than these Dumas boys.

They are walls of muscle and we are lean. So Luke has at least twenty pounds on me.

Even though his arms are folded like he's ready for an argument, he's got a smile in his eyes. His mother does that to him.

I really like his family. And even if I was bored of him—and I'm not—I would stick it out just to keep these Dumas people in my life. They have something special going on that street they took over.

"Determined to make Posie stay with us," I say, answering his question.

Luke sucks in a long breath and lets it out slowly as he directs his attention to Posie. "You can't fight us on this. We need to figure out what just happened back there and how it relates back to…" He stops. Because he can't say anything else. These are all secrets that only get revealed when absolutely necessary.

"Back to what?" Posie asks.

Luke doesn't answer and neither do I.

"What does any of this have to do with me? I mean, I get it. I lied about my name so they're all curious and shit. But it's not my real name. Just the byline I was gonna use." She glances at me, but just briefly. Then her attention is back to Luke. "And I'm not going to do the article. I think it's all a setup. I'm going back to Oklahoma. I still have a few friends there from college. I can start over. Maybe… get a job at… shit. There are no jobs for journalists. I don't know what I'll do. But I'll be fine. I don't need protection. I'm a scrapper. I'm used to taking care of myself."

Luke shoots me a look and I recognize it immediately. That looks says, *Change her mind, Zach. And do it quick.*

We've never used this look to change someone's mind about needing our protection. He usually throws this look out in the morning, after a hot night of dirty sex. The flavor of the week in bed with us, but already anxious to be on her way. Probably a little bit mortified about how dirty that sex got the night before. So this is the look Luke shoots me when he's in for one more time before it's over.

Of course, that's not exactly what he's saying in this particular situation.

He's telling me to distract her with sex and make her stop thinking about Oklahoma.

Posie is still on her stomach, her face turned to the side so she can see Luke. And she's still only wearing that green bikini. So all I really have to do is reach my hand over and place it on the back of her thigh.

She gasps a little as she looks over her shoulder at me. "What are you doing?"

I slide my hand up a little further and then massage her ass.

"That's not gonna work," she says.

"Oh, it is," Luke says. "Just watch."

Posie flips over real fast, foiling my move as she pulls her legs up. "I'm telling you right now, it's not gonna work."

I stand up and look down at her. "I think you've got the wrong idea."

Her face goes all crinkly in confusion as I cover the distance between Luke and me. He reaches for me as I approach, his hands coming up to my face, and we turn sideways so Posie can get a good look at our kiss.

And it's a nice fucking kiss too. I feel like it's been a while since I've kissed Luke like this. So I turn up the heat a little for my sake, not just Posie's.

"That's not going to work either," Posie insists. Defiantly.

But she's wrong. And she knows this.

She's already getting turned on. I can hear it in her voice.

I slide my hand down Luke's stomach and slip it inside his pants.

He's already hard. And Luke Dumas has one of the nicest cocks I've ever seen.

Mine's not bad either, but who cares about mine when I have his?

I actually chuckle at this and Luke stops kissing me. I compliment his cock all the time, so he's probably reading my mind. But he reserves his grin for Posie. "You won't be able to resist. Trust me."

"Trust you why?" Posie challenges. She's so out of her league. "Because you two have well-practiced moves?"

Luke and I look at each other and laugh. Then I pop the button on his shorts and pull his dick out.

She's seen it before. Obviously. But we were concentrating on her, not us. So she didn't see it *properly*.

I begin pumping him. Squeezing firmly as my hand glides up and down his shaft. He groans a little and when I glance at Posie, she's biting her lip. Watching my hand intently.

"You know you want some of this," I say.

"I can watch," she shoots back. "In fact, I'm quite happy to watch."

"Yeah. Go ahead. Watch," Luke says. "That's the point. It's porn. We're like porn, Posie." Then Luke reaches for the button on my shorts, pops it with practiced precision, and pulls my cock out too.

I watch him for this part. I like to pay attention to his expressions when we're messing around. I like the way his eyes go all heavy and half-mast. And his mouth turns down into a frown, even though I know he's having a good time.

We jerk each other off like that. Eyes locked. Heartbeats picking up. Breaths getting heavier.

And we're not the only ones.

Posie's eyes are also locked on us. Not our eyes though. She's watching our hands.

We've got her. She doesn't quite realize it yet, but it's very obvious that she's into this threesome shit.

And then, like our foreplay is some kind of sexy, coordinated dance—I push his shorts down in the same moment he pushes mine.

Now we're naked and we forget Posie and concentrate on each other. Our bodies pressing forward, our lips connecting again. One hand on each other's cocks while the other explores. Luke's comes up to my neck and his palm circles my throat while mine slips around to his ass.

He kisses me harder and his grip—both on my cock and my throat—tightens. My thumb is caressing the tip of his head and his palm has slipped down my shaft to cup my balls.

"Looks like you don't need me," Posie quips.

Luke and I smile into our kiss. Because she's there. Practically begging us for attention.

Neither of us answers her. We don't say a word.

Because the truth is—this *is* a sexy, coordinated dance.

We pull out of the kiss, let go of each other's cocks, and then turn to her.

She blinks at us. Mouth open, but speechless.

And then, before she can even consider the option of saying no, he's on one side of her and I'm on the other. We pull her legs open and begin kissing her neck.

"Oh, fuck," she mumbles.

Oh, fuck indeed.

I slip my fingers inside her little bikini bottoms and slide them up and down across her clit. Luke likes tits, and Posie has some nice ones. So he's squeezing those with his giant palms as he takes his mouth to her nipple and begins to nip at it.

Each time he does this she squeaks a little. He's nipping her too hard on purpose. He likes to make girls squeak.

And Posie's squeak is downright intoxicating. It's a mixture of pleasure and pain. A concoction of longing and rejection.

I get down on my knees in front of her. Then hook my fingers into the edge of her panties and pull them down, forcing her to close her knees so I slip them off.

Her eyes are closed. But when Luke and I open her legs back up she opens them and gasps.

I position back between them, two fingers pushing up inside her. She is slick and wet. So turned on. Panting hard, ragged breaths as Luke takes her hand and places it on the shaft of his cock.

It may be that her hand is small. But when she grips his giant dick and she realizes that her fingers won't reach all the way around, her eyes open to get a better look.

It is a very nice cock.

She stares at it for a moment. Then her eyes dart up to his and find him grinning.

I lower my mouth down to her pussy and lick it. Just once. From her opening to her clit. And she squeaks again, her other hand gripping my hair.

I take that as encouragement and lick her again. Just once.

"Jesus," she moans. "Don't stop."

Luke chuckles. He can't help himself. But this is his cue in our sexy dance. He leans back, grabs Posie by the hips, and brings her into his lap. She's facing him, so he kisses her. Long and hard. One hand fisting her hair, the other wrapped around her throat. It's a hard kiss. And I wait it out, watching.

Then, just as he pulls out of it, I get to my feet, pick her up, spin her around, and put her back down in his lap.

She's breathless. Her cheeks flushed bright pink as she looks up at me. Her green eyes bright and wide with expectation.

I don't disappoint. I kneel down again and lick her pussy as I grab Luke's cock and push it inside, right up next to my tongue.

Luke leans her forward a little so she can watch as I eat her out and then let my mouth drop down to Luke's balls.

His cock is amazing but his balls are world-class. Tight and hard.

"Fuck," Luke moans.

He really likes when I do this move. And his hips begin to thrust upward. Fucking Posie. She's moaning now. Short, gaspy moans with each pump of Luke's hips. I stand up, my hand still strumming her clit.

"Oh, shit," she moans. "Holy fuck. Oh, my God. Fuck yes!"

I think she likes it.

Luke stops fucking her and my hand goes still.

"What the hell?"

"Not yet," I say. "You can't come yet."

"Why not?"

"Because we have just begun to fuck."

She grins, her breath still heavy.

I straddle Luke's thigh and ease my cock forward, my balls dragging along the top of his leg. This makes him growl a little. And I know what he means. I like that move too. I like it when he's me, and I'm him, and he's the one easing his balls across my leg.

Posie looks down, watching as my cock pokes against her already-filled opening. I slide it back and forth alongside Luke's shaft. Then I reach down with my thumb and begin strumming her clit again.

She is so wet now, when I push the head of my cock with force, it slips inside her.

"Oh, my God. Oh… fuck!"

We did this last night. But it's different the second time.

I don't know why, I can't explain it, it just is.

The first time we're with a girl it's just sex.

The second time it's fucking.

And the third time… well, just like Luke said, we are porn. We are dirty. We take her ass and her pussy.

There is choking. There is sweat. There is begging. Mouths go places they never thought they would.

But that's next time.

This time we concentrate on her.

I hold her legs open, pushing her knees up to her chin as Luke and I both thrust in a perfectly coordinated, opposite rhythm.

He goes deep, I ease back.

He eases back, I go deep.

That's how we fuck her now.

And even though in the future, when we do it like this, we will take charge of her orgasms—we will control her, we will teach her to control herself, and the porn will turn into a dance that includes her—tonight we don't care about any of that.

Tonight is just... *fucking.*

She comes just a few seconds later. Unable to process all the sensations and feelings coursing through her body.

And I'm ready too. So I go next. I step up on the couch cushions, straddle Luke's legs, and shove my cock into her mouth while she's still trembling from her release.

She chokes a little, but she doesn't push me away. And that's all I was looking for. Just a little deepthroat to finish me off.

I come as I pull out of her mouth, spilling all over her chin, and her neck, and her tits.

"Fuck, yeah," Luke mumbles, his head tilted to the side so he can watch me.

When I'm done, with no warning whatsoever, Luke stands up, pushing Posie down onto her knees in the same moment, and then aims his cock at her eyes.

She turns her head and pulls back so it hits her in the neck.

Luke doesn't care.

Only the complete whores let him come on their eyes.

And anyway, I've got a hold of his cock, my hand over his, pumping as he comes.

Then I lean in and kiss him, pulling Posie up to her feet by her hair and pushing her between us so we can kiss her too.

And that's when Luke says, "You're staying with us. So get used to the idea, Posie Payseur. That's just how this ends."

CHAPTER FIFTEEN

POSIE

Luke carries me to bed.

But I'm so out of it—exhausted from the day and the sex—that I only realize this after he sets me down on the mattress. Then I catch a muted conversation between him and Zach and then a hot cloth is wiping my face and neck.

"We'll take a shower later," Zach says, climbing into bed with me. He slides one arm underneath me and we spoon. Just like last night.

I sigh. Unable to remember a time in my life when I was so tired, yet also thoroughly satisfied.

"I know you didn't agree to stay yet." Zach's words are a soft whisper that tickles my neck. "But you'll say yes, right?"

I hum something out. Tacit agreement. Because I'm already half asleep.

This must satisfy him because he sighs deeply and presses his face up against the back of my head. Then he kisses me. It's a gentle kiss. Something reserved for people who are intimate.

I am sleeping with Zach Boston.

He has his arms around me.

He kissed my head.

He's practically demanding that I stick around so he and his hot partner can protect me.

This… this… reality? Because that's what it is. It's even more of a fantasy than the one I was cooking up in my head two days ago.

There is a rational part of me that knows this is too good to be true, but I can't find her at the moment.

So I let it go.

I believe his promise.

(Or is it a lie?)

I believe it because I want it to be true.

I wake up in Luke's arms again.

"Hey," he whispers as we climb the stairs. "We're home."

He sets me down in the living area of the yacht. Then Zach comes over to me with a t-shirt. He tugs it over my head and then helps me push my arms through. "Here," he says, holding a pair of boxer shorts. "This is all we really have that will fit you."

I step into them and he pulls them up my legs, then folds the waistband over until they are no longer in danger of falling down.

"What's going on?" I'm so freaking sleepy.

"We're at the marina. We're gonna walk home. The cottage is just two blocks from here."

"Two blocks? Why can't we just stay here?"

"Because it's safer at home," Luke says.

I look down at my feet. "I don't have shoes." Then I look around the living room. "I don't even know where they are."

Zach turns around and points to his back. "Jump on. I'll piggy-back you."

I sigh, but jump, his hands grabbing under my knees as he hitches me up a little higher.

I rest my cheek on his shoulder and close my eyes as he hops onto the dock. Luke and Zach talk quietly as we walk. Something about that girl. Charlotte. And his brother Johnny.

And then all the bad shit comes back to me.

I groan. I don't want to think about it.

"We're almost there," Zach says.

I just keep my eyes closed until we're climbing some porch stairs. Then Zach lets me slip down his back and we wait for Luke to unlock the door. He holds the screen open for me and I go inside.

It's dark, so I just wait there at the door. Then Zach grabs my hand and leads me around furniture towards a bedroom.

Nothing more is said. We just climb into bed.

This time, Luke joins us. And now I'm in the middle.

Two men.

Two hot men.

With secrets.

This is a really bad idea.

I should get up, walk to my hotel, pack my shit, and run. I should run far.

But this was my fantasy.

If the fan club only knew where I was tonight, they would die.

And if these men want me to stay under their protection, who am I to tell them no?

I wake up to the hum of many faraway voices. At first it seems perfectly normal and it sounds like the bustle of the dorm back in college.

Then my eyes open and reality hits me again.

I'm alone in the bed. And there are voices in the house beyond the closed door. I crawl to the edge and get out, silently tiptoeing across the small room and pressing my ear against the door.

I recognize Luke's voice. Then there are several more that I don't. Then Zach. What the hell is going on out there? I turn the handle and then open the door a crack. It creaks and every single person out in the living room turns to stare at me.

"There she is," Zach says. He's sitting on the arm of a couch next to some other man I don't recognize. And he's shirtless, wearing only a pair of army-green cargo shorts. In fact, all four of the men in the room are shirtless.

Luke, Zach, and two others I don't know. There are two girls too. One blonde, one redhead.

Zach gets up and walks over to me. "We're having a family meeting. We didn't want to wake you. You were sleeping so peacefully."

He takes my hand and leads me over to the group. "OK," I say, looking around nervously. "But what's the meeting about?"

Please don't say me.

I get it. I lied to them and the crazy cult people, and now they're all on the lookout for some girl named Posie Payseur, but I'm really, really not in the mood to talk about all that shit with these strangers.

In fact, all my decisions this weekend are becoming suspect.

Really, Posie? You're figuring that out now?

"Well," Zach says. "It's… about you. Mostly."

Luke gets up and starts pointing to people. Brother. Girlfriend. Brother. Girlfriend. I don't catch any of their names. I'm too busy thinking about how I need to get the hell out of Florida and what might be the quickest way to make that happen.

I hold up a finger. "Excuse me." I'm looking at Zach, since he's closest. "I need to… um. Go. And… I have clothes. At my hotel."

"Oh, we did that," Luke says. Then he points over at the corner of the room where my suitcases are pushed neatly up against the wall.

"What the hell?"

"I called them," Luke says. Like this actually explains anything.

"How? I mean, how did you know where I was staying?"

"You said hotel near Mallory Square. There are nine bed-and-breakfasts over in that area but only one hotel." Luke shrugs. "I know everyone on this island. So I called up Gabriel and Dave—"

"Who?"

"They own that hotel?"

"Oh."

"I asked if you were staying there—"

"And they told you?"

Luke just shrugs again. "They think I'm hot. So I paid them to drop your suitcases off and check you out. You're all set, Posie."

"Umm." I force a smile. "Thank you?"

Luke winks at me. "No problem."

"OK, enough of the pleasantries bullshit." This comes from the dark-haired one leaning against the kitchen island. He looks a little bit like Luke, if Luke was mean. "I want to know her story."

"Don't mind Tony," Zach says, whispering in my ear. "He's a dick to everyone except Soshee."

But then the other guy—looks a lot like Luke, only bigger, if that's possible, and covered in mermaid tattoos—says, "Posie." Like he knows me and we're about to have a serious talk. "We're gonna need you to start from the beginning and not leave a single thing out."

That's it. I throw up both of my hands to ward them all off and say, "What the hell is going on here? I literally just woke up and only two of you people are familiar."

"Oh, sweetie." The blonde woman who is sitting next to the huge guy with all the mermaid tattoos walks over and puts her arm around me. She guides me over to the couch, waves a hand at Mermaid Man, and says, "Sit," as he moves over to make space.

I do sit. Well, she kinda pushes me to sit. And then I'm squashed between her and him, looking up at Luke, pleading for him to save me.

But he's got a remote in his hand and that's what he's focused on. He points it at a TV mounted on the wall and says, "OK, let's go through it one more time. Posie, take us through the house. Where were you?"

I feel like making a scene—standing up, stomping my feet, demanding coffee—but then I look at the mean one again and change my mind.

Clearly this is the Dumas family and they are not fucking around. So I go with it. I tell them where I think I was in the house. Then I get up and point as the drone moves. Luke and Zach both agree on the spot where they rescued me from the crazy lady. And we deduce where the dungeon might be.

"Why do we care where the dungeon is?" I ask.

"We might need to infiltrate," Zach says.

"No," I say, shaking my head. "Nope. I'm not going. In fact"—I smile real big and look at Luke, then Zach—"yesterday was super fun, you guys. Especially the ending. But I'm gonna be heading out. Soon." I pretend to check my nonexistent watch. "Or like… now." I head for my suitcases.

"Posie," the big one says. "Sit the fuck down. This is serious shit and we're about to have a conference call with Emma. And after that, we're probably gonna have to evacuate the fucking street because of you." He raises his eyebrows at me. "And that means we're gonna end up in the city and goddamned Johnny Boston will have to be brought in. So I'm not in a real good mood right now. And I for sure do not want to deal with any extra bullshit as we try to piece together what kind of fuckery you just unleashed on our family yesterday."

"Me?" I point at my chest. "What about them?" It's definitely not my best moment when I point to Luke and Zach. But I'm backed in a corner here. "It wasn't my idea to take a bunch of cult kids out to some stupid pop-up party that turned into a human sacrifice! All I did was tag along!"

"Now, now," the redhead says. She's tall, and willowy, and she's got a look to her that says, *Do not fuck with me, I know black magic.* "You did go snooping."

"Which we totally get," the blonde offers.

"We do," the redhead says.

"And you found some secrets," Blondie adds.

"And the whole world runs on secrets," the mean one snarls.

"And here's the thing," Luke says. Is he mad at me for pointing fingers? He might be. "We have our secrets, Posie. We weren't looking to know anyone else's."

"OK. So…" I shrug. "So we drop it!"

"We can't drop it," Zach says. "Those people are related to me."

"So do you see our problem?" Redhead asks.

I'm about to deny, deny, deny when a ping noise comes from an open laptop on the coffee table.

"There's Emma," Mermaid Man says. He grabs the tablet and accepts the call.

"Heeeeeyyyyy," a woman's voice says. "What's up, fam? Miss you! Wish I could've been there for taco night."

"Taco night," Zach laments. "Don't remind me."

Emma. That's the sister who is married to Jesse Boston.

"So listen, Ems," the mean one says. "We have a situation and we're gonna need to—" He stops to sigh. "I cannot fucking believe I'm saying this."

"We're gonna need to bring the Bostons in on it," Mermaid Man says.

"Oh." I can't see her. No one is sharing the laptop screen with me. But she sounds concerned. "OK. How bad is it?"

"Not bad," Mermaid says.

But the mean one contradicts him. "No, it's fucking bad, sis."

"It's not *that* bad, Tony," Mermaid counters.

"No," Tony says. "It really is." Then he shoots Redhead some kind of secret look.

Uh-oh.

Everyone in the room recognizes *that* look.

It says, *We know something. And we didn't tell you because it was need-to-know. And now you probably need to know and you're not gonna like it.*

"Shit," Emma says. "OK. So what's the prob? Should I send the jet?"

"That would be cool," Luke says. "But…" He winces.

"Mom and Dad have to come too," Mermaid finishes.

"Hmm." Emma sounds like she's thinking. "So we need a MOAB to get them up to the city without suspecting something's up?"

"Yep." Pretty much everyone agrees.

"What's a MOAB?" I whisper to Blondie.

"Mother of all bombs."

I nod. "Ooooh. Good to know."

"OK," Emma says. "I got one. Let me just send this text to Mom. And done. Now… cue the shrill, excited screams in five, four, three, two—"

And then, somewhere down the street, a woman really does start screaming.

"What did you just tell her?" Luke chuckles.

And even though I can't see Emma's face, I can hear that smile in her answer. "I told her I was pregnant."

So this is who they all are.

Blondie is Tara. She's with Mermaid Man, real name Alonzo. He's the oldest Dumas brother. Redhead is Soshee. I made her say her name three times because A, never heard that name before, and B, it's not only fun to hear, but fun to say. Kinda like Posie. Soshee is with the mean one, AKA Tony Dumas. Middle brother.

The screaming mom is called Silvia. And the dad is Jack.

Jack and his sons are the biggest men I've ever seen. So having all four of them around—plus spitfire Silvia, black-magic Soshee, and calm blondie Tara— well, let's just say no one is fucking with us at the airport as we make our way to the gate to board sister Emma's private jet.

Her jet is the first clue that this is no ordinary trip. Well, probably the first clue is the entire Dumas family, but the jet is a big 'whoa!' It's bright berry pink in color and the inside is… well. When I enter, it feels more like the yacht than a jet.

And then I just have to pinch myself because two days ago I would not have been able to make that comparison. Because I'd never been on a yacht or a private jet.

Luke leads us towards the back. The interior is divided into three sections. The first is like a first-class business suite. Conference table, giant chairs, large screen TV. It's probably where Emma works when she's in the air. The middle section is all seating. Huge chairs. I'm talking—nothing in here is economy class. There are three rows of pods then a bunch of table groupings. Four chairs to each table.

But Luke keeps going and we end up in the very rear of the plane, which is like a living area. Long couches on either side and a huge TV.

We flop down on the couches like we're a team. None of the others follow us back, and even though I think I will eventually like all these people, it's a little overwhelming at the moment.

So I enjoy the quiet.

Plus, I like that even though Luke and Zach could choose to sit anywhere but next to me, they don't. They are on either side of me, Luke with his back pushed up against one arm of the couch, Zach on the other end in the same position.

I slouch in the cushions and sigh.

"Sorry," Luke says, also stretching out a little more. "I know this is probably all very overwhelming, but shit is going down and we need to figure out where we all stand before we lose control."

"Jesus Christ." Zach groans. "You sound like my cousin Johnny right now." Then he looks at me. "Are you ready for this, Posie?"

"I'm not quite sure what I should be ready for."

"Neither are we," Luke admits. "That's the whole purpose of going up to the city. We need everyone together. Because I have a feeling that we might actually have all the answers, we just don't know it yet."

"Yeah." Zach exhales loudly. "Something is for sure going on."

"Like what?" I ask. Because he's been different all day. Kind of… subdued. Or… I don't know. Not exactly unhappy, but definitely… melancholy. "Why do you think that, Zach?"

He doesn't look at me. Or Luke, either. Just kinda stares off at the window as the jet begins to move away from the gate. Finally, he says, "I don't know. I can just feel it." Then he looks at me. But really, he's looking past me. At Luke. "I've been here before. A lot, actually. Ever since Emma showed up in Jesse's life." Luke doesn't say anything, but Zach puts up his hands like he's warding off an upcoming objection. "I'm not saying it's her fault. At all. But that was a trigger, Luke. I was there that night of the bachelor auction when Emma bought Jesse. I could feel it then too. Something was happening. You ever get that feeling?"

I look at Luke, wondering as well. He appears to be thinking. So I decide to answer instead. "I do," I say. "I get that feeling. I mean…" I pause to think about what I want to say. Because it's not logical. But Zach wasn't asking for logic. He was asking about a feeling. I turn my body towards him. "I started the Zach Boston fan club group when I was thirteen. It was just kind of a dumb thing, right? I never meant to get obsessed with you. And at first, I wasn't. It was a fun after-school distraction. I didn't have a lot of friends because… well." I point to my boobs. "I developed early. So I had these girls when I was in sixth grade. I was the only girl in my entire elementary school who looked like a… like a…"

Zach smiles. "Like a young Marilyn Monroe?"

I point at him. "Yes. Like a young Marilyn Monroe. In a few years, I'd love the way I looked. But looking like that at twelve? Um… nope. It was horrible. So I escaped to the socials and you were just there, I guess. I didn't want to follow the crowd. Everyone was so obsessed with Jesse, and I just wanted to be different. So I chose you. I made a group and didn't even tell anyone I made the group. But immediately, people started asking to join. So I let them in. And then… I don't know. They just kept coming. They just kept posting. And I was suddenly in charge of this group. But it all felt pretty fun and natural for a few years. Up until senior year in high school."

"Jesus Christ," Zach says. "It was still going off?"

"Yes. Zach, you would not believe how much it was going off. By the time senior year rolled around there were fifty thousand people in there. I only posted once a day with a little pick-me-up and some random photo of you that I just pulled from the search engines. But they never stopped posting. It was constant. It was this living, breathing thing, ya know? And I remember checking it during lunch just before the end of the school year. And from the time I started school that day until that moment I was having lunch, there were seven hundred posts. And I thought to myself, *What the fuck just happened?*"

"How many people are in there?" Luke asks.

I hesitate. Because this group is a little bit nuts and these men are going to think I'm a whole lot of nuts when I tell them this. So. I lie. "Last time I checked— which was a few days ago—there were like… seventy-five thousand."

"What?" Zach laughs. "That's nuts! What do they talk about? I'm like… legitimately not that interesting."

"Not to them, Zach. You are everything to them."

"Wow," Luke says. "That is kinda weird. All of it. But I get what you mean when you have to stop and ask what the fuck just happened."

I point at him. "But it wasn't in a bad way."

"Right," Zach says. "Yeah. That's a crucial point. Because bad shit is happening all the time. You expect it. But when something amazing happens… then…"

He trails off. But Luke picks it up. "Then you get suspicious."

He and Zach lock eyes. "Yeah. I'm fucking suspicious. Because I got dropped into this amazing family after that night Emma bought Jesse."

"Awww," I say, putting a hand over my heart.

"It's true," Zach says. "Everything changed that night. The world tipped or something. And now I'm here with you." His eyes find mine too. "And you too, Pose. Fuckin' fan-group queen. And I feel like…" He swallows. "I feel like I have a lot to lose."

"Yeah," Luke sighs. "Yeah. I've had that feeling ever since Emma came home and told us that she was officially a millionaire. I was like… *wuuuuut?*"

We all kinda giggle.

"And then everyone's business was booming. Alonzo had more clients than he could ever need. Tony's romantic sailboat thing took off. Couples were booking a year in advance. And Emma showed up with two speedboats for my twenty-fourth birthday. I had four jet skis to rent the previous summer. And then, the next summer, I had two speedboats, ten jet skis, and I was just getting into the hydroboards. It was…"

Now he trails off. And I pick it back up. "It was good luck."

We all look at each other, nodding.

"Yeah," Zach says. "Very good luck."

But he doesn't say it like it's a very good thing.

He says it like… I don't know.

He kinda says it like we cheated.

That's how we got that luck.

We cheated.

And now we're about to get caught.

CHAPTER SIXTEEN

LUKE

Here's a fun fact about my sister. When she invites you up to her lake house, she gives you the royal treatment. You get the pink jet. You get a stretch limo pick-up at the airport. You get champagne in the limo fridge, and little finger sandwiches, and a gift bag filled with Bright Berry Beach goodies. And she even makes sure that each of our gift bags has something personal in it.

She is just generous, and kind, and funny, and even though I don't really think Jesse Boston deserves her—she did kidnap him in a moment of insanity and that is how I met Zach.

Luck?

Is it really just luck?

The plane ride is long and we are all sleepy. So that's what we mostly do. Just sleep. Kinda piled on top of each other on the couch. Me on one end, Zach on the other, and Posie between us.

And even though it should be cramped and uncomfortable, it isn't. It isn't at all. It's... nice.

The ride from the airport to the lake house is long too. And by the time we get there the sun is setting and the water is bathed in a ripple of orangey-pink.

The car ride is mostly quiet. Everyone just kinda looks out the window or talks softly. Because this is what Zach was talking about.

That feeling.

We're all familiar with it.

Our family wasn't exactly dirt-poor growing up. But we weren't rich. We didn't fly in private jets or sleep in giant lake houses.

And we all know this. We know there's something going on here.

We just figured... good things happened to good people. And we're good people.

Aren't we?

The Bright Berry Beach lake house is really a retreat center for the business. So it's massive on a gargantuan scale. I've been across the lake to the house the Bostons own, and don't get me wrong—that's a very nice mansion. Spectacular mansion.

But Emma's house?

Nah. It's in another category of awesome all together.

For one, they own three lots. The mansion—
which is also where the conference room is—takes up
the center lot. It has ten bedrooms, fifteen bathrooms,
six living areas, and a view of the lake that almost
makes you want to cry. It might as well be a hotel.

There are two other buildings as well. Houses,
really. Two whole other houses. They each have four
bedrooms and when Emma and her partners have their
big yearly meetings, that's where they put the VIP's.

There is a team-building rope course in the woods,
there is a tennis court, a dock where they keep a nice
boat for entertaining, and a pool, which is closed up
for the winter now.

We stay in the main house when we visit and we
each have our own favorite bedrooms.

Once the luggage is unpacked from the limo, I
lead Posie and Zach up the massive spiral staircase to
the second floor.

When you think spiral staircase, you think tight
and cramped. But this staircase is twelve feet wide and
takes up almost the middle of the house.

We end up at the end of the hallway in one of the
master suites that has a balcony overlooking the
woods.

Zach is used to this kind of opulence. Their house
across the lake might not be this big, but this guy grew

up in the Bossy Building. He's no stranger to massive living spaces.

So when we walk through the house towards the bedroom, I watch Posie's face, not his.

She is in awe.

"Wow," she says. Her voice is soft, almost a whisper. Like she's in a public space instead of a private one. There are little interior gardens scattered throughout the mansion. Six of them total, I think. All spaced out on the first and second floors. They are like a combination between skylights and interior courtyards. And they are all temperature controlled, so there are some very colorful and exotic things growing in them.

When we get to our bedroom I stop at the door, turn the handle, and swing it open, waving her forward. "Holy shit." She steps into the room, walks to the center, and just spins, taking it all in. It's a modern room with a low king-sized bed and some sleek stainless steel furniture. But the really amazing thing is the view of the lake. And, funny enough, I can see the Boston lake house across the water from here. Posie lets out a long breath. "I'm having one of those moments."

I follow her in, then smile and turn around to look at Zach. He's got his back to me because he's shutting the door behind him. But when he does face me, I frown. "What's wrong?" Because clearly something is wrong. He looks... sad.

Zach shrugs and walks over to the bed, flopping back on it the way a sullen teenager might. "I don't know. I don't like this, you guys. It all feels wrong."

"How?" Posie says. She sits down on the bed next to his head. And then he does something really unexpected. He reaches for her. Just wraps his arms around her waist and presses his face up to her hip.

Posie looks at me with a pouty face.

"Zach," I say. "What's your deal?"

"My deal." He sighs. "My deal is..." He opens his eyes to look at me. "I don't live here anymore."

"Where?" Posie asks, which is the same question I have.

"This lake house. Our lake house. Johnny lives there now. Full-time. It's not even like I could throw a party or something because he's got a little baby and a weird woman I know nothing about. And I can't go to the city either. Because even though we still own the Bossy, none of us live there. And even if I wanted to go like... stay in my own suite there on Jesse's floor, I can't." He sighs. "I can't. Because..." He looks at me. "I don't think that place was ever ours, Luke."

"What is he talking about?" Posie asks. "I don't understand. Why can't you go to the Bossy?"

"Because they're watching us, Posie. And the sick thing is, I think they were always watching us."

"Who?" She looks very confused.

"The Way," Zach says.

Posie looks at me but I just shrug. "Dude. I don't know what you're talking about."

"I know," Zach says. "Because these are our family secrets. And they haven't touched the Dumas family yet. But I have a very bad feeling that they will." His face, man. He's so sad. "That's why we're here. This whole trip is about secrets, Luke. And when this night is over?" He shakes his head. "We're gonna be different people when this night is over. You too, Posie." He tilts his head up to look at her. She brushes a piece of hair out of his eyes. It's a tender moment of affection that takes me by surprise a little. "You're gonna be a different person tomorrow. All because you saw something you shouldn't have."

"Huh," I say. "Alonzo told me a little bit about what's really going on. And that's exactly how Tara got involved too. Not to mention Belinda."

"Who's Belinda?" Posie asks.

I wave a hand in the air. "Tony's ex from high school."

"Zach," Posie says, still smoothing his hair. "It's gonna be OK. I'm fine. So… don't feel bad about me."

"It's not gonna be OK. You guys don't feel it because you… you haven't *lived it* yet. You got good things when you got your weird feeling. Me? No. People die when this shit happens. And I don't have any extra people. This has happened to me three times now. Not just once. It happened when my father died, it happened when my uncle died." He pauses and looks at me. "And then it happened again when the Dumas family and the Boston family were tied together forever through Emma and Jesse."

"But that's not a bad thing, Zach," I say. I walk around to the other side of the bed and take a seat. Then I put my feet up and lean back against the plush headboard.

"No, not that part," Zach says. He rolls over and looks at me. "Of course meeting you was a good thing. Being with you and your family. Everything about you guys is good. You definitely made my life better. But don't you get it? The more you have, the more you have to lose."

"But you've always had stuff, Zach," I counter.

"Not stuff," he says, sitting up a little. "Love, dude. I have all this love."

I just stare at him, not really understanding where all this insecurity is coming from.

But then Posie says, "I get it."

"You do?" Zach turns to her.

"Yeah." She sighs. "I've lost everything too. We never had much to begin with. But my dad and I? We had each other. And then when he was gone it was pretty lonely. But you wanna hear something that's maybe a little weird?"

Zach nods. "Yeah. Tell me."

"You got me through those dark times."

He laughs. "How do you figure?"

"The fan group," Posie says. "It was..." She inhales deeply and lets it out slowly. "I maybe... downplayed it a little?"

"Downplayed it how?" I ask.

"Well..." She shrugs her shoulders. "It's not really seventy-five thousand members. It's... a hundred and seventy-five."

"What?" Zach and I both laugh.

"I'm so embarrassed," Posie says. "I don't know how it happened. And I'm actually on there all the time. And we all have little nicknames for each other. We call ourselves the Zach Pack and—"

I actually guffaw. Like... this is the biggest laugh I've had in months.

"You can laugh all you want," Posie says. "But those girls—well, they're not all girls. But they're like my family. They're all I have. So... I know I was stupid. I get it. But I really thought the Buzz Hollywood thing was legit. Because..." She takes a deep breath. "We're fucking legit, OK? We're fucking legit. And so what I'm trying to say is this. I get it. I get the more you have, the more you have to lose. Because I feel like that with them." She holds up a finger. "I'm not prone to panic attacks. I'm generally a very upbeat and positive person. But sometimes I have nightmares about losing my group. Like one day, the socials will be like, 'No more group for you, Posie Payseur. You're done. Bam. Canceled.'" She huffs. "So I get it. That's all I'm saying. They're my family and thinking of losing them makes me feel the way you look right now, Zach."

I look over at Zach and he's covering his mouth with his hand.

"Are you laughing at me?" she asks him.

He shakes his head no, but he's still covering his mouth. And it's very clear he's hiding a smile. Zach's eyes dart up to mine and I just shrug with my hands. "I don't know what to tell you, dude. You have a fan club."

Then we both bust out laughing.

"Your laughter does not bother me," Posie insists. She tilts her chin up defiantly, daring us to knock her down a peg.

"Posie," I say. Because Zach is still covering his mouth, too speechless to speak.

"What?"

"Come here." I grab her arm and tug her over Zach and into the middle of the bed. Then I put my arm around her and kiss her cheek. I can feel her smiling.

"What was that for?" she asks.

"You."

She looks at me and blushes.

"And I would just like to say that I've had two moments now. The first time when Emma got rich and we got rich with her. And two nights ago when Princess Euphemia stood next to me in a Miami club and told me that Zach Boston was out of my league."

All three of us laugh at that.

Then she says, "Wait. Who the hell is Princess Euphemia?"

"My dream girl," I say. "When I was fourteen."

Zach sits up and points at me. "I know her! She was on *Code Geass!*"

Posie pulls out her phone and looks the princess up. "Hmm. She's pretty."

Zach puts his hand out to Posie. "Can I see the fan group? Do you mind?"

She looks at her phone, then starts tapping on the screen. "Sure." She hands it to him. "Go for it. It's definitely going to cheer you up."

Zach takes it from her with a wide, slick grin and starts scanning the page. "And Posie? You are *so* Princess Euphie."

"Who is she?"

"*Code Geass* was a hugely popular anime series about fifteen years ago," I say. "And Princess Euphie was a major character until…"

I pause.

"Until what?" Posie asks.

"Oh. It's not important."

"The important thing is," Zach says, "you're totally her. She's good."

"Really?" She winces. "Because I feel a little… dirty right now."

"What do you mean?" I ask.

"Well. I'm only here because I was lying. And I feel like what I saw out there on that island was… I don't know. Karma, maybe?"

I know we should reassure her. And I know that we're not thinking, *Yeah, Posie. You totally deserved to be caught up in whatever the hell is happening right now.* We don't think that. It's just… I've had the same thought over the years. And I'm sure Zach has too.

We get what we deserve.

It's not true. Sometimes things are out of our control.

But it's not easy to buy that line of thinking when you're knee-deep in the bullshit and not heading for the shore.

Zach rallies and reaches up to swipe a stray piece of long pink hair out of her eyes, a tender gesture that mimics the one she just showed him a couple minutes ago. "No one deserves that shit, Posie. It was... just a set of circumstances. That's all. And you're totally Princess Euphie. She was good-hearted. She wanted the best for her people and then things just spun out of her control. None of what happened to Euphie was her fault either. It was just... wrong place, wrong time."

Posie considers this, but sighs. "I'm gonna agree with you. But." She holds up a finger. "'Wrong place, wrong time' is really like saying you didn't make decisions that got you here. But I did. I made all the decisions that got me here. So it's not wrong place, wrong time. It's a direct result of my own actions. It's on me."

"It's on all of us though," I say. "We all made the decisions that got us here. And if I can lighten the mood a little, it's really not that bad of a place to be."

This makes both of them smile.

"True." Zach laughs. "We could be a lot worse off than kicking back on a king-sized bed inside your sister's over-the-top mansion."

"I was just thinking that this whole weekend has changed my life," Posie says. "I spent a day on a yacht, rode in a private jet, and now I'm in a bed at the Bright Berry Beach retreat mansion with Zach Boston and Luke Dumas."

"Shit," I say. "Thanks for adding me. But you didn't even know who I was before Friday night."

Then she does something unexpected. And she does it without hesitation. She reaches for me. Her small, soft hand slips behind my neck, sending chills down my spine from her soft touch, and then she leans over and kisses me. Not on the lips. Just on the cheek. Just like I did. And all of a sudden it feels like the three of us are on the same page. In line. Hooked up. Together.

"I didn't realize what I was missing before Friday night," Posie whispers. "But I do now." She drags her fingernails across my neck as she withdraws her hand. Just a little bit of pressure. Just a little bit of possessiveness.

At least that's how I take it.

And I like it.

I like her, I decide. Zach likes her. She likes us.

Maybe… just maybe… this might all turn out OK.

"Holy fucking shit," Zach says. "Your groupies are dirty little deviants. They want to do very… interesting things to me."

I raise an eyebrow. "Define interesting."

"Well, this post pinned to the top of the group is called 'If I had Zach Boston all to myself for thirty minutes I would…' Dot. Dot. Dot." He laughs. "This one wants to suck on my balls while she fingers—"

"OK. That's enough." Posie tries to grab the phone away from Zach, but his arms are much longer. So he just grins and raises his hand out of reach.

"What?" He laughs. "What's got you all bothered?"

"You know damn well I'm in that convo."

"Yeah." He winks at her. "Your answers are fucking adorable."

"Oh, hell yeah," I say. "I wanna hear them."

"No!" Posie gets up on her knees, ready to grab the phone away. But I hook an arm around her waist and pull her back down.

"Settle down, Euphie. We wanna hear your dirty talk."

She flips over on her stomach and hides her face in the pillow, mumbling something.

"What's that?" Zach asks, still laughing. "You said you want to act it all out in real life?"

I grin too. It's been a pretty stressful weekend and this lighter mood is much needed.

"No," Posie says, lifting her head up. "I said I'm going to die of embarrassment."

"Why?" I ask. "It's just dirty talk, Pose."

"Because." She buries her face in the pillow again.

I look at Zach. Zach looks at me. And then our unspoken language kicks in and we grin. Wide.

Posie is wearing a short, tan, flirty skirt and a fuzzy pink cropped sweater. It's one of those start-your-day-in-Florida-but-end-up-in-upstate-New-York-for-dinner outfits. Zach and I are both wearing our own versions. Cargo shorts and hoodies.

But the only important thing about her outfit is the skirt.

We know just what to do with a girl who is face down on a bed between us wearing a flirty little skirt.

Our hands land on the back of her knees at the same moment. Posie gasps a little, then giggles. Because his hand is going up her thigh while mine is traveling down to caress her calf. The tension in her shoulders disappears immediately.

"What's wrong with a little dirty talk between you and your closest hundred and seventy-five thousand friends?" Zach says, cooing the words in her ear. He nips her earlobe and she lifts her head up, smiling.

"Oh, my God. What are you guys doing?"

"Just having a little fun, Posie. What did you want to do to Zach for thirty minutes? Hmm? Tell us."

She shakes her head and buries it in the pillows.

"I'll read it, how about that?"

Posie is about to object, but Zach flips her skirt up, rearranges her panties so her cheeks are bare, and then slaps her.

"Ow!" she squeals.

Meanwhile, my hand has slid up her leg and my fingers are in the process of pulling her panties aside so Zach's can slip inside her.

"Oh, shit," she moans.

Zach pulls his fingers out.

Posie lifts her head up and her half-mast eyes turn me on so much, my dick begins to get hard. "Keep going," she whispers.

"No," Zach whispers. "Not until you tell me what you want to do to me."

She tsks her tongue. "You know what I wrote. Just read it."

"I want to hear you say it."

"Me too," I say.

"Oh. My. God," Posie whines.

"Just say it," Zach says. Then he lowers his mouth down to her ass cheeks and begins kissing his way down to her thigh.

I join him, my lips fluttering against her soft skin. "Say it, Posie. Or we're gonna stop and you'll leave this room frustrated."

"Fine." She lifts her head up and looks over her shoulder at Zach. "Since you already know. I said I wanted to…" She sucks in a deep breath and moans. "I cannot believe I'm going to say this out loud."

I encourage her. "Just keep going, Pose. There are rewards at the end of this traumatic experience that you don't want to miss out on."

"I said…" She tries again, kinda huffing out her words. "I want to sit on your face and ride your chin until I come in your mouth."

Zach flops back, pulls her on top of him, and then says, "Take off her panties, Luke."

Fuck, yeah. This is gonna be fun. I get up on my knees, pull her panties down her legs, flip her skirt up, and then encourage her to scoot forward until her hips are positioned right over Zach's face.

Posie grabs the headboard with both hands and looks over her shoulder at me.

"Go ahead," I say, leaning forward to kiss her mouth. "We're waiting, Posie. Ride away."

She kisses me back, her eyes closed, her cheeks blushing a bright pink in embarrassment. But she lowers her hips down and Zach grabs her ass cheeks, the fluttery skirt all askew.

I pull her sweater up over her head and toss it aside, then take a moment to enjoy her lacy black bra cupping her large, round breasts as I tug my shirt over my head and toss it aside too.

Her breathing is more labored now. Long, panting, ragged breaths. And I love the way this makes her tits rise and fall. I scoot up and brace myself against the headboard, then take her hand and place it over the outline of my hard cock. She squeezes it. Then her fingers deftly pop the button of my shorts, pull the zipper down, and she's got it in her palm.

"That's it," I encourage her. And her hips begin to slide back and forth along Zach's face a little faster.

I glance down at him and find him jerking off, his cock hard in his palm too, his shorts halfway down his legs. I reach down and place my hand over his, helping him out.

Posie begins to moan as Zach's tongue works his magic. She squeezes my cock harder and this makes me squeeze Zach harder.

And then we're all moaning. Wanting more. Unable to keep the slow, easy pace going much longer.

I lie on my back, push my shorts down my legs, and again, it's like we're all on the same page. Because Zach pushes Posie off him and then he's up on his knees, positioning her on top of me.

She guides my cock into her dripping-wet pussy. And then moans when I stretch her wide so I can enter completely.

Zach pushes her down on top of my chest, straddles one of my legs and drags his balls up my thigh as he presses the tip of his cock against her ass.

"Oh, shit!" Posie says, suddenly realizing what's coming next.

"Yes or no?" Zach asks, licking her and spitting a little to get her lubed up. "We can do it the other way if you want. But this is better." He leans over her back, bites her shoulder, and says, "Trust me."

He's already got a finger inside her asshole, sliding it in and out. I can feel his finger against my shaft. I'm holding still, my cock all the way up inside her, and she's moaning.

"OK," she whimpers. "OK."

Zach and I exchange a glance. And I don't know what he's thinking, but I'm thinking… yeah. This is the first day of a very good relationship with Posie.

He withdraws his finger just as I hook both my arms around Posie's back and tug her tightly to my chest so her ass is up in the air.

Then I watch Zach as he pumps his cock and positions it at the entrance to her tight ass.

She gasps and tries to sit up, but I hold her still in a firm embrace. Keeping her in place.

"Relax," Zach says. "I'll go slow."

And he does. He's good at this.

We're good at this.

Posie hisses, and gasps, and moans—but in just a few minutes he's inside her. All the way inside her.

I can feel him, and he can feel me, and she can feel both of us. All at the same time.

And then Zach and I begin to move.

A perfect rhythm.

An easy, erotic, passionate rhythm.

We go slow at first, enjoying it as he slides out and I slide in, then I slide out and he slides in. We let the sensations wash over us as Posie adjusts to the new experience. But eventually she becomes comfortable and begins to move with us.

My grip on her loosens and I allow her to sit up. Her hands flat on my chest. Her long, pink hair dragging back and forth. Her eyes closed and her mouth open. Panting, and moaning, and biting her lip.

My hand goes to her throat automatically and in the same moment Zach gathers her hair up in his fist and pulls her head back. So her neck is stretched and I can feel her struggle to swallow and breathe.

His eyes lock with mine. That beautiful Boston blue. They're only half open, but he bares his teeth at me, growling a little. I reach up with my other hand, grab the back of his neck, and pull him down until his mouth finds mine and his teeth nip my lip as I kiss him.

Then we are an erotic mess of writhing bodies.

We spend endless years like this, lost in the ecstasy of each other. Until finally, Posie comes—her screams muffled by Zach's hand over her mouth. And then he pulls her off me, letting her flop down to the side, and takes my cock in his mouth.

I fucking lose it, my fingers gripping his hair as he sucks me off.

He's up on his hands and knees and Posie is jerking him off too. Didn't even need to be told. Just knew exactly what to do.

I come, he comes, and then we are nothing but a mess of tangled bodies.

And it's in this moment that I know we've got something real here.

We are going to be together.

We are going to be an us.

CHAPTER SEVENTEEN

ZACH

A strong knock at the door pulls me out of the best sleep I've had in years. Maybe ever. I resist that pull, insisting that knock was just my imagination.

"Goddammit, Zach! Open the fucking door!"

And then I recognize my cousin Johnny's voice on the other side of it.

"Fuuuuck," I growl, then throw the covers off and swing my legs out of bed. I vaguely remember last night. Sex in the bed. A nice hot shower. Sex in the shower. Then the three of us collapsing under the covers.

I glance over at Luke. He's got the pillow over his head, ignoring Johnny.

Posie is still sleeping soundly.

I sigh, then get up and straighten out my sweat shorts as I walk over to the door shirtless and pull it open. "What?"

Johnny's blazing eyes find mine. They dart to the bed, then back at me. "Get dressed and come downstairs. You've got five minutes. We're all having a meeting." I make to slam the door, but he puts up a flat hand and stops it. "Do not fuck with me today, Zach." He gives me a moment to let his mood sink in. "Do you understand me?"

"Fine. Fuck. Why are you such an asshole?"

But he's already walking away.

I push the door closed and find Posie sitting up in bed wearing a pretty lavender nightie, her pink hair all askew, rubbing her eyes. "What's going on?"

"Fuck. Him." That's Luke. And if I were Luke Dumas, I'd feel the same way.

But I'm not Luke Dumas. I'm Zach Boston. And when Johnny Boston tells me to get my ass dressed and be downstairs in five minutes for a meeting—well, that's what I do.

Jesse Boston is like my brother. Joey Boston is my cousin. Johnny Boston is… almost no one to me. He's pretty much a stranger and I can probably count on one hand the number of conversations I've had with him over the years. And most of those happened when I was much, much younger.

We are not close. He's just… well. The boss.

"What time is it?" Posie whines, clearly not awake. Not even close to being ready for this new day.

I glance at the clock on the wall. "Nine AM, it says."

"Really?" Luke mumbles. Then he pops his head up from the pillow. "Wow, we slept good."

He's a super early riser. Fucking ocean people are all like that.

Then he grins at Posie, probably remembering all the dirty sex we had last night.

I grin too. She's… a damn good… uh. Yeah. That mouth is magic. And the look on Luke's face is telling me that we're going to be enjoying her for years if he has anything to say about it.

I guess my plan was a pretty good one. Few bumps along the way, but nothing we didn't handle like champions.

"Come on," I say. "We really don't want to piss Johnny off, you guys. And I get it, he's no one to you, but he and I are in the same building, he's in charge of my life. Besides, if there's a meeting downstairs, then that means the Dumas fam is in on it. That's why we're here, right?"

"Fuck." Luke is not happy. But he gets up and so does Posie. We pull on some clothes—jeans and hoodies all the way around—and then drag our asses down the long hallway and hit the stairs.

Everyone is already down in the foyer standing around the staircase as we descend the spiral. The loudest voice echoing off the very tall ceiling is Silvia, Luke's mom.

"What do you mean you're not pregnant?"

"Aw, fuck," Luke grumbles. "I forgot we lied to her."

I glance at Posie and we both tuck down a smile. Because Silvia Dumas is a little bit like Johnny Boston. When she's in the room, she's in charge.

"I came all this way—" She's moaning to Emma about not being pregnant.

"Then why are we here?" Jack, Luke's dad, is saying. "Your mother made me cancel my day. I had four dives scheduled—"

I catch Jesse's eye and I know he's pleading with me to come save him from the fam shit, and I am just about to do that, but suddenly Johnny is in front of us at the bottom of the stairs.

He's got a hand up and he's not looking at me or Luke—he's looking at Posie. "Hold up. She's gotta go. We have a ride outside."

"What?" Both Luke and I look at each other. "What are you talking about?" I say.

Johnny glares at me. "This is family business. She's not family."

And then behind us is a loud thumping. Thump, thump, thump.

We all look up and find a creepy little blonde girl approximately the age of twelve, dragging Posie's purple suitcase down the stairs. She smiles at us.

This is Creepy Wendy. No one is really sure who she is or why she's always around when the shit hits the fan, but there it is.

This is the shit hitting the fan because Creepy Wendy has arrived.

"I got it all," she tells Posie as she pushes past us. "Don't worry. But if I missed anything, I'm sure someone will send it to you."

"What the fuck is going on?" Luke bellows. "Posie isn't going anywhere. She's with us."

Johnny drags his glare over to Luke.

Luke is a huge man. Not that much younger than Johnny, and easily two inches taller and twenty pounds heavier. So Luke doesn't even blink.

But then his older brother Alonzo steps between them, placing a hand on Luke's chest. "Sorry, bro. But she's gotta go. Family. Fucking. Business."

"But she knows—"

"She doesn't know," Johnny growls. "And she's the reason we're all in this mess to begin with."

"What is going on?" Posie asks.

"You're leaving," Johnny deadpans.

"She's not leaving," I say. "She's in danger too. And we're going to protect her."

"Is that right?" Johnny says. He comes right up to me. We're about the same height. He's maybe a little more muscular than me. And he's definitely meaner than me. Johnny is the muscle of our family and it shows. "She lied to you, Zach. She's working for Buzz Hollywood. She was sent to spy on you."

"We know all that," Luke interjects.

"And I quit, anyway," Posie says. "I'm not going through with it. I'm not writing the article."

Johnny doesn't even look at her. He looks at Alonzo instead. Then Alonzo looks at Tony, and Tony looks at Joey, and Joey looks at Jesse. Finally, Jesse looks at me.

And while all this is happening, I can hear Emma in the background leading the parents away while Joey's partners, Wald and Huck, follow with all the girls. So when I look over my shoulder there is no one there.

It's just us men. And Posie.

"Zach," Jesse says. "She has to leave. Right now."

"And go where?" Posie says, her voice shaky and loud.

"You're coming with me," Wendy says. And then she drags the purple suitcase past us and stops at the massive front door.

"Who the hell are you?" Posie snaps.

"I'm the muscle here," Creepy Wendy retorts. "Who the hell are you?"

I want to laugh at that. I'm pretty sure everyone wants to laugh at that. But then Creepy Wendy pulls a gun out of the waistband of her jeans and cocks her head. Like she's waiting for someone to disagree with her now. It's a massive gun. Like… it's got one of those silencer things on the end. It's something Jason Statham uses in movies. Not something twelve-year-old blonde girls carry around in the waistband of their jeans.

"OK, that's enough," a man's voice says. "Wendy, put that away. Take the luggage to the van and wait for us there."

We all look over to find Chek. Tall guy, yoked out, blue eyes, shaved head and tats. In fact, let's just say he looks a lot like Johnny with no hair. I'm not sure exactly how he became one of us either, but when Creepy Wendy is around, Creepy Chek is never far behind.

"What the hell is happening?" Luke asks.

Alonzo steps forward and Johnny waves a hand at him like… *He's your brother. You handle it.* "Luke," Alonzo starts. "We did a background check on her—"

"We already know," I say. "We've worked it out."

"You've worked it out?" Johnny growls. He comes right up to me, grabbing the neck of my hoodie. "You figured it out?"

"Dude," Jesse says, stepping in and pushing Johnny back so he has to let go of my hoodie. "Knock it off. He's just asking a question."

"The girl is a spy."

"I just told you, I'm quitting!" Posie protests.

Johnny pokes both me and Jesse at the same time. "This isn't up for discussion. There are lives on the line." Johnny snaps his fingers at Chek, and then Chek steps in and grabs Posie before anyone has a chance to react. Wendy is right there too. Standing in the open door, gun in hand, smirk on her face like... *Whatcha gonna do about it?*

"Take her out and put her in the van," Johnny tells Chek.

"No," Luke says.

But both Tony and Alonzo push him back with a force that says they are not fucking around. Then Joey is grabbing my arm, tugging me towards the interior of the house, while Posie struggles with Chek and Wendy stands guard as she is dragged out. Wendy waves her fingers at us, then kicks the door closed with a loud bang.

"Where are you taking her?" I yell.

"I'll fuck you up!" Luke is threatening.

And together, he and I are formidable. We could, for instance, take Johnny down. If we really wanted to. We could take all them down individually, if it were two against one.

But it's not two against one. I can see that now.

Jesse wouldn't fight. He's not that kind of a guy. But it's pretty clear that Joey, Johnny, Alonzo, and Tony are all on the same page here.

Posie is leaving and we are staying.

And that's the end of it.

"Chek will take care of her," Johnny hisses in my face. "She will be fine if she does what she's told. And we do not have time for this bullshit." Then he whirls around and points to Joey. "Maisy is in danger."

"I know that, you asshole! Posie was the one who found Charlotte!"

"What?" Joey says.

"That's why we're here," I say. "We found Charlotte."

"I already know," Johnny says.

"You do?" Joey asks. "What the fuck?"

"That's enough!" Johnny's yell echoes off the tall ceiling. He points at me and Luke. "Posie is fine. I've taken care of it. She will be safe. I got her story from someone else."

Luke and I both look at Alonzo.

He shrugs. "I told him last night. You guys were sleeping. He's seen the drone footage. We don't have time for this shit. There are serious things to discuss."

I don't know what to do.

I want to go after Posie. Walk away from this bullshit and just… live some other life where my last name isn't Boston. A quiet life with Luke and Posie. One that has no secrets and where we don't have to worry about accidentally stumbling into a dungeon filled with skeletons at a party.

"Zach," Jesse says, his voice softer than normal.

"What?"

"That skeleton your girl found?"

I look up at him. "What about it?"

"There are lots of dungeons like that. There are lots of girls like that."

"Megan was one of those girls," Johnny says. "If I hadn't accidentally stumbled upon her, she would be nothing but bones chained to a dungeon wall right now. And if we don't get our shit together, all the girls will end up like that. Not even I can save us by myself. I need you to listen to me."

I let out a long breath and look at Luke.

"She's safe though?" Luke says.

And then I get that sinking feeling in my stomach. The one where I know my life is about to take a turn and nothing about that turn will be good.

"She's safe," Johnny says. "I promise you. I have someone to take care of her."

"Creepy Wendy?" I snarl.

"No. I'll fill you in. But right now, I need you and Luke to go into that conference room, sit down, shut up, and let me explain just exactly what we're really into."

I shrug and Jesse tugs on my arm, leading the way. Luke comes on my other side, and then everyone else follows us.

Jesse leads me to a large room on the east wing of the house. It was probably a ballroom once upon a time. Inside is a long conference table. Sitting down are the parents, plus Joey's partners Wald and Huck and their girl Brooke, that weird Megan girl Johnny picked up in the Caribbean last year when he went looking for Charlotte, their baby Beatrice sleeping in her arms, Alonzo's girl Tara, Tony's girl Soshee, and my little cousin-niece, seven-year-old Maisy.

Emma takes the only empty seat at the bottom of the table as Johnny goes up to the front of the room in front of a white screen. The rest of us men just stand in the back.

"OK," Johnny says. "We all have secrets." He points to the Dumas parents. "We'll get yours last, but first things first. Zach?"

Yeah. That sinking feeling is back. "What now? What horrible fucking thing is going to happen to me this time?"

He points at Tony's girl. The redhead. "Soshee? Do you want to tell him? Or should I?"

"What?" I look over at Soshee. "What the hell does she have to do with anything?"

Soshee looks like she's about to panic. And Tony steps up behind her and places his hands on her shoulders. Then he looks at me. "Well…" He smiles. And I think this is a bad thing. Because Tony Dumas has never smiled at me. Ever. He hates me. "Surprise, dude. You two are related."

"What?" I just shake my head. "What are you talking about?"

"It's true." Soshee forces a smile. "We're siblings. Different mothers, same father. I didn't know how to tell you. Or even if you'd actually care so…" She forces a bigger smile and says. "Ta-da!" with manufactured glee. "Yay! Isn't this great?"

"What the fuck are you talking about?" I look over at Jesse.

He puts his hands up. "I just found out last night. I promise you. I would not have kept that secret." Then he glares at Johnny.

"It was all need-to-know, Zach."

"What was? That I have a *family*?"

"I'm sorry," Soshee says. "I really am. But we were sent away to Colorado to live with my mother's family."

Johnny pulls an envelope out of his back pocket and walks over to me. "I get it. Family is a big deal and you have every right to every feeling you're having in this moment. But we have bigger issues right now so you can read this later. It will explain everything. I just needed you to know this up front, but in the grand scheme of things, the fact that you and Soshee are related isn't important. It's just a detail that needed to be dealt with since she wasn't ever going to tell you herself."

"That's not fair," Soshee protests. "It was just..." She sighs. "Complicated."

I think I go a little numb in this moment.

I have a sister.

It's not that I ever specifically thought about wanting a sister, but I did think about wanting a brother. I know Jesse feels like a brother to me, but he's not. Not really. We're just... cousins.

So a real sibling. Even if it is this Soshee girl?

I meet her eyes. Find her looking nervous. And yeah, I think maybe this is kinda great. So I let out a long breath and shoot her my very best smile.

But before I can say anything Johnny is back in business. "It's all complicated, Soshee. And now we're moving on to…" He looks around the room like he's about to choose a target. His eyes land right back on Tony and Soshee. "Well. Might as well just keep it going."

"Keep what going?" Brooke asks. She's starting to look nervous too. And I don't blame her. She's like Megan and Charlotte—one of those girls who should've been chained to a wall and left for dead, but fate intervened.

"Tell them," Johnny says to Tony. "Tell them what you know. Start with Emma."

"What about Emma?" Jesse says.

"Yeah," Emma says. "I don't get it. I don't have a secret past. I mean, sure. We do run a family smuggling business, but it's all for the right reasons." She looks at Tony, her face still calm and sweet. But I don't have to look at Tony to know what kind of expression he's shooting back. Her smile drops immediately. "What? What's going on?"

"Emma…" Tony starts. "It's not like we were keeping this secret—"

I laugh. Because they weren't exactly keeping the last secret either.

"What?" Emma insists. "Just tell me."

"Bright Berry Beach…" Tony hesitates. "It's not what you think." Then he looks at his parents. "And our little family smuggling business? That's not what we thought it was, either."

"And that brings it all back to me," Johnny says. And then he does something weird. He looks at us. Like... really looks at us. One at a time. Like we are all a piece of some very confusing puzzle.

Then he sighs, waves a hand to the door—where a new guy is standing—and says... "I'm gonna let Nick Tate take it from here."

Nick Tate, whoever that is, walks into the conference room pushing a hoodie back from his head to reveal a nearly shaved skull—kinda like Chek, now that I think about it—and a neck covered in chain tattoos. He's got a scar down one cheek and this dude looks... well. Drug runner from Central America kinda springs to mind.

He smiles at us.

No one smiles back. No one says a word. We just stare at him in silence.

"I'm going to tell you a story," he says in a thick Central American accent. "And you're not gonna wanna believe it, but it's all true. And when I'm done, you'll all have to make a choice. No one gets out of this room undecided."

He pauses. And just like Johnny did, he looks at us one at a time.

When his brown eyes land on me a chill runs up my spine.

Finally, he sighs and says, "OK. Then let's go down this rabbit hole together, shall we, kids?"

CHAPTER EIGHTEEN

POSIE

The man called Chek drags me across the driveway to a black panel van. He's got a good grip on my upper arm and I'm pretty sure there will be a bruise later.

"What the hell is happening?" My heart is racing and I'm not proud to admit this, but I'm frightened. "What are you doing? Where are you taking me?"

Chek doesn't answer any of these questions. The little girl scoots in front of us, then opens the back door of the van and throws in my little purple roller suitcase.

Chek gives me a good, hard shove towards the van and says, "Get in."

I look inside and for a moment I'm so scared of what comes next, I start to get dizzy.

On the floor of the van are mattresses. In fact, the entire van is padded. Like a padded room you see in old movies about psychiatric hospitals.

And sitting on the floor of the van is a man holding a baby and a little blonde girl who looks a lot like mini-Creepy Wendy.

"What the hell is going on?" My voice is shaky and my legs are trembling. "Who are you?"

The man is youngish. Maybe Luke's age or a little older. He's got blond hair and even though he's sitting in the shadows, his brown eyes have a glint of light in them.

He's very handsome, actually. And he's smiling at me.

I'm just not sure if I should be afraid of that smile, or comforted by it.

"Come on now, Posie," he says, his voice low, and calm, and soothing. "Get in the van. We have a lot to talk about."

I look back at the front door of the mansion, hoping that it will fly open any moment now, and Luke and Zach will rush out to save me.

But it doesn't.

No one comes out that door.

"It's not really a request," the blond man says. "It's an order." And again, he says all this in a tone that implies there's nothing unusual about being abducted and thrown into a padded panel van.

"Tell me who you are," I say, my voice stronger now. But still, there's a little shake in my words. "Tell me what this is about."

The mini-Creepy Wendy sighs. "He's not going to hurt you. And we've been waiting here all morning. So can you just get in the fucking van?"

I just… gawk at her. She can't be any more than six.

"Lauren," the blond man says, his voice a little bit sterner now. "What have I said about swearing?"

"Sorry," she huffs, leaning into his arm. The arm not holding the little baby. "But I'm tired of sitting here. I want to go back to the house."

"I'm Nick Tate," he says. "And like I said, we've got a lot to talk about. So please get in the van so we can get moving and I can get these kids somewhere safe." He jostles the baby in his arms. "This one isn't mine and I'm not in the mood to deal with it much longer."

None of those words make sense to my brain, but I don't seem to have much choice in the matter since Chek and Creepy Wendy are his backup. What else can I do but crawl into the van and lean my back up against the side opposite him.

Chek slams the door and then we're alone in the dark.

Nick flicks on one of those industrial flashlights and points it up at the ceiling just as the driver's side door of the van slams closed. There's a partition between the front and back of the van, so I can't see what's going on up there. I'm just going to assume Chek and Creepy Wendy are in control.

The van begins to move and the four of us jostle a little from the turns.

Nick looks at me. No real expression on his face. Silent.

I try to wait him out, try to make him speak first, but my nervousness wins out in the end and I say, "What's this all about?"

He draws in a deep breath and then offers me the baby.

I… don't know what to make of that. So I don't do anything. Just stare at the little girl in confusion.

"Take it," he says. "It's not mine."

Feeling like I have no choice, I take the baby. She's not asleep, but she is quiet and doesn't object. Her eyes are blue too. Just like the girl called Lauren. Just like Creepy Wendy, actually. And she looks up at me as I situate her in my lap. Then she sighs and rests her head on my chest. She maybe even… *clings* to me. And this makes me want to hold her even tighter.

"Don't fall in love with it," Nick says. "I have plans for that one."

"What?" I hiss. Because one, she's a baby girl, not a baby 'it.' Two, why the hell would I fall in love with some random baby? And three—"What plans?"

"You don't need to know that. Just… don't fall in love with it." I'm about to say something about the 'it' remarks, but he starts talking again before I can. "I'm going to tell you a story, Posie. And you're going to listen to me. And when I'm done, you're going to know things you wish you didn't."

I parse all those words for a few moments, unsure what to make of them. "Then why tell me anything?"

"Because you've somehow got yourself involved at a very late stage of the game and I have to do something with you, don't I?"

"Do you? Why not just let me go?"

He rubs the space between his eyes and sighs. "Did I or did I not just say you've got yourself involved and I have to do something with you?" He pauses to look at me. Stare at me, actually. Then he says, "I hope I won't have to repeat myself often. I'm not in the mood for that either."

This Nick Tate looks like… I dunno. A surfer, maybe. Or someone at home on Key West. A golden boy. All-American quarterback type.

That's how he *looks*, anyway.

But how he sounds?

No. He doesn't sound like that at all.

He sounds… dangerous.

I suck in a deep, silent breath and then carefully let it out in a controlled way. "OK. I'm listening."

"Good. I'm gonna start with me. But there are a lot of people in this story, so don't stop me if you get confused. Just let me go until the end. Trust me. You will have a lot of time later to ask all the questions you want."

Implying, I realize with dismay, that he is taking me somewhere. He is taking me somewhere and I won't be going home any time soon. He's going to make me stay there.

He's… kidnapping me.

I nod. Because I don't trust my voice to say anything back.

"Good." And then he sighs. Like this is an actual relief. "Like I said. My name is Nick Tate. I am…" He pauses, like he needs to think about what he is. "I am in control of a lot of people at the moment."

"What kind of people?" Then I realize I promised not to ask questions and want to take it back. I want to keep him calm. I don't want to see the dangerous side of him lurking below the surface.

But he doesn't chastise me. "Bad people," he says simply. "A lot of very bad people. And those two families back there?" He nods his head at the van's back door. "The Boston and Dumas families? They're part of it."

"Oh, fuck," I mutter. Then I look at Creepy Lauren and say, "Sorry."

She shrugs. "I've heard worse."

"'Oh, fuck' is right," Nick continues. "They are all tied to some very fucked-up shit. But." He holds up a single finger. "They don't actually know it yet. You see, right now, in this very moment, there is another me back there, telling them this same story." I must make a face of utter confusion. Because he says, "I know it doesn't make sense. How could there be another me? But there is. And it does. Got it?"

No. Not really. But I nod anyway.

"I grew up"—he stops and makes a two-fingered gesture at his chest—"*we* grew up on a superyacht on the ocean. We have a sister too. Her name is Harper, by the way. Triplets we are."

"OK."

"One set of identical boys. And one fraternal girl."

"That's... interesting."

He nods his head. "It really is. And it gets better. But one thing at a time. We are part of a long bloodline of people who run a secret shadow government called the Company. Have you ever heard of it?"

I shake my head.

"Well, it has a lot of other names. The Way? The Silver Society? Any of those ringing a bell?"

"No."

"Good. That's actually good. How about… Snake and Apple?"

"Snake and Apple?" I repeat his words back dumbly. "Um. Yeah. We took some people out to an island yesterday. They were wearing shirts that had a snake and an apple on them."

Nick points at me. "That would be them. And now you see how we have a problem."

"I don't know anything about them."

"Don't you? I was told you stumbled into something you should not have seen?"

"Yeah, but"—I sigh, blowing hair up over my eyes—"I don't know what it means. I'm not going to say anything."

"It doesn't matter if you say anything. They have, by now, figured out that you trespassed. That you went down into that dungeon. That you saw the dead girl's bones."

"How though? No one saw me. We got away."

"No one gets away, Posie. And they have cameras. Trust me, they know all about you. They've always known all about you."

"What are you talking about?"

He actually laughs.

So does Creepy Lauren. And she's the one who answers. "You're one of us." She snorts. "Can't you see it?"

"See what? I'm not even joking. I don't know what you're talking about."

"What color is your hair?" Nick asks. "When it's not dyed pink?"

"Blonde," I say. Then I lift up a long strand of it. "That's the only way to get pink this bright."

"And what color are your eyes?" Nick asks.

"So?" I say. Because I see where he's going with this. "There are billions of people on this planet with blonde hair and blue eyes."

"Billions?" Nick cocks his head at me. "No. Only about two percent of the world's population has blonde hair and blue eyes."

"You don't have blue eyes."

"No, I don't. Neither do my siblings. But that was all part of the plan. The point is, you are one of us. I know your history. So what I'm gonna tell you now isn't some magic trick, OK? I looked you up. Do you have a mother?"

I let out a long breath. "If you looked me up, then you know I don't."

"How common do you think it is for children to grow up without a mother?"

I shrug. "I dunno."

"In America only eight percent of households have a child with no mother. Of those eight percent, only a small minority are due to divorce. Most of the mothers are dead or just plain missing."

"I don't know where you're going with this, but OK."

"My point is, it's a rare thing to grow up without a mother. Unless, of course, you are Company. Then you have a ninety-eight percent chance of never knowing your mother. Because we use them up, Posie. Or we just outright kill them. Growing up without a mother does a thing to a child. It makes them suspicious. It isolates them from other children. Because their situation is such a rare thing. Especially children who never knew their mother. I'm not talking about adoptions, either. Kids who grow up with only a father learn to trust men. They have issues dealing with women. Both the boys and the girls. And this," he says, waving a hand in the air, "this is why we, the Company, do it this way on purpose. We need these kids. Badly. For all sorts of reasons. And we need them in a certain state of mind. We need them to see the world differently than the people outside the Company. This is a plan. Do you understand what I'm saying?"

"I guess. But I'm still not sure what this has to do with me. My mother died giving birth."

Creepy Lauren laughs. "All our mothers died giving birth."

I look at her, then him, trying to decide if she is his. He said, *This one isn't mine and I'm not in the mood to deal with it much longer*, when I got in the van. Meaning the baby, not the little girl. Letting me assume that Lauren is his. Even though she has blue eyes and he doesn't.

Nick nods to Creepy Lauren. "Yes. She's mine. No, she has no mother. Yes, it's a problem."

"It's not a problem," Lauren objects. "I'm fine."

Nick ignores her. "You're one of us, Posie. I'm sorry about that. It's not something you can change. You didn't have a choice in the matter. You were simply…" His eyes dart to the baby in my arms. "You were simply born that way."

"I don't know what you want me to say."

"I just need you to accept this as truth."

"Why? Because something really horrible is about to happen?"

He nods. But his words come out as a sigh. "Yeah. Something horrible is about to happen. Unless we intervene."

"We?" I ask. "Who is this we?" I point to myself. "Me?"

"You're part of it now."

"Part of what?"

"The Company."

"I'm not part of any Company. I'm just… Posie Miller. Patty Ann, actually. Patty Ann Miller. That's my real name. I went to Oklahoma State and majored in journalism. And then I got a lucky break because I just happened to be waitressing—"

"Let me stop you there, OK? Because not even Lauren here is buying the shit coming out of your mouth right now. They got to you a long time ago, Posie. Who do you think took you in after they killed your father?"

"Killed—they didn't kill my father. He died of kidney failure when I was a freshman in high school."

Nick laughs. Then puts up a hand. "I'm sorry. I know it's not funny, but the lies they tell. God, they have no shame."

"What lies?"

"Kidney failure? No, Posie. He didn't die of kidney failure. They stole his fucking kidneys, OK? Your father was what we call a harvest. He was… *stock*. They took his fucking kidneys. One at a time. You probably didn't even know that he only had one kidney while you were growing up, did you? They took the first one when he was a teenager to save the life of some rich Company higher-up's child. That's the only reason your father was born in the first place. He was bred, Posie. To harvest. To save someone more important than himself. He didn't die of kidney failure—unless you call *lack of kidneys* kidney failure."

I... can't even think. I have no words. "That's not true. That's simply not true. What you're saying? That's illegal. It doesn't happen. It's an urban legend."

Lauren laughs. "Wow. I guess I didn't realize how hard the normies bought into this shit."

"Lauren." Nick turns his head slowly to look at his daughter and says, through gritted teeth, "If you swear one more time in the next forty-eight hours, I will wash your fucking mouth out with soap. Do you understand me?"

She pouts and crosses her arms. "Sorry. Geez. But she's just being stupid."

Nick stares at her for another moment. Then his gaze slowly migrates back to me. "She's not being stupid. She's simply parroting back what she's been told." Then he looks back at his daughter. "Just like you, when you think about it."

Lauren shakes her head furiously. "Nope. I'm not a parrot. I know better."

"Good," Nick says. "And in a few weeks, Posie will know better too. But right now, she needs our help to understand."

"Hold up," I say. "Maybe this is just all a misunderstanding? Hmm? I mean, I'm fine. I'm happy.

I'm well-adjusted. I have a good thing going with those guys back there—"

"Those guys back there?" Nick says. "Well, I'm glad you brought them up. Because the story I'm about to tell you? It's not about us. It's about them."

"Wait. There's more?"

"The story hasn't even started yet. I'm not going to go all the way back to the beginning, that would take forever. I'm gonna start close to home. With Zach first. Because he's interesting. Then Luke second, because he's just a side note." Nick holds up a hand. "But it's all important in the end. So if you're thinking that maybe Luke will be the one to save you from this truth I'm about to tell?" He shakes his head. "No. He won't. Because by the time he walks out of that mansion we just left, his world will be crashing down around him."

He pauses. And the seconds tick off into minutes. But I barely register this time passing because my mind is playing those words over and over in my head.

Finally, he says, "Ready?"

I look at him in the eerie shadows cast by the upturned flashlight. But I don't respond. And he doesn't wait. "That redhead back there?"

"Soshee?" I ask. "What about her?"

"She's Zach's sister. Last name Ameci, but she's really a Boston. Her mother never married. The Ameci family goes back hundreds of years. They are—they *were*—one of the untouchable families before Zach and Soshee's great-great-grandmother, Sedonia, tried to leave the Company and started blabbing to all the wrong people. She was killed and her family was kicked out. Not of the Company, mind you. Just out of the upper tier. The ruling class.

"Soshee's grandmother was resourceful. She had children out of wedlock, her line went on, she got away with the help of her people back in Sicily. Until Zach and Soshee's mother met up with good old Chuck Boston. And that was a problem, you see. An Ameci crossed with a Boston is what we call a pure bloodline.

"No one cared about Zach. It's not the boys they're after. It's the girls. So Soshee stayed in Colorado with the reinvented Ameci clan and Zach was sent to live with Chuck."

He stops talking. And I wait for him to continue, but he doesn't. "OK. Should I have opinions on that?"

"He's one of them. One of us. That's the point."

"Fine. Got it."

"Now let's go to Luke. His story is much less complicated. His people are Dumas on the father's side and de Gama on the mother's. French Portuguese. They started out as fisherman. Then they became explorers. Then pirates. Today they are smugglers."

"What?" My laugh bursts out with my words. "Did you say… smugglers? Luke? That nice family?"

"They smuggle kids out of Haiti. Cuba. Coastal parts of Central America. Sometimes the kids even come from as far away as Africa."

"I don't understand. What are you trying to say? They traffic children?"

"No. Well, not knowingly. They think they are saving them. And they are. Let me be clear here. The Dumas family does not sell children. But."

"But? What do you mean, but?"

"But they cover for the FBI, CIA, and a whole slew of other three-letter-word government organizations. This is how it works. People are like drugs. They are worth money. And the younger they are, the more they are worth. But how do you sell people without attracting attention?"

He waits. Like I'm actually supposed to answer this.

I let out a long breath and stretch my neck a little. I'm very tense. And I don't want to be here, or answer these questions, or learn the truth. I just don't.

"Go ahead, give it a try, Posie. How could one sell children without attracting attention?"

"I don't know," I huff. "Adoption agencies."

He points at me and flashes a smile that looks very wicked in the crazy shadows cast by the upturned flashlight. "Very good guess. That's the best-case scenario. Selling children from other countries to desperate American families. Very lucrative. They pay a lot for those babies. But not all humans have that kind of worth. At least to the traffickers. Some of them are only worth a few thousand dollars. Still, it's easy money if you think about it."

"What the hell is your point?"

"The slave trade is my point, Posie. The slave trade runs the world. Always has, always will."

"That's insane," I scoff.

"Not any more insane than your father being harvested for organs."

I get a sick feeling in my stomach. And I want to tell him he's wrong, but I can't seem to get the words to come out. Because my father wasn't sick. I did know he only had one kidney. He was always at the doctor. And he prepared me for his ultimate demise. He never hid the fact that his time was coming.

But the months before his death, he was fine. He was great, in fact.

His death was so sudden, I didn't even have a chance to think about it.

And I don't have time to think about it now, either. So I tuck all that away for later reflection, because Nick is still talking.

"They have other ways to sell people. The list is long. And not important. The critical take-home point right now is that the Dumas family—which includes

Luke—they are all going to prison very soon because they were a cover organization."

"What?" My mind has literally been wiped clean. I cannot think straight.

"Like the adoption agency?" He asks. Trying to be patient with me. "They were a cover organization."

"You just told me the Dumas family are child smugglers. How is that a cover?"

"It wasn't a cover for them, it was a cover for the black ops inside the FBI. Think about the world we live in, OK? Satellites, and GPS, and facial recognition. Not to mention all the global agencies who have access to that kind of tech. If the CIA or FBI wants to sniff out your slave trade business, they will. It's a done deal. There is no possible way that slave traders remain in business through sheer cunning and luck."

"What are you saying? The government is behind human trafficking?"

"How could they not be?"

"That's insane. You're insane. This whole thing is fucking stupid and insane!"

He takes a moment. Pauses as he watches me. Finally, he says, "Think about a crime scene. Think about how we catch criminals. We have so many ways to track things down. So many databases. We have one for tire treads. We have one for fingerprints. Facial recognition. DNA, of course. We have one for shoe soles, one for glass, and one for ballistics. Hell, we even have a database for paint chips, Posie. If someone is murdered today and the crime is not solved, it's because the agency involved doesn't have the time, or the money, or the will. That's the only way criminals go free in this day and age. There is no possible way that none of the major government intelligence services on this planet are unaware of the human trafficking problem. They know. They know everything. And they cover it up."

"But why? Why would they do that?"

"Money." The whispered word comes from Lauren. Quiet this whole time until now.

"Money," Nick agrees. "I know what you're thinking. That doesn't make sense to you. But the reason it doesn't make sense to you is because you don't understand why they need the money."

"Why do they need the money?" I ask.

"War. They need the money for war. Because war makes more money. War keeps people afraid. Fear is how they control us. Fear. It works every time."

"But—why? Why do they want us to be afraid? That doesn't make sense."

"Doesn't it?" Nick cocks his head at me.

I don't know what to say, so I say nothing.

"Let's not get hung up on this," Nick says. "We're just getting started. Child smuggling is just half of the

Dumas problem. Emma? That amazing cosmetics company she runs? That's all a front for illegally obtained ingredients."

My mouth drops open. "What kind of ingredients?"

"You don't want to know those kinds of details, Posie. Trust me. She's on her way to prison for that too. As are her partners, because they have no idea that the three-thousand-dollar age-defying facial cream they're selling contains human DNA obtained from missing children."

Out of nowhere the baby in my arms begins to whimper and squirm. I hold her a little tighter and she nuzzles her head into my chest. "Her?" I ask, motioning to the baby.

Nick nods. "Her. She's nothing so ordinary as a harvest, don't worry about that. She's like…" His eyes dart to Lauren, but he doesn't move his head. And then his words don't match his motions, because he says, "Like Wendy up there," nodding to the front of the van.

"What *is* Wendy?" I ask.

"Let's just put it this way. If that girl tells you to do something?" He pauses here to make sure I'm paying attention. "You do it." He points to the baby in my arms. "This one, left alone with the people who were raising her? She would be Wendy by the time she was six."

I glance up at the front of the van. And even though I can't see Wendy in the front seat due to the partition, I can picture her. She is probably… I dunno. Thirteen? Fourteen?

And yeah. I don't know that girl but everything about her is creepy.

I look down at the baby, then back up at Nick. "What will happen to her?"

He shrugs. "I'm not sure yet. I'm still trying to decide if it can be saved."

"What do you mean? She's like four months old. She can't even crawl yet. Of course she can be saved."

Nick is shaking his head. "She's not what you think."

"She's like me," Lauren says.

"She's not anything like you at all," Nick snaps. "And we've had this talk a million times. So no more out of you."

Lauren's eyes drop to the floor and she doesn't say another word.

"Back to the story," Nick says. "No lotion is worth three thousand dollars. Bright Berry Beach Cosmetics is a way to package up these illegal ingredients I didn't mention and then launder the money made by other companies in the network. It's a circle, you see. It's all connected. This one makes money by stealing children. This one makes money by harvesting children. This one makes money by using those ingredients to make a product. This one sells the product. And on, and on, and on."

"Wait a minute. Emma Dumas is laundering money?"

"No. Of course not. She's a nice girl. She would never do that. But she's the CFO. She's in charge of the money. Her suppliers are doing the illegal shit. She's just an unknowing participant at the end of the chain. The final step. But it won't matter in the end. She's still going to prison. The whole family is fucked. Alonzo's girl, Tara? Also one of us. One of you, I should say.

"Now, let's skip over to the Boston family, shall we? And since we're talking about the women, let's start with them. Brooke. This is Joey Boston's new thing. She's one of us. Just like you and just like Tara. Comes from a harvester. Megan, Johnny Boston's baby mama? Well, she's like a hundred levels above you girls. Not quite untouchable, but damn near close. She's a chemist. We'll get back to that in a minute. Because that is the endgame here, Posie. Megan and Johnny are not going to jail. In fact, none of these Boston boys are going anywhere. They are in it until they die. There is no getting out for them unless we get to that endgame.

And we're not gonna get there now. Not after you went and fucked everything up on that island. Because now I have two loose fucking ends called Bart and Chandler Conner. Which is a problem for me, Posie. Because I was counting on the Conners staying out of shit. And now…" He pans his hands wide. "They have to choose sides."

His pause, after all that, is long. And I swear to God, it lasts for several eternities.

Finally, my brain catches up with all those words and I suddenly get what he's saying.

"OK." I swallow hard. "I understand, I guess."

"You guess?" He sneers at me. "Let me spell it out for you then, Posie. Because I don't have time for guessing. I have two options here. One, I kill you. And them. All of them, except Johnny and Megan, of course. Because I need them for a future play."

Fuck. I let out a long breath. "Or?"

"Or"—he bites his lip, like he's thinking—"or you do exactly what I tell you, when I tell you. And maybe you end up like that baby you're holding."

I look down at the baby.

He hasn't decided if he will let her live. He said that to me. No hesitation. That's why he's calling her 'it.' She isn't real to him.

And neither am I.

"Maybe," Nick continues, "just maybe… I find a place for you. A place where you can't fuck up my plans."

The van stops. And then the passenger doors open and slam closed. The back door is yanked open and Wendy and Chek stare back at us as the girls and I shield our eyes from the sun.

Then Nick says, "But that's a very big maybe."

CHAPTER NINETEEN

LUKE

The rabbit hole this Nick character takes us down is deep, and twisted, and—quite frankly—unbelievable. And the objections begin almost immediately.

Emma is first. "What the hell do you mean our company is laundering money? That's ridiculous! Who the hell do you think we are?"

She has a point. My sister is the CFO of Bright Berry Beach. If her company was responsible for laundering money, she *should* know about it. And not only is my sister not stupid, she's not a criminal. Aside from that time she kidnapped Jesse Boston, she's pretty much the most honest person I've ever met.

So there's about a ten-minute stretch of time after he starts talking where we're all pretty confident that this Nick dude is full of shit.

But then he points out the fact that Bright Berry Beach has a luxe line of facial creams. A very popular line. One that accounts for nearly ten-million dollars in sales each year.

I'm sorry. Did he just say... *ten-million*?

Did it ever occur to Emma, Nick asks—rubbing it all in—why this specialty item is so popular?

Well. It just gets worse from there.

Emma and Bright Berry Beach are just the beginning. Because it turns out that my only sister isn't the only shadow criminal in this room. Our entire family is secretly part of some global child trafficking scheme. Never mind that we've been saving kids for decades, it was just a front for the evil smugglers.

Do we object to this characterization? Of course we do.

But then Tony stands up and says some Creepy Midnight woman showed up in Colorado last spring while he was meeting Soshee and told him all this.

All these years while our little family was smuggling in a few dozen Caribbean and Central American kids into the US each year so they could have a shot at a better life, the Company was smuggling thousands of them all over the world to be sold as sex slaves or worse.

We were the cover. All eyes on us.

Most of the FBI agents involved probably didn't even know about the Company's business. They actually thought they were helping us save these kids.

That's how they make this black-ops shit work. Everyone is in on something. Most of them think they're like… I dunno. Batman, maybe? The vigilante outlaw. When the boss tells them to ignore that boat. Let it go. They actually think they're helping kids.

Just like we do.

But a much smaller percentage of those crooked FBI agents know the truth.

They know we—and lots of others like us—we're nothing but a distraction. And if the FBI stopped protecting us—and they have, thanks to that Madrid bitch Alonzo and Tara dealt with last winter—and anyone got caught in the future, we're the fucking fall guys.

They set it up this way.

If their child trafficking ring is interrupted and/or the general public gets wind of it and, worse, actually starts believing it, then all they have to do is blame us and we're all going to prison. Because we really *are* smuggling kids.

Creepy Midnight instructed Tony and Soshee to go home and forget everything they saw because she assured him that they 'got this.'

Do we ask Tony what he saw in Colorado? Of course we do.

He saw some dirty FBI agents and found out that Fort Collins is some kind of witness protection program haven that hides random people involved in their secrets.

Which makes our boy Nick up front smile in satisfaction, because his entire day-of-reckoning speech was based off this assumption.

The FBI is compromised so bad, it's nearly impossible to fix it.

And we're all going down if anyone finds out.

Now we're all just kind of numb.

And Nick is *still* talking.

"We did it once," he says. "About ten years ago. We took them out. We killed more than two hundred elite Company higher-ups."

"What?" That's my mom. "What did you say?" She's been taking this pretty well. She was pretty upset that Emma wasn't really pregnant, but this whole time she's been sitting down with a stoic look on her face. "Two hundred people? You killed two hundred people?"

Nick is not fazed. This guy is, well, tore up. That's the only way to describe him. The tattoos. The shaved head. The look in his eyes. Not to mention the Spanish accent when he is so very, very clearly not any kind of Spanish. "Two hundred is nothing. As we soon figured out. Two hundred was enough to slow them down a little, but only because those two hundred were very high up in the chain of command. Even so, they were back in business in less than a year. They just reorganized. Started splitting up the Company into many different factions with many different names. You know them as the Way. But they are all the same. And the point is—they've regrouped. They came back. And now they are almost one hundred percent in control of the FBI. We basically have one guy on the inside. And he doesn't even know he's on our side yet. We're still working him."

"What do you mean he doesn't know?" This is Tara asking. "How could he not know?"

"He's the son of the black ops project coordinator who works directly for the Company. Adopted son, actually. They steal kids from everywhere. Some of them are sold and some of them are placed. This guy was placed in Max Barlow's home along with a couple other boys, but only two made it into the FBI to work under their father. And now we have one chance to take this Max Barlow out and you people"—he points at us—" all you people are in the way."

I catch Zach looking at Johnny. In fact, we're all kinda looking at Johnny, waiting for him to step up and say something. Anything. Just—tell this Nick dude to fuck off. We don't need his help. He's not in charge of us.

But Johnny doesn't move. He stands in the back of the room, leaning up against the wall with his arms crossed and his face blank. Just… listening. Like the rest of us.

And he's the boss as far as the Bostons go. So Jesse doesn't say anything, and Joey doesn't say anything, and Zach doesn't say anything.

Finally, Alonzo clears his throat and the entire Dumas clan relaxes a little bit because—well, he's our Johnny. Alonzo speaks for us. But all Alonzo says is, "So what do you want us to do?"

"What do you want us *to do*? Alonzo, first of all…" I hold up a finger because I'm making a list. "Chains here"—I motion to Nick—"he's not in charge of us. Second of all, *do*, Alonzo? We're not doing anything with these people. Emma is gonna discontinue her freak line of overpriced money-laundering cosmetics, we're gonna track down every single kid we've ever smuggled into the US and make sure they're cool, and then we're gonna lie low and wait this heat out."

"That might've worked," Nick says, directing his attention to me, his eyes narrowed and mean, "before you and your boyfriend over there decided to team up with the Conner brothers for their monthly let's-burn-someone-at-the-stake pop-up party two nights ago."

"We didn't team up with them," Zach protests. "It was a day charter, that's it. We weren't even there when that happened. It's all drone footage."

"Did Posie or did Posie not see a dead Charlotte Kane chained to a wall in a dungeon?"

"She did," Zach says. "But she wasn't a part of it."

"Well, she is now. They know. They've pulled the footage of her sneaking around."

"How do you know that?" I ask.

Nick snarls at me. "My last name is Tate. I *am* the fucking poster child for the damn Company. I know everything."

"Good," Tony says. "If you're so important, then just put an end to it. Problem solved."

"That's not how it works," Nick says. "You don't understand how many people are involved. Let me put it this way. We—and I'm including all you people here because like it or not, you are with us now—we make up less than one percent of the population. The total population of the world right now is seven point eight billion people. One percent of that is seventy-eight million. Those involved in the Company are less than one percent. But one percent of that is seven hundred and eighty thousand. Let's call the true number one half of one percent of one percent and that gives us three hundred and ninety thousand people involved in this shadow government called the Company." Nick pauses to let that number sink in. "Three hundred and ninety thousand. We took out two hundred and that was a Herculean effort that involved cashing in favors to an entire army of gang members, not to mention sacrificing myself"—he pauses to seethe for a moment—"in order to save *one* girl. There is no way in hell we can take down the Company completely. All we can do is cripple it one small piece at a time. And we were in the middle of doing that"—he says that last part through gritted teeth, and then his gaze finds Zach and me again—"when you two dumbasses decided to take a gossip reporter from Buzz Hollywood down to a Company ritual and let her snoop around until she found some actual real-life motherfucking skeletons in the closet."

Nick stares us down. And I have to admit, I'm like three inches taller than this dude and I've easily got thirty or forty pounds on him, but he's... kinda terrifying.

"Look. Let's all take a breath." Finally, Johnny fucking Boston decides to speak up. "There's a lot more to this story than you know, Zach."

And don't you love it how he only talks to his cousin? Forget the rest of us. Zach is the only one who matters to him.

"What about Posie?" I say. "Where is she? How does she fit in? What's going on with her? Is she safe? How do we contact her?"

"Luke," Alonzo says. "There really is more to this story. Forget about that fucking girl."

"No." Zach and I both say it at the same time.

"We're not gonna just forget about her," Zach says.

"And I want to speak to her right now. I want to know she is OK. Or I swear to God—"

"Luke!" This time it's my father. "That's enough." And I'm so stunned that my easy-going—albeit criminal—father is raising his voice, I actually do shut up. "There are things going on here you know nothing about."

"Then tell me," I say. "I might be the youngest in the family, but I'm not a fucking kid. I deserve to know the truth."

My mother, of all people, takes over. "Girls, why don't we go to the kitchen and make some food."

"Are you fucking kidding me?" Brooke says. "I'm not being relegated to the kitchen like some... brainless woman."

But Joey Boston taps her on the shoulder and says, "Brooke, I'll fill you in later. But right now, we need to talk to Zach. So just take Maisy out of the room and Huck and Wald will go with you."

"Emma will go with you too," Jesse says.

"Wait," Tony says. "Do I need to know about this?"

"Come on," Alonzo says. "There's no rush, Tony. We're all gonna know what the real crisis is soon enough. Let's give the Bostons a few minutes to discuss in private."

"Well, I'm staying," I say.

Alonzo glares at me. "No, Luke. You're not."

I glance over at Zach, but he's not looking at me. So I find Johnny's eyes instead. He doesn't say anything. Doesn't need to. It's pretty clear I am not staying.

And this, I think, is the moment when I realize all this is real.

And I'm about to lose everything.

CHAPTER TWENTY

ZACH

The room is cleared except for me, Jesse, Joey, Johnny and Nick.

I am sitting now, having taken Emma's chair. My arms are folded over my chest, my legs are stretched out under the table, and my eyes are fixed out the window on the lake.

My cousin-brothers all take seats around the table. Jesse and Johnny are across from me and Joey sits next to me.

Nick leans against the whiteboard at the top of the room. "Well," he says, "I believe the floor is yours, Johnny."

Johnny clears his throat. "OK. Nick here has already explained the FBI's part in all this. It goes deeper, Zach. Much, much deeper. But that's not the part that really matters here. What I'm gonna tell you next?" He pauses. Waits for me to look him in the eyes.

"What I'm going to tell you next is not something you can repeat. To anyone. Not even Luke."

"Why?" I ask.

"Because," Joey says, "they could kill Maisy if too many people find out."

"They'll kill more than Maisy," Nick says. He walks around the table and stands behind Jesse and Johnny. "Thousands of people will die, Zach. Not because we took them out, though. That's the important part. They'll die because they will become a liability. And little Maisy is one of those liabilities."

"What the fuck are you talking about?"

"It's a long story," Johnny says. "And it starts with Megan."

"Megan." I sneer her name. "Your baby mama."

"Don't call her that." Johnny doesn't say those words with malice. His tone is neutral and low. Almost soothing. But I have known this man my whole life and I hear the threat underneath. "She is my partner. She is the mother of my daughter. And she will be the one to save all our asses in the end."

Before I can say anything, Nick speaks. "Here's the problem though. We're not ready for Megan to save anyone's ass at the moment. That plan is years in the future. We were biding our time. Johnny here was given a year to produce offspring with Megan and they did their part."

"Whoa." I hold up a hand. "What does that mean?"

Johnny lets out a tired sigh. "Our mother came to see me last year while I was down in the Caribbean searching for Charlotte."

I look at Jesse. "You knew this?"

"I knew," Jesse says. "He told me after Beatrice was born."

"You didn't come home to meet her," Joey says. "So you missed out on the little Boston brothers' come-to-Jesus moment."

I look at Johnny and suddenly feel ashamed of myself. "Sorry. I honestly didn't think I'd be missed."

"It's not about my daughter," Johnny says. "It's about all our daughters in the future. And whether or not we will allow these sick fucks to use them to experiment on."

I expect more after that. Some kind of explanation. But Johnny goes quiet. "And?" I say. "What the hell does that mean? What kind of experimentation?"

"They're developing a drug," Joey says. "To extend life."

I scoff.

"Laugh all you want," Nick says. "But it's true. Megan Machette comes from a long line of Company scientists. She and her father were working on a longevity drug. And they found one."

"A fountain of youth?" I don't scoff again. But I really want to.

"You can call it that if you want," Johnny says. "The point is, it appears to be working. It definitely worked in rats. Megan gave the treatment to a rat twelve years ago. The damn thing is still alive." He pauses for a moment to let me work out the full meaning of his statement.

Twelve years. "Huh."

"Huh," Nick says. "Twelve years is at least four times longer than the average lifespan of a rat. If we only doubled the human lifespan, we could live to be two hundred years old."

"Fuck," I say. "I'm not sure humans *should* live to be two hundred years old."

"Especially the ones who could afford it," Joey adds.

I turn and point at him. "Yeah. No shit. Good point." Then I look back at Johnny. "But what's this got to do with Maisy and Beatrice?"

"Here's where it gets tricky," Nick says. He pulls out a chair next to Johnny and takes a seat. "Because Megan and her father weren't just working on a fountain-of-youth drug. They were working on a way to take the Company down as well."

"O-kaaaay," I say hesitantly. "Not sure I like where that's headed."

"Good instincts," Nicks says. "They came up with a sort of trap. So to speak. A pre-drug cocktail was introduced to the Company elite to"—he does quotes in the air—"'prepare them for the upcoming final drug.' But it was more than that. It was a way to selectively, and efficiently, *kill* a whole lot of bad people. Elites sounds really exclusive, but remember how many people we're talking about here, OK? Three hundred and ninety thousand total. If the elites are one percent of that, then we're left with about four thousand people on the pre-drug cocktail."

"This would've been fine," Johnny says. "I don't think any of us have an issue taking out four thousand scumbags, right? They have killed millions and they will kill billions more if they get their way. So who gives a fuck, right?"

"I'm getting the feeling there's a catch," I say.

"There is a catch," Joey says. "They gave the pre-drug cocktail to all the Company kids. And Maisy is one of those kids."

I let out a breath. "OK. So I should assume that's bad?"

"It is," Nick says. "Because it was a trap, remember?"

"Megan and her father made a drug that will rewrite your RNA. And before you ask me what that means, I'll tell you. The RNA creates proteins. Proteins do all kinds of things in the body. And in this case, they do very bad things."

"In this case," Nick says, "they kill you."

"What?" I look at Joey. "But Maisy is fine. She was just in here. Sitting in the back listening to music on her headphones and playing a game on her phone."

"She is fine," Johnny says. "As long as she gets the pre-treatment cocktail every month."

"But if she misses a dose?" Nick says. "She will die a very painful, horrible death. And once she passes a certain point, even if she did get the drug, it wouldn't save her."

I lean back in my chair and let out a long breath. "Wow. OK. But"—I point at Johnny—"Megan made the drug. So she's cool, right? She'll just keep giving it to Maisy and Maisy will be fine."

"Yep," Nick says. "That's all true. Maisy will probably be OK. Live a long—possibly unnaturally long—life because her auntie is the mad scientist who came up with this shit. But there are hundreds of other kids getting this treatment. Maybe even thousands. We're not sure. And they will all die if they don't get the drug. As horrible as this sounds, it gets worse. You see, the Company is perpetuated by bloodlines. They keep very careful records of the bloodlines. Even the nobodies in the Company—like your girl Posie? Even her bloodlines can be traced back at least a thousand years. So here's our dilemma. If we eliminate the bloodline, we eliminate the Company. That's what Megan and her father were trying to do."

"Not with kids," Johnny protests. "She didn't know about the kids."

"Right," Nick says. "The kids. Are we willing to kill hundreds, maybe even thousands of kids to eliminate the threat?"

"Ummm. No?" I ask. "We're not?"

"Don't sound too sure of yourself," Nick says.

"I'm not. I mean, if a few hundred die but billions are saved?"

"Yeah," Joey says, sighing. "Trust me, we've had this conversation hundreds of times over the past several months."

"Here's the bottom line," Nick says. "We're taking out the FBI in about six weeks. Give or take a week or two, depending on how fast Max Barlow's boy in black ops makes his move on our target and then figures out his father has been playing him and he does the right thing. It's all been planned. We're doing some clean-up of the creepy girls. Wendy excluded. She and Chek have been working with us for years now, so she gets a free pass. But there are others out there who can't be left behind."

"What are they?" Jesse asks.

"They are bred," Nick says, "to kill. You don't ever want to find yourself the target of one of those girls. They are… not right."

"Then why let Wendy live?" I ask.

"I just told you. She's one of us. We're loyal, Zach. You think my name is Nick Tate, and it is. But there is so much more to that story than you can possibly imagine. I'm not gonna live to see Christmas. It's not in the cards for me. I'm going to die taking down the FBI so I can save someone else who will play a bigger role in the endgame. It's a sacrifice worth making. We are loyal. We live and die with one goal in mind. Leave this world a better place than how we found it. And Wendy has a role to play in the future. She lives because she must."

"There's more," Johnny says. "The longevity treatment has another purpose. It's a way to make a vaccine."

"What kind of vaccine?"

"One day, maybe soon, maybe not, a terrible disease will be released. It will kill billions of people. Decimate the Earth's population."

"Oh, fuck. Please tell me this is not going where I think it's going."

"It's going there all right," Nick says. "That's their endgame. The Company wants to depopulate the Earth. And this longevity treatment will make them immune to the disease."

"But it's not ready. Not even close," Johnny says. "So…" He sighs. "They need lots of little Company babies to test this on. To make antibodies."

"Human drug trials?"

He just nods.

"OK." I'm so tired right now. "Is there anything else?"

"Beatrice," Johnny says.

"Shit. Did they give her the drug?"

Johnny shakes his head. "Not yet. But they will. If we don't make sure that Nick's plan works, then they will. And one day"—he points to Jesse, then me— "one day you two will have kids. And they will be girls. And those girls will be just like Maisy and Beatrice. They will be bloodlines. They will be test subjects."

"Unless Megan and her father find a cure for what they've done."

"That's why Megan works for Emma at Bright Berry Beach," Johnny says. "She's running a secret lab there. Trying to make this right and making enough of the cocktail that Maisy won't ever have to go without it."

"But if she finds the cure," I say, "that's good… but. The bad guys live then, right?" I look at each of them in turn. "That's what that means, right?"

"And now we're back," Nick says. He folds his hand on the table and smiles at me. "You, Luke, and Posie are a problem, Zach."

"How the hell do you figure? I'm not involved in any of this!"

"Posie saw things on that island," Jesse says. "They know, Zach. They know. And she's connected to us through you."

"They're gonna look very close, Zach," Johnny says. "They're gonna look at everything we're doing."

"And if they look too hard," Nick says, "they're gonna find things."

I get it. I do. I see it all. I even understand it. But they can't be saying what I think they're saying. "What are you saying?"

"We have to walk away," Jesse says.

"From who?"

"All of it," Joey says. "All of it that leads back to the Dumas family."

"What?"

"Emma," Jesse says. Then he sighs.

"You're not walking away from Emma! That's fucking crazy! You married her five fucking times in one day last Christmas!"

"What am I supposed to do?" Jesse is pissed now. And he's not that kind of guy. But he stands up and pounds his hands on the table. "Huh? What am I supposed to do? Let the Dumas clan go to prison for child sex trafficking? Let Emma's company be implicated in some freak raid that connects her to atrocities I can't even fathom? Walking away from them is the right thing to do!"

"Fuck that!" I say. "We fight back!" I look at Johnny. "You're willing to walk away?"

"If it saves Beatrice and Megan, then yes. I am."

"And you?" I look at Joey. "You'll what? Just walk out on Maisy?"

"If walking away means she will live, then yes. Huck, Wald, Brooke and I would move back to Japan."

"Fuck you people! Fuck all you people! We are the motherfucking Boston brothers! We do not walk away from a fight!"

"You're not understanding," Nick says. "In about six weeks shit is going down. Lots of evil people will die, but more importantly, this will be a huge disruption. Lots of people in the know will be dead."

"And that means," Johnny says, "that the Dumas family has a chance to become less visible. Everyone knows that Jesse and Emma are married, that can't be helped. But we can manage that situation. The people who really know what the Dumas clan are up to will die if everything goes to plan. And the ones in the Company who take their place will be in the dark about certain things."

"Certain things like the Dumas family smuggles children as a cover for the FBI," Joey adds.

"They will be left behind," Johnny says. "And some of them will be happy about that. There are a lot of people in the Company who just want out."

"So that's great!" I say. "We lie low for a while and then when that's all over—"

"No," Nick says. "It's not that easy, Zach. We would need a literal army to keep taking out the people who rise to fill in the positions. The leftovers won't stay clueless for long. They will regroup and reorganize. And we don't know who might come out on top. What you're proposing—a fake out until the heat is off? It could work, but we're not talking weeks or months. We're talking years—maybe even a decade—before we're ready to take it all down for good. When we took them out last time we got gang members to fight for us. Hundreds of them. But it came with a price. That's how I became"—he pans a hand down his body—"this guy. I gave myself up to save the girl I loved. I gave myself up to give her a second chance. And they turned me into this. So I understand what you're saying, Zach. I really, really do. But we don't have an army big enough this time. It would take… hell, I don't know. Thousands of people. And we can't start a literal war in the Caribbean. We can't just go in and kill them. It won't work this time. This time all we can hope for is to disable the black ops inside the FBI and then live to fight another day."

I pace the room, back and forth along the length of the long conference table as my cousin-brothers watch and wait for me to say, *OK. Fine. I'm on board.*

But I'm not on board.

Because I will not walk away from Luke.

I need to know where Posie is and if she's safe.

And what is the fucking point of living if you can't make a stand?

But really, the reason I pace is because I just know there's another way. I just know there is.

Then I stop pacing and look at Jesse. Just stare at him.

"What?" he asks. "Why are you looking at me that way?"

I look at Johnny. Then Joey. And then, finally, my eyes rest on Nick.

"What if there is another way? What if… we *do* have an army? And what if we had a way to make them *fear* us?"

CHAPTER TWENTY-ONE

POSIE

When I got out of the van, I found myself at an airfield. A small jet was waiting nearby, but other than that, there was no one around. No other planes. No small terminal. In fact, if I hadn't worked at one of these places, I would've never recognized it as an airfield.

The first thing I did was go looking for my phone in my suitcase.

It wasn't there. I think I left it in the bed. I don't know. I think Zach had it last.

So I was just about to put up a fight and let Nick know that I would not be getting on that plane when an argument broke out between him and Wendy.

Well, no. It wasn't an argument. It was a fight. He was giving orders, that guy she was with was nodding his head, and then all of a sudden Wendy was furiously protesting.

This was happening near of the front of the van and I was still in the back of the van trying to keep the baby out of the wind with Lauren. I started to walk that way to see what was going on, but Lauren grabbed my hoodie sleeve and shook her head. "Don't interfere. It's none of your business."

They were still just arguing at this point, but then Wendy struck Nick in the head with her fist.

He took her down so fast—her back hit the pavement so hard—for a moment I thought for sure he'd broken her.

But she started kicking and screaming and by this time I was backing away. The baby did not move in my arms. She didn't startle or make a single squeak.

And this is when I started figuring out that there was something wrong with these children.

Even Lauren. She was calm and unaffected as well. Like it's normal for grown men to have fistfights with teenage girls.

But Wendy somehow wriggled her way free from Nick and then they were a blur of flashing kicks, and elbows, and knees.

The next time Nick got Wendy on the ground they were both bleeding from the mouth and Chek was screaming at Wendy to stop.

Not Nick. Not the grown man. But the small blonde girl. She was the one out of control.

Finally, Lauren said, "We should get on the plane. He's going to be in a bad mood when this is over."

And in that moment getting on that plane felt like a pretty reasonable thing to do.

It wasn't a big plane. Just four seats aside from the cockpit. Two on the left and two on the right, both sets facing each other.

I took a seat, still holding the baby. Lauren sat across the aisle. And when Nick arrived, he sat across from her.

The pilot closed the door before Nick was even seated, and before I knew it, we were taxiing down the lonely runway.

I looked over at Nick, ready to start asking questions, but I caught the warning in Lauren's eye. So I shut up and clung to the baby, who wasn't asleep, but didn't seem to be awake either.

It was a long plane ride. At one point Lauren got up and found some snacks, but I didn't take anything. The baby was far too young to eat snacks, and I started wondering how I was gonna feed her when she finally got hungry. But we landed before that happened.

There was a car waiting. No driver. So Nick drove. Lauren sat in the front and I sat behind her so I could keep my eye on him as he drove.

This is when he told me about Megan Machette and Johnny Boston.

This is when I realized… evil was the right word after all.

He told me about the drug. The trick Megan and her father played on the Company. How they wanted to kill them all, and they were about to do that, but then they found out the elite children were on the drug as well and all plans needed to be changed.

He went on and on and after a while I did my best to tune him out and stop listening. But there was no way not to hear the things he was telling me.

This drug needed a cure. And my Nick, this one with me, it was his job to buy time so Megan and her father could make that cure. So that the Company could be taken down, once and for all.

Then we were pulling up to a gate that looked like maybe, at some point in the past, it might've been a nice gate. But right now, it was old, and the iron was rusty, and squeaked fiercely as it rolled open after Nick punched in a code. We drove on. Down a long, winding driveway that was pitch black on either side.

I wouldn't figure out where I truly was until the sun came up the next day, but I could smell it. The heavy air of a bog. The thickness of the humidity even in late October. The incessant sound of insects.

I was in the South.

After that we found ourselves in front of an unassuming house made of light brown bricks. I knew there was water nearby, but I couldn't see it. I could only hear the signs of it. We got out of the car, went inside, and finally—finally—this baby decided to have an opinion.

I was so relieved that she was crying, I didn't even care why.

And even though, if someone had asked me just a few hours before if I thought Nick would have a nursery in his house with all the things babies need, I would've said hell no—he did have a nursery in his house.

And it creeped me out.

Why did he have this nursery?

It was so very, very clear that this baby wasn't his. So what was I supposed to think?

There was only one thing to think.

He brings babies here often.

At any rate, I bathed her, changed her, fed her, then put her in the crib. She didn't complain one bit. So I picked her back up and held her instead. I couldn't bear the thought of her being alone right now.

When I found my way to the kitchen—because by this time it was late and I was hungry—I found Nick and Lauren sitting at a table eating sandwiches.

"There's one for you," Lauren said. "It's in the fridge."

I looked at Nick and he said, "Do not fall in love with it," meaning the baby. "It's not yours," he reminded me.

"Who does she belong to? Where did you get her? Surely, she has parents. Am I part of some sick kidnapping plot now?" That's what I said.

It was Lauren who answered. "She doesn't have any parents, Posie. None of them actually have parents."

"None of who?" I looked around. "You have more of them?"

"Not here." Lauren scoffed through a mouthful of sandwich.

Then Nick looked at me with those savage eyes of his and said, "You don't want to know what that baby is, Posie. It would break your heart. And the only reason I didn't put her down when I took the others in the facility was because I have a sister."

I just stood there. Not understanding. Trying to wrap my head around the word *facility*.

"So. I'm thinking about it. That's why I'm telling you, do not get attached to it. It's not yours. Either it will go to my sister or I will kill it."

"That's what he was fighting with Wendy about," Lauren said.

"The baby?" I asked, turning to her.

"No." Nick was the one who answered me. "She has a friend. Much like herself. The Dumas brothers were involved with smuggling this friend out of the Caribbean several months back and Wendy knows where she is. I need that information from her before we can move forward. I cannot—I will not—leave a loose end like that when things go down."

"What things? What's going down? Who the fuck are you people?"

I sigh loudly in the here and now. It's been weeks since that first night in the house. Weeks of knowing things I wish didn't know.

I kept pestering him that night. Kept demanding answers. More and more and more. And I didn't even realize that I should stop. That I shouldn't know these things. That this information he was spilling to me was even worse than what I saw out on that island.

Because he said, "These girls aren't girls, Posie. I've already told you that."

"But what are they? I don't understand. Why are they so different? Why does this baby scare you so bad?"

"Because if she grows up, and there's no one there to stop her, she will kill people."

"That's utterly absurd! That's not how it works!"

And then he was tapping on his phone, pulling up files from some secret server, and I was watching his proof.

I was watching little girls like his Lauren, doing the most atrocious things. And one of them... was Wendy.

I dropped the subject.

Fuck it. I don't understand.

And besides, yesterday three more little girls showed up. I don't even know how they got here. I just woke up, did my thing with the baby, then went into the kitchen to get a bottle ready and there they were. Three little blonde girls sitting in front of the TV watching cartoons.

The oldest one—Daphne, age five—filled me in on their exciting adventure and explained that they came from some place in Wyoming. The middle one—age threeish—is called Avery. And they had a baby too. Lily. About one and a half, I'd guess.

I would've asked Nick what the fuck was up with them, but he's gone. I'm here alone with five little girls, none of whom belong to me, all of whom have been kidnapped by a psychopath.

So today I decide I am not in control.

There is nothing I can do about this.

I have no say in anything that is happening to me or these kids so... whatever, I guess.

I'm just his… babysitter.

But the days pass.

Then a week goes by.

Then two weeks.

Then three.

And then, one morning, the girls and I wake up to screaming.

We're all sleeping in the same bedroom. The house is not big. Maybe three thousand square feet. But it's on a large acreage and if you walk far enough, you come to a wide river. There's no one around, but the whole setup is creepy. I'm pretty sure even the baby thinks the place is creepy. So we pushed a second bed into the master bedroom and that's where we sleep. All piled together on two beds.

But on this morning, the screaming wakes us.

All the girls—except for Lauren—are looking at me for an explanation, which I cannot provide.

"It's just another girl," Lauren says, wiping sleep from her eyes and swinging her legs out of bed. "That's all. A new one. They almost always scream like this."

Jesus fucking Christ.

She creeps me out. I can't help it. I don't want to be afraid of her, but I am.

"What girl?" Daphne asks.

"It's Angelica. We've been looking for her." Lauren glances at me. "She was the one Wendy was hiding."

"Shit," I mutter. "So now what?"

"Well." Lauren frowns. It's the first time I've seen her frown, so I get a really bad feeling in my stomach about it. "I guess we're done here."

"What does that mean?" I want to shake her. But I don't dare.

"It means it's time to go."

We all turn, gasping, and find Nick in the doorway. He's got the new girl by her long, blonde hair. It's all wound up in his fist. She's about... twelve, maybe. Tall for her age. Her bright blue eyes are blazing with wild rage. Her hands are tied, there's a piece of duct tape over her mouth, and she's breathing hard through her nose.

"Go where?" I'm so done with this freaky shit show. My voice is trembling because I want to threaten him. I want to tell him that if he wants these girls, he'll have to go through me first.

And I can't say that. Because he *will* go through me to get to them.

I don't even matter here.

I am the fucking babysitter.

"Pack your shit up, girls," he says. "We're leaving."

"Where are we going?" Daphne asks.

And I expect Nick to be short with her. To snap at her. But he's not. And he doesn't. "We're actually going back to Wyoming, Daphne. I found you a home."

"Back to our home?" She asks this with hope in her voice.

"No," Nick says. "Everyone at your house is dead now."

"For fuck's sake," I say, scrambling to get out of bed with the baby in my arms. "Don't tell her that shit. She's five years old."

Nick raises an eyebrow at me. Then he pulls out a knife and cuts the zip tie around new girl's wrists. He points his finger in her face. "I'm not gonna tell you again. This is how it shakes out. And you're gonna do as you're told. Got it?"

It's pretty clear she's not on board. She might even be growling.

But Nick ignores her and instead reaches for the baby in my arms.

I do not give her up. I cling to her and she clings to me and begins to whimper.

But Nick looks me in the eyes and says, "Let go, Posie. Or I'll make you let go. I told you not to fall in love with her. She is not yours."

I sigh, wanting to cry. Because I can't change any of this.

I concentrate on the fact that he called her 'her.' 'She.' Not '*it*.'

But I need more than that as reassurance. "What's the difference?" I ask.

"What are you talking about?"

"Between these girls and those elite kids you can't bring yourself to kill in order to take down the Company? What's the difference?"

Nick sucks in a deep breath, then lets it out slowly.

"You want to kill these kids," I say. "And save those."

"They're not the same."

"Tell me why. I need to know why they're not the same."

"I already told you. Those elite girls are well-bred. They have a nice pedigree. They were bred, but only in the nominal sense of the word. Their parents were matched. But they lived in homes, and they went to school, and they have been living a pretty normal life. One day, of course, they will figure out that's not really true. But their hell is a secret." He points to the blonde girl he brought with him. "Ask this one if *her* hell is a secret."

I look at the new girl and I don't need to ask. It's written all over this girl.

Pain. Suffering. Maybe even torture. She could be the next skeleton chained to a wall.

"No," Nick says, like he's reading my mind. "They were never going to chain this one to a wall or walk her into a fire. They have done much, much worse to this girl already. But here's the difference." Nick leans in a little. Like he's going to tell me a secret. "The difference between Angelica here and Charlotte Kane, who died chained to a wall, is this." He points at Angelica and straightens back up. "*She* can take it."

Then he takes the baby from my arms without asking. And there's nothing I can say or do to change that. So… I let him. He hands the baby to the new girl. "Take her, Angelica. She's your sister now. And if anything happens to her before you two make your way to your final destination, I will hold you personally responsible. And trust me when I say this." He points a finger in her face. "If I hear you're being an asshole to the people I'm leaving you with, I will do something about it. And should you ever hear rumors of my unfortunate demise, well. Don't believe rumors. Ever."

I take one last look at the baby before Angelica turns her back to me and walks over to the window to look out at the front yard.

It has been easy to love that baby. Because she clings to you. She *needs* you. And it's very clear that Angelica needs her too. Because in less than ten seconds, they are clinging to each other.

My heart hurts in this moment. It's dumb. That child is not mine. None of these girls are mine. But I suddenly don't understand what life looks like without them.

"Posie," Nick says, bringing my attention back to him. "You have a phone call." Then he hands me a phone and I take it out of habit. "Go outside and work it out." And he nods his head in the direction of the back yard.

I push past him and start walking down the hall towards the back room where the patio door is when Nick grabs my arm. He leans in, whispering, "Remember what you saw on that island?"

I look up into his eyes and nod.

"All the girls I've taken"—he nods his head towards the bedroom—"they were all gonna end up that way, Posie. All of them. Eventually."

"End up how? Being chained to a wall? Walked into a fire?"

"Worse than that. Those two girls? They were nothing like the girls I've been taking."

And it's in this moment when I realize—he's had a lot of little blonde-haired blue-eyed girls in this house. And now… they are all dead.

Because of him.

"It would've been much worse than that. I promise you. I shouldn't let any of these girls live, but we've had enough. And we know people who can handle them. If I let you have that baby, Posie, she would kill you one day."

"What?" I scoff.

"You don't believe me. And that's OK. But it's true. She has been *bred*. They have done things to her. You *know* this."

"She's not even six months old."

"They've *done* things to her. She is so damaged already, there is almost no way she will be normal. But my sister will take her." He nods his head. Like he's trying to talk me into thinking this is a great idea. "My sister can save her. She will be with people who understand who and what she is. It's either that, or I kill her. Do you understand me?"

I don't. Not really. "But what about the others?"

"Same. They are going to people like me. People who understand how to raise them. And listen"—he shakes me by the shoulders—"even Lauren is going. She's mine, but she can't stay with me."

I look over my shoulder, ready to protest.

But Nick shakes me again. "She knows. We've been talking about this day for years. Now I need you to go outside, have your little phone call, and decide what you will do next. Because our time together is over."

Then he lets me go and walks away.

I just stare at his back for a few moments.

Unable to move, feeling incredibly alone and sad.

I'm not even sure why.

So what else can I do?

I walk outside, put the phone to my ear, and say, "Hello?"

"Posie?"

His voice is my last straw. Everything that's happened over the past month catches up to me in this moment. All of it crashes down on top of me and my heart is suddenly crushed.

"Luke?" And now I'm crying.

"Walk towards the river. Posie? Do you hear me? Walk towards the river."

I walk towards the river because I can hear Nick giving soft orders to the girls in the driveway on the other side of the house. They are leaving me behind.

They are getting in the car and in mere moments they will be gone and I will be lost.

"Posie?"

Luke sounds worried. So I wipe my eyes and sniffle. Trying to be strong like Lauren. "I'm here. I'm OK. I'm walking."

The car doors close. One. Two. Three of them.

And that's it.

My life here has been over for mere minutes and I'm already desperately sad.

CHAPTER TWENTY-TWO

LUKE

I keep the phone in my hand and listen as Posie makes her way through the woods. She stumbles a few times but she doesn't say anything else. Just breaths heavy and sniffles like she's crying. The two Nicks both assured us that she was fine and I believed them right up to this very moment in time.

But there is nothing to do about it now but move forward.

Zach has jumped out of the yacht's little tender boat and is walking towards her as she emerges from the woods, still holding the phone to her ear like she's on autopilot or something. When Zach reaches her, he takes the phone and pockets it. Then he grabs her shoulders and looks down at her. I'm still on the yacht about twenty yards off shore, and the call has ended, so I don't know what he's saying, but I can take a good guess.

Brad-Pitt Nick—that's what I've been calling the other guy who is not Chains—mentioned that she might get attached to the girls she's been looking after, and that Zach and I should reassure her that they are going to be OK when we get her back. So I figure that's what Zach is doing.

She's nodding at him. Wiping the back of her hand across her nose. But she keeps looking over her shoulder at the woods. You can't see the house they've been staying in from here, but that's what she's really looking at.

Zach says something to her, then she looks out across the river. At me. I wave and smile.

She takes a deep breath and then lets Zach help her into the tender boat.

I hop down the flybridge stairs and wait on the bathing platform for them. The little inflatable dingy bumps up against the stern and I hold out a hand to help her out.

She sighs as she boards. Looking around.

"You OK?" I ask.

She presses her lips together and stares at the forest of trees for a moment. "Yeah. I'm good."

"They're gonna be OK," Zach says. Meaning the girls, I presume. "Nick promised us. He told us to make sure you understand that." He steps onto the platform and then he and I attach the tender to the winch to lift it out of the water. "Take her inside," Zach tells me. "I've got this, Luke."

I nod and guide Posie over to the stairs that lead to the aft cockpit, and then we go inside to the saloon. She flops down into the soft cushions of the couch and pulls her knees up to her chest. "What's going on?"

"Well." I take a deep breath. "Shit is about to get very interesting, Pose. And I hope you're up for it. Because a lot of people are counting on you right now."

"Me?" She points to herself. "What the hell? I can't do anything. I don't have the power to help anyone. Those girls—"

"Those girls, Posie, are going to be fine."

She's not convinced. "I get that they're... different. Whatever that means. I've seen it in their eyes. The way stress doesn't affect them. Their lack of emotion. Even the baby was apathetic. And if you had asked me a month ago if I thought babies were even capable of being apathetic, I would've said no. But I was with them. I took care of them—"

"Posie." I say her name sternly. Trying to get her to pay attention to me. "Listen to me. Those girls are going to good places."

"How do you know? That Nick, he was crazy. He's insane."

I scoff just as Zach comes into the saloon. "No, he was the sane one. You didn't even meet his twin, Chains. That dude." I shake my head. "Now, if we're leaving the kids with him, I might have another opinion. But Brad-Pitt Nick, he's different."

"He had a fist fight with that Wendy girl when we landed here." She looks around with wild eyes. "Where is *here*, anyway?"

"Mobile," Zach says. "We're just outside of Mobile on the Dog River."

She narrows her eyes. Thinking about that and momentarily distracted. Then she shakes herself out of it. "They had a fist fight, Zach! Like—punching each other in the fucking face!"

"Well," Zach sighs. "That's Creepy Wendy for you. The girl is not all there. And she's definitely part of the secret society shit my family is running. So, forget about her. She can take care of herself. The important thing is, Nick is very grateful that you helped him out by taking care of those girls when he hunted down the last one. He told us to tell you that. And it's OK to miss them—" He stops here because Posie is crying again. Not sobbing or anything. Just quiet tears running down her face.

I sit down next to her and pull her into a hug. "It's OK to feel like this. Nick said—"

She pushes me away. "Nick said? Why do you believe him? He's crazy!"

"You're not listening." Zach sits down on the other side of her. "We're all crazy. We're all mixed up in something really fucking bad, Posie. He's doing the best he can."

"And," I say, trying to steer the conversation back to where it needs to head. "You trust us, right?"

"That's different!" she insists.

"It's not," I say. "It's really not. I mean, yeah. Maybe my family is pretty normal. But those Bostons?"

Zach laughs. And then Posie, against her better judgment, lets her guard down. Just a little.

"It's a fucking shit show," I say. "But we've got a plan."

"And it's a good one," Zach says. "But we need you."

"I've already told you," Posie objects. "I don't have any power. I can't do anything about this. I'm just… going along. That's all I've ever done. I just go along."

"Well then, now's your chance to change that."

She makes a face at me. "How?"

Zach pulls her phone out of his pocket and offers it to her. "Make a post."

"Make a post? Where?"

Zach grins. "In the fan group. I've been in there getting them all excited for the past two weeks but they need to hear from you. They keep asking—"

"Hold on." Posie puts up a hand and sits up straighter. "What the hell are you talking about?"

"The group," Zach says. "You left your phone behind and—" He shrugs. "I had it. So… I've been in there a little. Talking to my fans—"

"A little?" I ask. "Shit. Don't let him lie to you. He's addicted to your group."

"Wait." Posie shakes her head like she's trying to understand something complicated. "What?"

"The plan," Zach says.

"What fucking plan?"

I laugh. "The plan where Posie Payseur's Zach Boston Fan Club Army saves the world."

Despite her confusion and sadness, Posie laughs too.

"Hey," Zach protests. "It's not *that* funny. It's not a surprise that half a million women wanna congregate in a social group to celebrate me. I'm a charming, likable, handsome little fucker."

I point at him. "That you are, Slick. That you are."

Posie giggles and even though her face is a little blotchy and her eyes are still red, she looks a million times better. "Wait. Half a million? We only have a hundred and seventy-five thousand members. And not all of them are women."

"We *did* have a hundred and seventy-five. A few weeks ago. But I've been in there every day since we've been apart and…" Zach shrugs. "Well, they flocked to me after I showed up. I have Top Fans now."

Posie sits up on her knees. "Half a million?"

"Yep," I say. "It's an army."

"An army." Zach points to her. "Ready and willing to help a girl out."

"What girl? What help?"

"You," I say. "They're gonna help you out."

"Help me do what?"

"Start a new gossip magazine, of course. Not one corrupted by the Company the way Buzz Hollywood was."

"What?" She bursts out laughing.

"I was thinking we could call it Posie's Possie. What do you think?"

She squints her eyes at Zach. Points her finger and says, "Nope. That's not gonna work. But forget about the name. What the hell happened while I was stuck in Mobile babysitting a handful of creeping beautiful girls?"

"A plan happened," Zach says. "A gorgeous, perfect, morally questionable—but incredibly effective—plan happened."

And then he drags her into the kitchen and starts explaining while I go to the helm, set a course for Key West, and guide us out of the Dog River, through Mobile Bay, and out into the Gulf of Mexico so we can meet up with our new army in Miami.

CHAPTER TWENTY-THREE

ZACH

"What is the job of a reporter?"

Posie is sitting at the bar eating a sandwich when I ask her this. "Is that a real question?"

"Yes. It's real. You're a reporter. You went to school for this shit and everything. So what did they tell you the job of a reporter was?"

"Well." She chews her mouthful of sandwich. Thinking. "To ask questions."

"Exactly," I say. "What else?"

"To... look for answers."

"Snooping," I say. "Something you're good at. What else?"

"Um. Well, present your findings to the people. Otherwise, what's the point?"

"Yes." I point at her.

"OK. So what's this have to do with the fan group?"

I shoot her a thoughtful—but still charming—look. "Do you think that reporters these days do those things?"

She shrugs. "To be honest, I don't really watch the news."

"Why not? You are a journalist. You have a degree. This is what you wanted to devote your life to. So why don't you watch the news?"

"Well, because I guess they really don't do a great job. Or." She points at me now. "That's not really true. Maybe they do a fine job, but the things they report on? I'm just not interested in it. They ask all the wrong questions. They go looking for the wrong answers. And most of them are just... obnoxious. They are more about their on-screen personalities than they are the truth."

"Ding, ding, ding," Luke says from the helm.

"So how can we change that?" I ask her.

"I don't know. But I'm going to assume it's got something to do with your fan group since you're supposed to be telling me why they're involved in this plan of yours."

"It does. And I'm getting there. But I have to present it the right way, don't you think? So you understand the first time. So you get it and don't become confused. Because most people have a pretty short attention span."

"Yeah." She sighs. "Tell me about it. People like bullet points."

"Exactly. So these are my bullet points. Are you ready?"

"I'm ready. Hit me up."

"We all know there are bad people in the world, right?"

She pouts a little. "I wish I didn't know that, but yes. I've seen it first-hand."

"So... what are you gonna do about what you saw? Tell everyone?"

She scoffs. "Tell them what? My story is crazy. And even if someone did believe me, by the time anyone got to that dungeon to look, all the evidence would be gone. There's really no point of telling anyone. Besides you guys, of course. Because you were there and you get it."

"Because we also saw it with our own eyes, right?"

"Yes. Exactly. But if I just went on TV or whatever, claiming that this super-rich family pushed a girl into a fire and had literal skeletons in their closets, I would be the crazy one."

"They need to see it," Luke says. We're in the Gulf of Mexico now and he's got us on auto-pilot, so he takes a seat next to Posie at the bar. "With their own eyes."

"Please tell me we're not taking the fan group down to the island to show them the truth. Because that would never work."

"Why not?" I ask.

"You know why. The evidence is gone. They're not going to find anything. I'm sure they're on high alert right now. Probably hunting us down as we speak."

"You're right," Luke says. "It's too late to show them what we saw. But think about it, Posie. They didn't just throw that party together."

"It's wasn't a pop-up," I add. "It was planned."

Posie thinks about this for a moment. "Ahhhh. So they're gonna do it again. When?"

"Who knows. That's why we need to be patient. You know all about the crazy drug Megan and her father unleashed on the world?"

"Yeah," Posie frowns. "Nick mentioned it. It's very fucked up."

"We need time, Pose," Luke says. "We need to keep these people away from Megan and Johnny so she has time to come up with a cure. But at the same time, we need to keep people safe and do two other things so when the end-game comes, we're ready. The world is ready."

"We need to watch them," I say. "Very carefully."

"And document everything they do, as efficiently as we can," Luke adds.

"But it all has to be legal," I continue. "If we collect evidence, we have to collect it legally. That's the only way we can present it to the world. That's the only way normal people who do not believe some rich-fuck families are out there throwing girls into bonfires will accept this as truth."

Her eyes go wide. "We... *become* the reporters."

Both Luke and I smile.

"What have you done?" she says.

"Oh," I say. "Just... invited all our fans down to Key West so we can crash a pop-up party."

"But that won't work. We just—"

"It doesn't matter," I tell her. "It doesn't matter if they're doing anything wrong. And they're not going to be there anyway. *We* just need to be there. Every time they turn around, one of us has to be there. We need to be everywhere."

"With a cell phone camera," Luke adds. "Asking questions. Getting it on the record."

"While others follow them. Get close to them. Learn more about them. Become their friends, and confidants, and lovers."

"You're setting up a... a... what? A global spy network under the guise of journalism?"

Luke and I smile.

"That's crazy!"

"Why is it crazy," Luke asks.

"Because. It's like... a total... infiltration. A secret... invasion. We can't—"

"Why can't we?" I ask.

"Because... can we?" Her confusion morphs into a wide, grinning smile. "We can, can't we?"

We can.

And we do.

We *become* the news.

Twenty-four hours later there are five Buzz World operations in play.

Posie hated the name I offered up for her—no, *our*—new media company.

Posie's Possie, yeah, OK. It was lame and just an off-the-cuff option.

Besides, we needed to troll the "legitimate" media just a little, right?

So Buzz World.

Buzz to troll Buzz Hollywood and to let all the other media outlets know that we're closer to an online gossip magazine than we are the nightly cable news. We wanted to make sure the people who mattered understood that our methods won't be... *traditional.*

We will look everywhere.

Under every rug.

Behind every closet door.

No one is safe.

And the World part—well, because we *are* global.

The fan group is spread out all over the world and every single member already owned the tool of our trade.

A cell phone with a camera and an internet connection.

Ironic that one simple piece of tech, made by the very corporations we will definitely be looking in to, was all we needed to start changing the fucking world.

The first Buzz World operation is taking place right now at a sandbar pop-up party between two private islands that coincidentally happens to be at the very same place where Posie found her first skeleton.

No one is here.

There is no ritual scheduled for tonight.

There are no rich people to ambush.

There are no drugs being sold and no naked people painting themselves up with weird symbols.

Just a small crew of full-time security.

But that was the point.

We took over both islands in less than twenty minutes. And the best part was—we had an invitation.

The fucking flags.

God, I still laugh about it now.

When we left the pop-up party all those weeks ago the security team never collected our flags. So we pulled right into the channel and eighty-five of our closest sailor-friends, from Key West to West Palm Beach, sailed in with us—carrying a half a dozen brand new Buzz World employees, cell phones in hand.

We took over the house first, of course.

There is no Satanic temple. No closet with a secret door to a secret dungeon. They actually bricked over it. There are no clues here. In fact, one of the security dudes who recognized us from the last party said the Conner family left the day after the bonfire and haven't been back since.

But we are all over this island. Photographing, and videoing, and having a pretty good time, to be honest. A few pontoon snack boats came along for the fun and it's basically a big old ribbon-cutting ceremony for Buzz World.

I'm standing in the same spot where Bart and I were kicking back. Shielding my eyes from the sun as a helicopter approaches from the north.

I don't know who it is. Yet. But I will soon.

There are four other operations happening today as well.

Johnny bought the estate next to the Kane-Conner family estate north of the city.

Well, *bought*… eh. That's a strong word. He definitely owns it. *Now*. But there was a little blackmail involved to get that deed. We moved in about fifty new Buzz World employees. Emma and her crew from Bright Berry Beach are handling this part. They are experts in corporate retreats for new management hires. They are, at this very moment, horseback riding in the woods between the two estates, making friends with the Kane-Conner family teens.

Keep your friends close and your enemies closer. That's what we always say.

And we *are* close.

Maisy isn't living at the Kane Estate anymore. Joey just never handed her back to her step-dad, Michael Conner. And that bastard never even called looking for her. He *knew* we knew what they were up to. He *knew* we would never hand her over again.

He *knows* we're coming for him. For all of them. And he is so weak, and pathetic, and selfish—that he didn't even *try* to fight for Maisy.

So fuck him. She will never step foot onto that estate again.

We wish we could've gotten our half-sister, Malinda, out as well. But that's why we bought the estate next door.

We're keeping an eye on those fuckers.

Literally. Since we sent Wendy in to hook up some closed-circuit cameras so we can spy on them.

One day all the Company kids will be free.

One day.

The third and fourth operations happening today are out on islands just southwest of this one. We don't actually know who owns them, and so far, no one has popped up to kick our people off, but it's all Company. The first one is where Johnny found Megan and the Buzz World crew on that one is just taking pics and vids. Documenting the cells and the dungeons.

Most of the main house on that island is a burned wreck, but they didn't clean up these dungeons.

They just never thought to do that.

How smug does one have to be to leave behind evidence of dungeons?

I mean, I get it. We all get it.

It doesn't matter how much footage our new reporters come back with of that island, no one will give a fuck. They won't believe it. How could they believe it? It looks like a movie set.

And if we make any of that footage public, that's what they'll say. It's a movie set. It's a set up. Whatever. The Buzz World employees taking that footage are part of the secret team.

We figure—fuck it. If the ruling class can have a secret society dedicated to evil, then we can have one dedicated to cleaning it up.

The other island is a much more delicate operation and the crew on that one is all wearing hazmat suits. Johnny is on that team. Along with Alonzo, Tony, Chek, and Johnny's friend, Logan, who helped us out with our FBI skirmish last winter.

There is a lot of evidence out there.

Lots of things that Megan can use to find our cure.

And the last operation is out in Kansas. At that very same airfield where Posie was working as a waitress.

If everything went according to plan, Chains is dead now.

But one girl is alive because of his death.

The one girl the Nicks needed to save above all others.

I hope she was worth it.

The Buzz World group up there in Kansas will be our hard-hitters. Turns out, the Zach Boston fan group actually had about three dozen legit reporters on the roster. They cover the serious shit and then they turn it in to us so we can pass it out to the more serious aggregators.

We. Are. The news.

The helicopter lands. Dust and sand swirls in the air as the rotors wind down.

I'm actually sorta surprised that they're turning the helicopter off.

Maybe they do want a fight?

Chandler appears. I thought maybe it would be Michael Conner, but no. That bastard is too big of a pussy to own up to anything.

By the time Chandler makes it out to me most of the dust and sand has settled down.

He looks like he walked off a tennis court about ten minutes ago, that's how pretentious his clothes are. But he's smiling and lifting his sunglasses up to his forehead as he approaches. "Zach Boston. I should've seen this coming, actually."

"Yeah. You probably should've."

He stops about six feet short of me so I figure we're not gonna greet each other by shaking hands. "So." He looks around. Puts his hands in his pockets. "What's all this?"

"This is the only warning you'll be getting."

"Friend—" he laughs.

"That would be a mistake, Chandler. We're not friends."

He's still smiling. Playing it off like he and his ilk aren't fucked. "OK. So what can I do for you?"

"These islands are ours now."

His words come out past a laugh. "Is that so?"

"And so is the one with the lab, Chan. We've got boots on the ground right now. We've got samples, and scientists standing by, and an entire hard drive with all the data on it."

His mouth gets very small as he sucks air in through his nose. "What am I supposed to do with that information?"

"Whatever you want. It's all ours now. We want deeds, Chandler. Deeds. For every single island connected to this Caribbean shit show. You got away with it for a long, long time. But that's over now."

He's still laughing. "You Boston bastards are very fucking sure of yourself. But I gotta tell ya, Zach. For your own good, mind you. That you have no idea who you're really fucking with."

"Is that so?"

"Yeah, that's so. These are dangerous people. And I'm telling you this as a friend, even though we're not friends. I really am."

"When's the last time you talked to your people, Chan?"

"What?"

"The last time you talked to your people?"

"Like… half an hour ago. When I left the yacht."

"You might want to call them again."

"And why's that?"

"Because your world just ended out in Kansas, Chandler. We got Nick Tate. He's dead."

"What?"

Oh, yeah. I forgot to mention. The Nicks? They were playing both sides. And only our side knew that. In fact, only our side actually knows there are *two* of them. Chains is the only one people see. Chains was the Company assassin trainer. He was the one who lived down in Central America with the drug lords. He is the one who ran the training camps. He is the one responsible for every single blond-haired, blue-eyed creepy girl born in the last ten years.

Brad-Pitt Nick, on the other hand, is a secret only one girl who is not part of our operation, knows about. Just the one girl.

So Chandler here has a very confused look on his face right now as he attempts to process this information. He's trying to figure out how to respond. And in the end, he goes with, "Bullshit. No one *gets* Nick Tate. That sociopath is the best assassin this world has ever seen."

"No one?" I scoff. "The best, you say? Have you ever heard of a girl called Sasha Cherlin? Her name ringing any bells to you right now, Chandler?"

I almost feel sorry for the guy.

Almost.

Because his Caribbean-tanned face goes pale white. "What?"

"Yeah," I say. Sighing with satisfaction. "Sasha Cherlin shot him—" But before I can even finish my sentence, my sat phone buzzes. "Ah, here it is." I smile at Chandler. "The evidence. You got a number? I'll message you the vid so you can take it back to whoever your master is."

"Bullshit." He says it again. This time through gritted teeth. "That's *bullshit*."

"Take a look, *friend*."

I hold the phone up and press play.

I haven't seen the vid, so I'm not even sure what's on it, but our new Buzz World hard-hitters out in Kansas don't disappoint.

She shot him in the head.

Blam.

Chains is dust.

"What the fuck?" Chandler isn't taking the news well. "What the actual fuck? Do you have any idea—"

"Of course, I do," I say calmly. "We know exactly what we're doing. So like I said, we're gonna need the deeds to every island the *Company* owns in the Caribbean or a whole lot of people from the *Company's past* are gonna start showing up again. Gonna not only start taking interest in what you people are doing, but also *why* you're doing it."

He's opening his mouth to say something back to me, but when I say the word *Company*, he closes it up right quick. Add that to the word *why*, and yeah. Chandler might just throw up on his pristine white tennis shoes.

"And after we get that," I continue. "My sister Soshee and I are gonna need our trust fund back."

"What?" This snaps him back. "I don't know what the hell—"

I pull the envelope out of my back pocket, slip the piece of paper out, and snap it open. "Seventy-five million dollars. That's the amount of money our father collected for us. And when you people murdered him, after he tried to get me out, you assfucks took it back. So, yeah. That's part of the price for you leaving this island alive today, *Chandler*."

He just stares at me.

"You've got it. We all know you've got it."

"That's… that's not our money," he stutters.

I know this. None of this money is technically ours. It's all stolen from somewhere. And then laundered by any number of bad people doing bad things, all across the globe.

"None of that is my problem. So you go do that, friend. And send it all to Johnny. He says you've got forty-eight hours."

Chandler glares at me.

"And if we ever see any of you again—we'll take out Bart first. Then your mother. Then you. Then everyone else who lives at that mansion. And let me be very clear about this next part, OK? If anything happens to my half-cousin-niece, Malinda? And I do mean anything. If that girl gets so much as a hang nail. If we even get a *hint* that she, or one of our loved ones, is being fucked with or they hurt, whether it's your fault, or not? *Blam.* Chandler. That bullet goes right in the head. And if you people think you're going to be walking any more girls into a fire or chaining them up in your dungeons, you better think again. We have thousands of people watching you. You cannot go anywhere without being seen. You won't even be able to walk down the street without being photographed. One step out of line and that's it. No second chances. You got me?"

I suddenly feel a lot like Johnny.

It's an act, though. I'm not the one who will explode heads if these people fall out of line and give us trouble.

Chandler has dropped his indignant look and is now properly scared.

Not of me. Just… us. All of us. Everything, probably. This whole fucked-up world we were born into is enough to give even the most hardened soldier nightmares.

But he nods his affirmation.

"Good. Then go on, now. Get. I'm gonna need that helipad in about five minutes. And trust me, you do not want to be here when *Merc* arrives."

"Wha—" Chandler is incredulous "Where the fuck did you find *that* guy?"

"Well, I'd tell ya. But then I'd have to kill ya. Seriously, though." I point up at the approaching helicopter. "Merc's up there. And he's got a rifle. I'm pretty sure he could pick you off from here, so…"

Chandler looks panicked. Scanning the sky. Shielding his eyes so he can find the helicopter. And just as he does that, a shot hits the dirt mere inches from his feet. Sending up a cloud of dust that Chandler has to wave away.

"He didn't *miss*, Chan. That was your only warning shot. I'd start running for your ride home, if I were you. Merc don't like to wait."

That's all he needs to hear. Chandler turns and runs back to his helicopter as the other one circles above us.

I smile and wave as they take off and disappear from view.

Then I look back at the new arrival just in time to see Other Nick jump out holding a massive rifle with a sniper scope attached.

He's smiling as he runs towards me. "Did he buy it?"

"Fuck yes, he bought it. I don't know who this Merc guy is, but Chandler ran like the scared little Conner pussy he is."

Nick smiles. "Merc is one fucked-up dude." Then he sighs. And when he looks back at me, the smile is gone. "Thank God, he's on our side."

I study him for a moment. "You OK?"

He considers this a real question, because he takes his time before he answers. Finally, he says, "I lost my daughter and my brother today. And I know they are both in a better place, but walking away from them was the hardest thing I've ever done. And I've done some pretty hard things in my life, Zach."

I don't doubt it. And I wish I could say I understood, but I don't.

I *get* it. We took down a lot of FBI today in the Midwest. Lots of them. But not *all* of them.

Chains had to die so future Sasha Cherlin can take down the remaining Black Ops people in the FBI from the inside out. And Lauren needed to go live with Sasha. Nick is not the kind of man who should be in charge of raising little girls. She needed a mother and Sasha was his first love, even if it never went beyond friendship and can't go anywhere now. Sasha is the only one he trusts with his daughter.

Lauren is right where she belongs.

But I would never, ever agree to let my cousin-brothers die to save me. And even though I don't have kids, I can't imagine what it would take—what kind of selflessness it would require—for me to give up my daughter to save her at some distant point in the future.

So I just clap him on the back, take the rifle from his hand, point to the helicopter, and say, "Let's get you home, brother. We've done our part for today."

And I think he likes that idea.

Not the home part.

Nick Tate has no home. He's dead now and he'll be living on the run for the rest of his life. But he'll stay with us on Dumas Street tonight. He's earned that much.

No. He liked the part about us being brothers now.

Because that's what we are.

In it together.

Forever.

POSIE

FOUR MONTHS LATER

The Dumas backyard is filled with people because it's Saturday night and when you're a part of the Dumas family, you show up for dinner at seven o'clock *every* Saturday night.

I've heard this was sorta optional before I came along and crashed the family, but not anymore. These days, it's mandatory.

Silvia, the Dumas matriarch, gives no fucks at all if your names are Jesse and Emma and you live two thousand miles away. She expects you to get on your corporate jet and fly your ass down to Key West for dinner every single weekend.

And everyone does that. Even if their last names are Boston instead of Dumas.

Even Joey, Brooke, Huck, Wald, and Maisy show up.

Hell, even Johnny, Megan, and Beatrice make it for Saturday night dinner these days.

And no one misses taco night anyway. Zach has been talking about it all week. He made Luke and me knock off work at noon today, just to make sure we weren't late for taco night.

But… we all love it.

Especially if our last names aren't Dumas.

None of us ever had a real family. And this Dumas clan, they are as real a family as they come.

It's the perfect ending, really.

Me, and Zach, and Luke all live in our little cottage down the street. Two doors down from Alonzo and Tara. Across the street diagonally from Tony and Soshee. When Emma and Jesse are in town, they live next to Tony. And when Joey and his clan show up, they live between us and Alonzo and Tara. Johnny's family lives next door to Emma when they stay overnight.

So the whole street really is one big, happy family.

And I'm totally happy.

Zach, Luke, and I started out as a fling. Then we turned into partners in crime. And then, ironically, we became actual business partners. Buzz World isn't turning a profit yet, but it's close. It's booming. The fan club has been so great. And we really are the news now.

People started taking us seriously after our reporters broke the story of the FBI safe-house murder of infamous criminal mastermind, Nicholas Tate.

It was the scoop of the century.

So it's all good.

It really is.

Today is my birthday and even though I wasn't supposed to know that taco night is actually a surprise party, I knew. It's pretty much my job to know. I am one-third owner of Buzz World, after all.

So this dinner is perfect.

There's food, and family, and cake, and singing, and laughing.

In fact, it's the best birthday of my life.

Still. There is this nagging feeling that something is missing.

I've felt it for a few weeks now. But I can't figure out what it is.

Zach and Luke are incredible. I don't know if we're like... marriage material, or whatever. Not that that's even legal. But... there is something there. Something very special.

I know we started out as a one-night thing. And the whole let's be criminals together is probably not the best way to start a new relationship. Especially a complicated plural one. But it works for us. It really does.

We have dinner on someone's porch most nights. We take turns and we all bring a dish to share. So it's like Dumas family dinner almost every single night.

And even though the king-sized bed is a little bit cramped for three people, I'm pretty small and I'm not gonna lie, being squished on both sides by these two men isn't something I'll ever complain about.

I have the best job ever, too. My dream job, in fact. I'm a real, legit reporter. For my own media company. Our corporate office is on the yacht, so every day Luke, Zach, and I get up, walk down to the marina together, and work from the yacht. We don't do long-distance charters anymore. And Luke has people to manage the adventure biz, so it's perfect. It's like I'm living in a literal fantasy world where I have everything I ever wanted.

Emma has told me that she's never seen Luke so happy.

And Zach is always smiling.

Me too.

I'm *totally* happy.

But is there something missing?

I would not say I think about this missing thing a lot, but I often get this feeling during family dinners.

I just don't understand why.

"Ready for cake?" Emma asks. She's sitting across from me. This family is so big that in order to have everyone together for meals, we have to push four picnic tables end to end in the family-home backyard.

"I'm ready," I say.

Emma just smiles at me. In fact, everyone is smiling at me.

But that's normal. It's my birthday. I'm the star of the night. And we all just ate tacos.

But… "Why are you all looking at me that way?"

"Presents," Soshee says. Shoving a gift wrapped up in a silk scarf at me.

"We love presents," Tara agrees.

Which OK. I get that. And they do give nice presents. There is a beautiful bracelet inside the scarf that Soshee made herself. Tony even found the seashells on a nearby beach. Emma and Jesse give me a spa day on Little Palm Island. Tara and Alonzo arranged for us all to go diving at a secret reef before all the tourists arrive. Silvia and Jack have named their new boat after me—which is a big deal. That's how you know you're really part of the family. Joey, Brooke, Huck, and Wald let Maisy pick my present, so I get a new bikini from them. She makes me laugh. But every girl can use a new bikini when you live in Key West. And Johnny and Megan give me a new cell phone of all things.

I… just look at it. "Um. Thanks! This is awesome! The new model!"

Everyone is just looking at me. Still. Smiling.

"What?" I say.

They just keep smiling.

"Come on." Zach gets up from the picnic table and takes my hand. Luke is accepting a tray of leftover cake from his mother and holding a brightly-colored bag filled with my gifts in the other. And then I'm pulled down the side of the house and out onto the sidewalk.

"What are you guys up to?" I ask. Zach turns and walks backwards in front of me. And I know that grin. I know all his grins. "You're up to something.

"Up to what?" he plays innocent.

"We have to give you our present," Luke says. "It's private."

"Hmmm. That sounds interesting."

"Oh, you're gonna love it," Zach says. Turning around to walk up the porch steps. "Just wait."

Luke herds me inside and I don't know what I was expecting. Maybe some decorations? Balloons, streamers, some presents on the table?

But the house looks the same way it always does.

Small and a little bit cramped. But mostly it looks comfy.

Luke pushes me in the direction of the couch. "You're gonna need to sit for this."

"O-kay." I laugh and take a seat. "What's my present? Are you guys gonna do a little strip tease for me?"

Zach points at me. "Probably later."

"But first," Luke says. "This." He takes the phone out of the gift bag he was carrying and places it on my knee.

"What are we doing?"

"Just wait." Zach is grinning.

"It's your gift," Luke says. "Because we know you're not all here, are ya, Pose?"

"What? What do you mean? Of course, I am. I love being here."

"We know that," Zach says. "But your thoughts are other places."

"Like where? I mean, no they're not. I'm totally, one-hundred percent here. My life is amazing and—"

The phone buzzes on my knee. I glance down to look at it, but it's not a call.

It's a text.

A picture, actually.

I gasp and pick the phone up to look at it closer. "Is this?" I hold the screen up. Biting my lip, because my chin is suddenly trembling. Both Zach and Luke remain quiet. Just look at me. I glance back down at the picture.

"It's Daphne," I say. Starting to cry. She's smiling big, wearing pink arm floaties and hanging on to the side of a pool. Her blonde hair is plastered against her head. Her bright blue eyes are shining with happiness. The phone buzzes again and another picture appears. This time it's Avery sitting at the top of a pool slide, mouth open and I can practically hear her wail. She's crying her eyes out. A message appears. *I'm told she's very afraid to go down that slide. So that's why she's crying.*

I hold the phone up gain. "Who is this from?"

"Nick," Zach says. "I told him you missed them. So he got some pics for you."

"Oh, my god." And I'm really crying now. Then another pic comes in. Lily sleeping on a hammock. All sweaty like they live somewhere hot, but not tropical.

"They look… happy." I sniff and look up at my men. "Thanks, you guys. I don't think I understood how much I missed them. And it's stupid but—" the phone buzzes again and this time it's Angelica and the baby.

Now I really lose it. I just start bawling.

They are sitting on a beach with palm trees in the background. Both of them in profile and lit up from the glow of an orange-y red sunset. Solemn faces, but not sad ones. Angelica's hair is tousled and bleached from long days in the sun. She's resting her chin on the baby's head, which is covered by a pink and yellow floppy hat, and the baby is sucking her thumb.

Another message comes in under the pic. *My sister named her Hannah.*

And that's it. My tears are out of control.

But the phone buzzes one more time and it's Lauren. She is sitting on top of a palomino pony surrounded by other girls her age, also on top of equally beautiful ponies. She's got the full formal riding gear on. Black velvet helmet. Those special pants riders wear. She even has the tall, black boots.

Those are her new cousins, this message says. *Her pony's name is Buttercup. And I'm not crying, you are.* Then one more message. *Happy Birthday, Posie. I just want you to know, they are loved and so are you. Your friend forever, N.*

I text back hurriedly. Because I don't want to miss him. I don't know if he's going to throw that phone away or what. But I have something to say to this man.

Thank you. You're loved too. And we all need you to know that. Love, Luke, Zach, and Posie.

He sends one more text.

Just one word.

Soon.

I don't know if I'm laughing or crying now.

I just know… I feel better.

Then Luke and Zach are hugging me.

Hard.

Like never gonna let me go kind of hug.

And then… even though nothing is quite right in this world…

Every one of us are right where we *need* to be.

END OF BOOK SHIT

Welcome to the End of Books Shit. This is the part of the book where I get to say anything I want about the story. And wow—series over! So that means I have a bunch of stuff to say.

So here we go.

Well, first—the Bossy Brothers Series isn't one-hundred percent over because Zach Boston will host the Happily Ever After book once I'm ready to write that. Also, if you've been paying attention you know that this story is actually happening on two timelines in two different series. So the story of Nick and Wendy picks right back up in the upcoming Gorgeous Misery—which is book three in the Creeping Beautiful Series.

I'll get to more about that in a moment, but first… wow. I was a little worried about this ending because I have been building this mystery for SEVEN books now. So that comes with a little bit of stress, right? Gotta deliver that ending.

But this series wasn't too bad. It was nothing like coming up with Wasted Lust (also another book taking place with some of the same characters on another timeline). Wasted Lust was the last book in a thirteen books series that included Rook & Ronin, The Company, Three, Two, One, and Meet Me in the Dark. And now the Bossy Brothers has slipped into that series as well, but as a spin-off. It was much harder to pull the mystery together at the end of Rook & Ronin series because the plots were a lot more complicated.

I feel like most of the Bossy books are at least 60% fun. Like at least 60% of the story in each book is about the romance, and the banter, and the sexy times and only 40% is about the mystery. Some of them came in way less than 40%. Bossy Bride is like 90% fun and 10% mystery. And I think the Dumas brothers were easier to keep on the fun side because their family wasn't as complicated as the Bostons. The Dumas fam wasn't hiding deep, dark generational secrets like the Boston family was.

So it's been pretty fun writing about the Dumas clan and this Bossy Luke book was pretty easy as far as the author struggle goes. It did take me a while to write but that's because it's 2020 and every time we look around, we get distracted by weird shit. So it was super hard to write this year, just in general. And that really had nothing to do with this book.

I really—like REALLY—fell in love with Posie. She started out as a conniving little trollop but I warmed to her pretty quick and toned all that stuff down. Posie is just a nice girl trying to find to find her way in the world without doing too much damage. And I think that a lot people are like that. But her character matured really quickly once she realized she was inside a mystery. And even though she wasn't the "hero" in the end—that was probably Zach—she played her part and it was not insignificant. None of these boys could have gotten to their ending without Posie.

In fact, everyone in both families got their second chance because of Posie's teenage crush. And that's no small thing.

As far as Zach and Luke go—well, we all knew these two were together. I don't remember exactly when I started dropping hints about Zach and Luke— maybe Bossy Bride?—but they've been in this weird, sorta-committed, plural-ish relationship for a few books now.

They've got a thing going. They are living together. Zach doesn't work for Luke, but he does work with Luke. So this relationship they have is showing all the signs of commitment. And then Luke starts overthinking things. He suddenly realizes that he's maybe ready to settle down. His business is going great, he's making money, he's expanding, he owns his own house—Luke appears to be living the dream. And that's all fine, but when your partner is still in his early twenties, it's pretty normal to wonder if they're on the same page.

And then those doubts creep in.

Posie did help him out in this regard. She was only there to get her story and this was before her big character shift, so that was her job.

Zach was the one who liked to spice up the relationship with "extras". He was always bringing in a third. And this made Luke feel a little insecure. Is Zach looking for a third because that's his normal? Or is Luke boring?

That's the first question in the book.

So I started the story with Luke as the insecure one in the relationship and Posie was his way of keeping Zach interested. And then she became this destabilizing force because Luke figured out he had a big 'ol protective-alpha gene hiding inside him. He's the one who rushes to protect Posie on the island. He's the one who has her back.

And at the same time that this is happening, she's starting to piss Zach off. He was kinda tired of her after their one-night stand and then she got dragged along on this charter trip. But after she outs him to the Conner boys, he was done. And he starts wondering if his relationship with Luke might be stagnating.

So I thought that was kinda fun. That Luke and Zach switch places in the middle of the book and Luke becomes the one who needs to keep Posie around—not for Zach's sake and not to save their relationship—but to keep her safe.

And then, of course, we have to get Zach back on board because now he's having doubts about his relationship with Luke. He's wondering if Luke likes her better than him. There is nothing unusual about this dynamic. A threesome relationship is, almost by definition, unequal. And to keep one going long term you really have to know where you fit in. And I think by the time this story ended each of these characters understood that what they bring to the relationship was unique and the three of them together worked. Zach and Luke were probably always solid. The problems they perceived were mostly in their heads. Were mostly just insecurities. And they realized they were solid. They were so solid, there actually was room for a third.

Yeah. I think that's the theme of Bossy Luke.

They were so solid, there actually was room for a third.

Even though the Boston and Dumas families have found a happy ending and they've wrangled control over their futures, this story isn't over yet.

The really cool thing (at least I think so) about this world is that we already know how it ends. We already know that the Company goes down. What we don't know is how and we don't know how long that lasts. Now, if you're reading all the books in this Company world you know that we've taken the Company down three times inside the stories I've already written and one more time in a story I'm in the process of writing.

We took them down in the very first Company book.

We took them down in Wasted Lust (and at the same time in Bossy Luke)

We took them down in The Misters (which happens way in the future).

So there's one more thing that needs to happen in this world and that's about the drug that Megan and her father made. So all that side of the story will play out in the Creeping Beautiful series.

That series is darker—on purpose. The Bossy Brothers was like... JA Huss "lite". Keeping it fun and sexy for the most part.

I give no fucks at all about fun and sexy in the Creeping Series. That series is all drama. It looks at all the dark secrets, exposes all the evil truths, and no one gets out unscathed.

I saw a review for Creeping Beautiful in a Facebook group and this reader said—"Well, it wasn't a romance, but it was a love story."

I think that sums up that series perfectly.

There are many ways to find love in the end and the romance route is but one.

Up next in the Creeping Series is book three, Gorgeous Misery, and that is all about Creepy Wendy and Nick Tate. Not to mention Sasha and Merc will be back for real. I did a little fake out with you guys in this book with Merc, but he will be back for real in Gorgeous Misery.

And honestly, I think this is a story you're gonna want to hear.

End of series sads? Yes or no?

Mmmm... I'm gonna say no sads for this one. Not the way it was for Wasted Lust because I really thought that was the end of those people. I thought I was leaving them behind and I would never see them again and Bossy Brothers still has a HEA book coming. Crazy weddings are my specialty so that's gonna be super fun.

Plus, ending are really nothing but new beginnings.

New beginnings are unpredictable and often times scary, but so very, very necessary.

New beginnings are like adding Posie to a Luke and Zach sandwich.

OK, I'm done here. I hope you enjoyed all these Bossy Brothers and I hope keep going in the Creeping Series. There are many, many more stories to tell about these people.

Thank you for reading, thank you for reviewing, and I'll see you in the next book.

Julie
October 31, 2020

ABOUT THE
AUTHOR

JA Huss never wanted to be a writer and she still dreams of that elusive career as an astronaut. She originally went to school to become an equine veterinarian but soon figured out they keep horrible hours and decided to go to grad school instead. That Ph.D. wasn't all it was cracked up to be (and she really sucked at the whole scientist thing), so she dropped out and got a M.S. in forensic toxicology just to get the whole thing over with as soon as possible.

After graduation she got a job with the state of Colorado as their one and only hog farm inspector and spent her days wandering the Eastern Plains shooting the shit with farmers.

After a few years of that, she got bored. And since she was a homeschool mom and actually does love science, she decided to write science textbooks and make online classes for other homeschool moms.

She wrote more than two hundred of those workbooks and was the number one publisher at the online homeschool store many times, but eventually she covered every science topic she could think of and ran out of shit to say.

So in 2012 she decided to write fiction instead. That year she released her first three books and started a career that would make her a New York Times bestseller and land her on the USA Today Bestseller's List twenty-one times in the next five years.

In May 2018 MGM Television bought the TV and film rights for five of her books in the Rook & Ronin and Company series' and in March 2019 they offered her and her writing partner, Johnathan McClain, a script deal to write a pilot for a TV show.

Her books have sold millions of copies all over the world, the audio version of her semi-autobiographical book, Eighteen, was nominated for a Voice Arts Award and an Audie Award in 2016 and 2017 respectively, her audiobook, Mr. Perfect, was nominated for a Voice Arts Award in 2017, and her audiobook, Taking Turns, was nominated for an Audie Award in 2018. In 2019 her book, Total Exposure, was nominated for a Romance Writers of America RITA Award.

Johnathan McClain is her first (and only) writing partner and even though they are worlds apart in just about every way imaginable, it works.

She lives on a ranch in Central Colorado with her family.